AMAZON SEVEN

BOOK ONE:

Mission Queen

AMAZON SEVEN

BOOK ONE:

Mission Queen

ALEX JAMES

Also by the author:

Out Now:
Dark Streets – Book One: Agents of Fear
Terraguard – Book One: Maker of Rules
The Pandora Sequence
Venus I.A.

Amazon Seven – Book One: Mission Queen

Cover design by Michal Dutkiewicz and Alex James
Cover Illustration Copyright © 2015 by Galexy Tales
Cover Art & Illustrations © 2015 Michal Dutkiewicz

Book production by Ingram Spark
Editors: Stan James, Melissa Sheldrick
Editorial Consultant: Gretel Newman-Sugrue
Text layout: Adam Dutkiewicz

Galexy Edition 2.1 (Revised and expanded from the original ebook)

Dedication

This book is dedicated to Terry Nation, Chris Boucher
and Robert Holmes.

'For what it is worth, I have always trusted you.
Right from the very beginning.'

PROLOGUE: CONFESSION

Whenever she was in town, she liked to sit on the steps of the Sydney Opera House and look out over Port Jackson. There was nothing quite like the sight of the Sydney Skydocks and their enormous, airborne shipyard platforms as they hovered high over the ocean harbor. Some were very far out over the water but others were much closer in, even seeming to edge toward the outer corporate towers of Sydney City.

Not for the first time she thought of her grandmother, who'd been a Qantas airline pilot, and wondered what she would have made of the Skydocks.

It had all happened so quickly, at the end of the last century; so many people had struggled to…

Whatever.

It had happened.

The Sydney Skydocks were now included as an extension of this part of the world's human-created iconography. They were as beautiful and impossibly majestic as any grand-scale industrial monument, especially when they glistened in the sapphire-blue sky on a clear winter's morning such as this.

She kept staring up, mesmerised, letting her mind wander.

Although the Sykdocks seemed to hover in essentially fixed positions, she knew from experience that over the course of the day they actually curved in slow, wide arcs. She found it engaging, soothing sometimes, to wait until she could tell which of the massive shipyard stations were arcing clockwise and which were not, before she once again set off on her business.

Sometimes her business was up there. Sometimes, up there, she found time to gain a view, and she would look back down to the Opera House. She would stare back at the steps where she'd been sitting. Remembering what she had been thinking.

She'd known a few skyworkers in her time.

From down here, some of the skyworkers were visible, along the edges and upon the platforms of some of the closer, lower docks.

As easily visible as…

She looked down at the surface of the Opera House steps, by her feet, for the cliché.

Yes; as visible as the ants that were bustling along, right there, where someone had ditched a half-eaten burrito.

She moved along a bit, and sat down again.

Then she reassessed her surroundings.

There were only a few people on the steps this morning.

It was quite early.

She gazed out, contented once again at the view.

A kid arrived and sat on the steps beside her.

She glanced at him, and he glanced back. He'd given the kind of slight, precocious nod a child gives, when they are growing up perhaps a little too quickly for themselves. He was nine, she guessed.

'My Dad says they'll never get it to work.'

She took a while to consider a response; you never knew these days. People got upset at the slightest things.

'You're talking to me, aren't you kid?'

'Yeah.' The kid rolled his eyes. 'I don't just, like, sit down and start talking to myself. I'm not mental.'

'That's not a nice thing to say. There are all sorts of minds who think all sorts of things. Almost none of them can help it and most of them are fine.' She raised an eyebrow. 'Especially if you just leave them alone.'

The kid didn't take the hint.

'Well, my Dad says they'll never get it to start.'

'Her. They'll never get *her* to start. Ships are shes.'

'Mum says that's sexy.'

'Sexist. You mean sexist.'

'Whatever. It… *she* looks cool though, doesn't she?'

She found herself allowing the kid a smile. 'She sure does.'

They looked at the largest of the massive floating docks, perhaps two kilometers out over the water, and maybe five hundred meters high. There were seven other spaceships being built. She counted an explorer, a freighter and a colonist ship amongst them. Too soon to tell what the other three were, but they were always building something up there.

But the closest was something else.

Unlike anything else.

'They're going to stop building it.'

'What?' She was stunned at this.

'My Dad, he's up there. He says they're going to stop.'

'Why?'

The kid leaned in. 'He says that really, if you ask him, they finished building it a year ago. But it doesn't work.'

'It doesn't?'

'Doesn't at all, Dad says. It was supposed to be new. A whole new kind of ship. But, the man who made it all up, he's mental.'

She sighed. 'Really? After I told you that's impolite?'

'No, I mean, really mental. He's locked up somewhere now. Mum says it's all really embarrassing, so they just keep pretending to build it. But, someday soon, they're gonna stop. Dad says they might as well just unhook it and let it drop into the bloody ocean. For all the good it's worth. He says, unofficially, they're gonna leave it up there another year while it still brings in the tourists.'

The kid looked at her.

'Are you okay lady?'

She held her breath a few seconds, before speaking again.

'Yeah...' She could hear the emotion in her own voice.

'You sure?'

She sighed. 'You're gonna see grownups cry eventually, kid. It was bound to happen sooner or later.'

They were quiet again as some people walked by. Thinking she was mental. Some unstable young mother and her poor kid, growing up too quickly.

'Sorry if I upset you lady. It's just, they're so cool, the way they just float up there. My grandpa says in his day they never dreamed that there would be floating space docks above Port Jackson.'

'My boyfriend used to say that, too. Well, my ex-boyfriend.'

'I've got an ex-girlfriend.'

'You have?'

'Yeah. I just… came to school one day and she said I was a pig. Wouldn't explain it. Don't know what went wrong.'

'You'd better get used to that, kid.'

'That's what Mum says. She's got a girlfriend now. But it's okay. My Dad likes her. They all watch movies together. I have to stay quiet, on the other side of the house and do my homework.'

'Oh. I see.'

'I know, right?'

She smiled at him. 'There's no growing up any more.'

'Dad says that. Mum says that every generation says that because every generation starts further along.'

'They're both right.'

They sat and watched the floating shipyards and the Skydocks while a school of joggers trundled past, up and down the steps for a while, then on again.

She rolled her eyes as they jogged away and the kid laughed.

Then they were quiet again for a while, as the furthest platform to the right caught the sunshine and glistened so brightly they had to shield their eyes.

'Wow…' She said, quietly.

'Yeah…' The kid responded, kind of laughing.

When it was over he looked at her curiously for a second, a little precocious, a little curious, but mostly earnest.

'Did your ex-boyfriend used to come here with you or something? Is that why you cried before?'

She gave him a sideways smile.

'It was just a couple of tears. It was a long time ago.'

'But… did he?'

'No. I always come here on my own. When I'm on Earth.'

The kid stared at her immediately wide-eyed.

'On Earth? Oh my God, are you, like, a pilot or something?'

She smiled at him again. 'Something.'

'And you, like, come here to look at the ships you're going to fly?'

She smiled again, broader now.

'Can I make a confession, kid?'

'A confession?'

'Gotta promise not to tell anyone.'

'Okay! Sure! I won't tell!'

She leaned in and whispered.

'I don't come here to watch the ships being built that I'm going to *fly* one day.'

'You don't?'

She smiled, wide and wicked.

'No. I come here to watch the ships being built that I'm going to *steal* one day.'

The kid stared at her, right in the eyes, so he could tell she wasn't lying.

'That…' The kid guffawed. '..is – so – *cool*.'

'I know!'

She stood up.

'I mean…' She shrugged. 'Sure. The man who designed it might have been mental and sure, maybe they did lock him up for being mental, but…' She leaned down and spoke in a low, conspiratorial tone again. '…he *did* name the ship after me, after all.'

She stood.

'What else am I supposed to do? If they're just going to chuck it in the water?'

She gave him a little salute.

'See ya kid.'

She started walking off.

'Wait! Lady! Hey wait! Can I help!?'

She turned around and beamed the biggest, broadest smile she could, one he would always remember.

'You just did kid! More than you know!'

PART ONE
ASTRA SOLARA

CHAPTER ONE

The party was over and Astra Solara was, as usual, the last one standing.

Or sitting, as it were, in a comfortable outdoor chair, on a large patio balcony.

She was admiring a cat, a cat who knew it was being admired.

Astra Solara could tell that the cat knew by the way the young and healthy creature, sleek and dark chocolate-brown, had come out of the darkness and approached the long, dark-wood banquet table. The cat would do well. The party had been over-supplied and under-attended and the spoils were aplenty. But just before it had reached easy pouncing distance, the cat had stopped suddenly, then slowly and elegantly seated herself. Even though she was scavenging for scraps, and there was quite clearly the prospect of an unguarded bounty directly above her, the cat had posed before Astra, and Astra had formed an instant admiration for the little feline.

This was a regular party setting with which Astra was comfortably familiar. The patio was enclosed but the open balcony extended from half way. The banquet table was centrally positioned, just under the edge of the patio roof, so that guests could mingle around the entire circumference, or break off to one of the settings along the balcony rail. The whole space, in Astra's keen estimation, was a good thirty meters wide and ten deep, enough for a small family back in the city. Roughly two hundred people had mingled comfortably here, just a few hours ago, their numbers peaking between eleven and one. Now, around three, it was just her and the cat.

When everyone else had gone, Astra had seated herself at the setting furthest from the table, with her back to the bluestone corner where the patio ended and the balcony began. Although she was relaxing, it was a perspective from which she could still remain completely but unconsciously aware of her entire surrounds, but if necessary become instantly, consciously alert.

Along the inner, original bluestone wall were lined four evenly-spaced french doors, above which extended a modern corrugated-iron veranda. The doors all led back into the homestead, the central section of which had been restored as a function hall. People had wedding receptions there, or birthday parties for ages that ended with a zero. It was a decent space, even out here, in about as 'Rustic Australian' circumstances as things got these days, at the end of this, the most bizarre twenty-first century.

Astra smiled at her own thoughts as the cat allowed herself to be admired a few seconds longer. It… *she* must have seen from afar that across the length of the table there was much more than scraps on offer. There was actual food, untouched by human hand. But cats being cats, she had been happy for a moment to pause, with nobody else around; at least no threat, no competition, and to take in some soft energy from a burst of human admiration before feasting at leisure.

Then the cat leaped gracefully on to the food table. She nimbly avoided empty bottles and glasses, slinky as she negotiated the scattered remains, delicately picking through and quietly chewing over some leftover sausage cuts. Then she was content, as Astra was content just to watch.

This vigil was not the first of such solitary, post-party remembrances Astra had allowed herself since she'd quit drugging. But in some ways, these days, this; being alone but still on the scene after everyone else had gone, was the best part of any given social gathering. Astra found now that by simply sitting within or just outside of the scene of the crime like this allowed her to perform a kind of social post-mortem. It helped her visualise the continuity of the night that had just passed.

These kinds of parties were never what they seemed. Nor were the attendees ever who they seemed, or even who they were being paid to be. This gathering in particular had been a veritable masquerade ball of misdirection and misrepresentation. Almost all the conversations tonight had been generally and massively subtextual. At least half the conversations she'd been lured into this evening had contained overtures for her to accept another secret assignment, her tenth such endeavour, or to sign on for another covert long-range exploration. Of course, they were the same thing really. Four offers had been from one or another of the various continental Earth governments, another few from one particular country or another, then a few from independent states. Three had been corporate – but deeper down they had all been some unspoken combination of all three.

She smiled at the symmetry of it; ten offers for her tenth mission.

It was a little eccentric perhaps, but she liked that kind of thing. That was part of it. It was within these quiet party codas, sitting alone and surveying the scene of the aftermath, when she found herself able to join all the dots and see the whole picture, and enjoy remembering even the small, silly details. In that way, these solitary moments were not only the best part of the party, they had become invaluable to her. An hour or so disconnected from the grid, the feeds, the news and the hype. Just herself, with her own thoughts, her own vision, and her own sounds. Her own processes, her own ideas and feelings. Her own inner monologues and demons, her own angels on her shoulder, whispering in her ear, her own crises to create, her own messes to sort out, her own decisions to make and solutions to divine.

Just Astra Solara, alone with herself.

And her own secret missions.

She assessed the bluestone walls again, admiring the rocky texture, calm.

There was always something here, on the weekends. For people like her. And them. She'd gotten to know a few of them; the pilot club, the mission clique.

The regular VyTel event, the VyTel crowd.

She hadn't even checked, this time, what or who it was for. It might even have been a 'Welcome Return' for her, for all she'd known. Certainly, enough people had incorporated that sentiment into their conversation.

'Nine executive missions! Six Indie! Surely that's some kind of record!?'

Maybe. The numbers were right. People seemed to know that about her. She'd graduated, been accepted aboard the *Rosetta* as Lieutenant, and gradually been promoted until she commanded her. When she took her first executive missions, it was as Commander of that ship. It was not until she'd gone Indie that she'd found the *Hightail*.

But more likely the event had been to mark the occasion of the colonization, or claim, or discovery of another habitable, minable, or even slightly approachable Goldilocks planet, or moon, or celestial body, or what have you, that was now available to VyTel. She looked to the cat.

They were alone on a patio balcony, and she was certain that the restored colonial homestead itself was empty. To the other side, over the balcony, was a beautiful view down a long, descending valley, at the top of which the homestead had been built, stretched across a short divide. Twenty feet below her, out from the ground floor of the homestead, an expanse of lawn flowed down the first, gently sloping section of the valley floor, toward a restored Edwardian pool house. The pool house in turn was set above a decent-sized lake, much further down. All she could see right now of the pool house was the moonlight on the glass but down in the distance the reflected moon was bright across the lake, like streaks of quicksilver. These were all locations of previous VyTel parties, sites of promotional events or corporate gatherings. The trusty old homestead, the twinkling crystal pool house, and the gossamer lake.

As Astra gazed down, she remembered from the VyTel tourist info that two centuries ago the pool had once been a squatter's dam, and was in fact supplied by the underground stream that came out right there, the water having been collected even higher up, in the mountains behind the hills, behind the homestead. The dam, now a freshwater swimming pool, was constantly replenished, feeding on into the lake below, even attributing to a river that supplied the artisan farmers in the lower valley.

She'd been a little surprised that the pool hadn't been open on such a humid night, but also pleased. On other occasions, especially when she'd been open to drugs and especially alcohol, she had thought nothing of stripping down to her underwear and diving in. But now… after Amazon Seven, she wondered what would happen if she were to do something as simple, as innocent, as to dive into a body of water. Probably nothing. But certainly, nothing she would do in public untested. Still, there would be time for all that later. Not a lot of time, but… tomorrow at least.

She returned her attention to the patio balcony, as the cat moved to another untouched platter. She recalled that over there by the furthest of the four doors that lead back inside she had spoken to this person about one thing, and over there at the table near where the massive barbeque still sat, cleaned and closed, she had chatted with that person about another. She had been standing over there and looking across to there when that *thing* had happened, and she had been sitting over there and talking to her friend when the others had arrived. And at the end of it all, just over there, *he* had clearly hit on her. And so on.

Having remained level and sober throughout it was now simple for her to sit here and recall her movements, to trace the pattern of the night as the other guests had become more and more intoxicated. As they opened up they told her what she needed to know, then departed none the wiser.

Astra fondled the stem of the wine glass she had carried around with her all night, then spun the crystal stalk and gently skimmed the beautifully curved receptacle across the table top. She was calm as she sat with one long leg crossed firmly over the other, one slender arm crooked across the table, balancing the spinning glass with an open palm. But she was becoming just slightly more puzzled as she ruminated over several of the clear yet formally unstated propositions she had received. She was favoring none of them, but their intent represented dots in the emerging picture as to how she was perceived… now.

Now that she had returned to Earth.

Returned to Earth, again.

Proved herself beyond a doubt, surely in the eyes of the elite.

Earned her right, equally as surely, to claim a stake.

Astra Solara was as good as she could be now. She was as good as they could make her, and then as good as she could make herself, which was better than they knew. Five times over she was supposed to have died out there and yet here she was; back yet again, as good as it gets. Here tonight, every commission she had been offered was a suicide mission, disguised as, 'a mission only you could accomplish', 'a commission we've never offered anyone, because we never thought anybody…'

…anybody what?

Lybrand had finished the sentence with a wicked smile. Was good enough? Mad enough? Would be stupid enough? Could prove themselves worthy? Brave? Skilled enough? Powerful enough within her still-Independent status to be expendable enough to be offered an insane suicide mission that she *just might complete*?

She'd told them all she'd think about it.

But here was the trick.

She was supposed to be –

A glass smashed on the dark wood. The chocolate cat remained up on the table. She stared across the patio at Astra, their eyes almost level. Then the cat looked to the next glass. There were several, arranged in a ragged row. Someone must have collected them, half-heartedly, at the end of the night, thinking they were being helpful. The cat reached out a deliberate paw and gave the glass a tiny swipe. It fell also, on the patio beside the other.

Another smash.

– she was supposed to be dead.

Conformity dictated that you took your corporate commission after the third executive command mission, even as an Independent. That was the way. No rogues, no loose ends. Tied to a pay scale, a percentage and a royalty rate. But not everybody did that, not every Commander conformed to the corporate path, and she hadn't. It was a risk but it was a path, a legit path, to go completely Indie. You could still accept government missions and corporate missions of course, but you could also accept private missions, and if you wanted, you could embark upon personal missions.

Accordingly, the missions Astra had been offered, even at the start, had become more distant, longer and more dangerous. The idea was that if she completed them, fair enough. Job well done, worth paying for. If not, she became a potential rogue element who had been dispatched cleanly, through official channels.

'Very sad but… they're like that, those types.'

Astra had taken her three executive command missions and thus earned the title of Colonel Commander. Jojoba, the Colonel Commander who had served as her Earth controller throughout those missions, hadn't the first clue that she'd intended to go full Indie. Nobody had. When that intent had first crystalized in her mind, she'd not exactly advertised the fact.

'Independents, freelancers…' Jojoba had literally looked down his nose at her when he'd spoken about the very idea. 'They don't want to be tied down to one service, one corporation, one military arm. They can't commit. They value freedom over conformity. They eventually become like those secret agents or assassins in war time…' Jojoba had snorted smartly to himself. '…well, official wartime anyway; the kind who keep taking the missions, more and more dangerous, further and further behind enemy lines, longer and longer shots, until one day they simply fail to return.'

Astra remembered that moment. She would never forget the thought that had struck her, and the realization that, with that thought, her decision had been made. Had already been made, some time ago, in the back of her mind, without her fully knowing.

Astra had thought; not me. I will not fail to return.

'That's not to say I don't know some Independents. Work with some. Even… *like* some of them. They have stories, after all. Tall tales, high drama. But you see, each time one of these Independents return, they inevitably exhibit signs of being less stable, less integrated. And if they are running official missions, they inevitably know more. More about the enemy, and therefore, about their masters. Or rather, their ex-masters.'

Jojoba was an Armada General now, a position his guidance and promotion of Astra had gone some way to achieving. He had been good to her, and she had waited until his promotion to Commodore had gone through, before pulling the plug on her Earth Interstellar military career. His promotion… and of course, her own as well.

'Furthermore, many of them seem to seek to understand the nature of the government, in whatever form, that hires them. Either that, or they learn the nature of their employers quite naturally as a consequence of their mission results; they return here knowing more, sometimes more than is good for them, about the cycles of war and the nature of power… and it becomes too much for them.'

It will never become too much for me, Astra's heart had told her.

'In the end, it's almost always a blessing in disguise that these agents of non-conformity, eventually, do not return. While we are grateful for all they do, all they learn and achieve for us, all they *sacrifice*, the more missions they take, the less likely they will be able to find a place back in *our* world, to stop and settle and belong when they are done. And, it follows, the less likely they are to be content with our society if they did.'

Astra had understood. These people were never done. And one day, it was implied, and certainly assumed, if not outright expected, an Independent Colonel Commander would fail on a mission, out there somewhere. And that was a good thing.

'In all, the potential threat of radicalization that their antisocial tendencies represent increases exponentially each time they return. An unfortunate demise on a high risk mission will inevitably contain that risk. There is, as well, the added benefit that such a dispatch of the said 'unstable security threat' would be a clean one, in the sense that it would occur unseen and 'out there'.'

Alone.

'Then there is the third inherent benefit, in that the death of any Independent, be they Captain or Colonel or Commander, who might find themselves in such an alienated state, any one of whom, it must be said, is firmly believed to be unable to ever earnestly repatriate into elite society...' The long nose had leaned in. '...let alone the substrata where radicalization would surely catch hold and ferment...' And leaned back. '...in all, would surely be a blessed release.'

The implication here was, it was firmly believed, that the non-conformist, deep down, had always wanted to die. In the same way, it was assumed, that promotion meant nothing to them. There were no Brigadiers or Generals, no Marshals or Admirals, nor any of the relatively modern combinations of those ranks that were recognized by Earth, within the scattered ranks of the Independents. Colonel Commander was as high as it went, no matter how much further you advanced the cause, no matter how many missions, nor how dangerous. Not even the results mattered.

And a glorious death, somewhere out there, furiously inevitable, resolutely anonymous, was almost always, it was assumed, 'what they wanted'.

But Colonel Commander Astra Solara was different.

She kept coming back.

She had never failed to return.

She would always bring her ship, the *Hightail*, and her crew, back to Earth.

Maybe not undamaged; she had lost and blasted both hardware and personnel in any number of ways, but she herself always returned, her missions always executed with maximum zeal, accomplished to the utmost satisfaction of her employers.

Very few before Astra had reached a tenth Independent Executive Command. Only a handful before her had gone further, and only one other, still living, had done anything like significantly more. But things would be different this time. Many of her most loyal crew would not be with her. Some had disbanded, some had –

The cat smashed over another glass.

– some had outright gone, and some, some had been left behind.

The cat stared at her again. Astra hadn't seen the chocolate feline move further along the table. She had moved up to the next cluster of wine glasses and gently swiped over the closest one.

Astra was sure the cat was a she.

The way it pondered, then swiped. She was mad about something. In heat maybe. A she.

Trigrick had hit on her.

Right over there by the middle balcony door.

Huh.

Representatives from six of the eight corplexes had approached her with insane suicide missions.

Five of the nine bitexes and all seven of the pharmies had done the same.

Massive risk, gob-smacking commissions.

Then, near the end of the night, when all was said and done, she had added them up and realized that some of them had been the same missions. Not that unusual. Competitor of my competitor, enemy of my enemy, mutually beneficial, that sort of thing. But in the end, the offers had distilled down to ten. Ten for ten.

And she'd told them all… she'd think about it.

But still, Trigrick had hit on her. An LCI, a HoliNeg, who had made no bones before about his desire for them to confirm as potential primary co-retirees, and assured her that he would never suggest anything casual, despite his clear sexual attraction to her, before that option had been exhausted. Astra had never closed the door on that option. In fact, quite the reverse. Astra had always thought, and felt, that Trigrick would make an excellent co-retiree. That feeling possessed no true spark but she would nevertheless be pleased to ease him, to pleasure him, down the line, in return for his easy-going nature and wit. But that would still be some time away. She had to assume that he would think, even at a conservative estimate, and without even knowing the truth about her, that she would want to risk at least two more missions, and accept at least two more big executive commissions. They'd discussed the possibility, so far as he knew in theory, and agreed that she could pretty much name her price for the next one, and if she came back again, unheard of but if she did, she could name it again, and triple it. But as they'd said, that meant she would not be free for at least another two more Earth years from now. That was, after all, the payoff for the continual high risk; she remained an Independent, and she retained the massive commissions with no government penalties.

Two more. After two more executive commissions she could retire well, at the calendar age of forty, biological age ten years younger, with the life experience of someone five times in advance of anyone even remotely close to either of those ages.

And yet, this evening, Trigrick had been… unromantic, uncharacteristically, in the face of that.

Trigrick had always been gallant with her.

But not tonight.

Therefore…

The only conclusions could be that…

She sat up straight, involuntarily.

Six of the eight corporate complexes, five of the nine biotech complexes, and all seven branches of Earth military wanted her dead, as soon as possible.

She had made a huge mistake, making them all wait.

Just one night, even one hour, had been suicidal.

Now, they would not take any chances.

They would not have her simply depart.

Independent Commanders like her who simply *departed*, to *explore* often never returned. Or even worse, they *did* return. Jojoba had been clear on that, all those years ago. There was no break for someone in her position. You kept going on elite commissions until you died, or you retired with a stake and joined the elite. And she did not yet have that confirmed. She had not yet plotted a stake… she hadn't even made it clear she wanted a stake. She had planned that move for when she had returned… from mission ten. After she'd spoken more seriously to Trigrick, maybe to Essy, perhaps Ijean or even Gerrelikrix. But Trigrick first. Alone, she could make a stake on a moon, of course. But together, with a cabal of co-retirees and a primary like Trigrick, a green continent was a possibility.

She had something in mind for mission ten, something important, but the last mission, eleven, was the key.

That had been her mistake.

She had kept her mind on eleven. Sure, ten would be hard, but all that mattered was that she was offered the mission she desired, made it back, and didn't get caught.

But to *them*…

A tenth mission was a huge deal.

Damn.

Sure, she was a non-conformist. But in their eyes, in which there was no such thing as non-conformity, in which there was conformity even within independence, she had not conformed to the Independent path. Or maybe, the way she had, had suggested something other than what she had intended…

She sat up a bit more.

She'd slipped up, badly.

She should have accepted any commission tonight. Any one, then simply changed her mind when she was offered the one she really wanted. But she had given the impression she was not going to accept anything, without having made it clear she was angling, at least down the line, for a stake. In their eyes, she was totally rogue!

You always took the next job straight away, so they knew where they stood.

So they knew; you just wanted to keep going.

When they didn't know exactly what you wanted they got concerned. They liked knowing. In fact, they liked it so much, they insisted upon knowing.

Think, Astra. She had to *think*. She had taken more commissions from VyTel than any other complex but that was just three within the nine she'd completed. She had made no formal corporate alliance, done nothing to suggest that a bid for a stake might even be on the cards.

Wait.

She saw it now.

When Trigrick had hit on her, he had been warning her.

Somehow he'd gotten wind. It had been his way of telling her.

Time was running out.

Although, had there been something else? Maybe it wasn't just a signal, a suggestion that she, that they, had no future if she pursued her present course and did not accept a commission. It had come at the end of the night. After she had told them all, *I'll let you know.*

Maybe he'd hit on her to warn her – *there was a hit on her.*

The cat smashed another glass, then another.

Yes. One after the other after the other. Crash, crash, crash, with each new proposition.

Arse.

But there had been something else, hadn't there? True, she had been trying to draw out another kind of mission. One that would better suit her own purposes. And she had paid for that casual calculation. But there had also been this:

She had to know.

In the end, it had been that too. She had to know. Given where she had been, what she had seen, on her nine executive commissions, would they allow her to live? Even a while? Even through one more mission?

She hummed aloud, thinking, low and ominous.

This changed things. But one thing remained. She still had to get back. Regardless of anything else. She still had to get back to Amazon Seven. She clenched her jaw and, at that thought, looked up, unconsciously, to the stars. To the familiar constellations of the Southern Hemisphere, her shoulders tense, like marble all of a sudden, unsurprised at how her body had reacted to the realization, how instantly tense she had become.

Think it through, she told herself. There may still be a way out of this without bloodshed.

The party. The party had been ordinary, just a few hours of her routine, the stuff she did to appear normal each time she returned to Earth. The kind she could attend without an invite and find people who would be pleased to see her. Not friends especially, but people she knew who could be relied upon to be entertained by her presence, her stories, her notoriety.

Colonel Commander Astra Solara.

Earth's current 'Mission Queen'.

So she had attended, waited it out. She had listened politely with formalized interest to the propositions. She had chit-chatted. That was okay. She could chit-chat. All simple and pleasant enough.

But it had also been a trap.

Her one advantage was that she had remained afterwards, here, now, like this.

Disconnected.

You didn't hear that much anymore. It was a bit like those other words you never heard any more.

Online. Internet. Technology, even.

It was all invisible and ever-present now. But she could *just* recall when there had been screens like walls, even devices people carried in their pockets, in their bags. God, remember when people had *bags*? You wouldn't even question it now. 'Is the electricity working? Is it on?' She laughed to herself. She had friends who still did, coming to think of it. Carried things, in bags and pockets. Eccentrics!

Then there was Hylar of course. Poor Hylar. Goddess, she missed her.

Karmada was an excellent pilot. Nice girl, good shot, good company. But these next two missions… should they still be viable… there was no-one like Hylar Moondarla.

But in the end, after all was said and done, she *was* Astra Solara.

She had come this far without anybody knowing. Not even her executive crew. She'd shared secrets, and they had all been through… what they'd all been through. But not even Hylar or Swish or Galilea had known everything. Not Spar, not Indigo… maybe Zoe and Tiger had an idea that there was something bigger, but even Chens could not get every secret out of her, and she'd found out about the shorgs.

Maybe the elites were *right* to be afraid of her. But she had been careful to subvert all that. She was sure that they didn't know where she'd truly been, what she'd actually done on their ridiculous spy missions. They suspected nothing that was real, or concrete. This was pure ruling paranoia; they were afraid of the kind of thing someone like her, who had seen what she had seen, might have truly done, or become, and then do. Presumably do now, when she was back. Therefore now was the time to strike, when she was unsuspecting, before it was too late.

Well, so be it then.

Now all she had to do was wait, survive the inevitable assassination attempt, and then complain, vigorously and righteously, at the insult. The main thing was; she had to survive, and that in turn meant; it was now all about who they sent. Because once Astra knew who they'd sent, she would know who *they* were. And once she knew that, she would know if there was any chance of getting back on track. Of mission ten, mission eleven. Maybe a chance of just one. One last assignment with the weight of Earth behind her.

She sat up fully now, feeling the fury build in her.

Damn, she did not want to do this tonight.

Damn and arse and spit.

It was *nice* here.

It was *nice* to be here, and disconnected.

But what would they do?

Well, first, they would assume that she had gone home. Around three with the rest of the guests. Maybe with Trigrick. She hadn't thought of that. Maybe his sexual advance had been a suggestion that he accompany her, for safety. But Trigrick would not know who they would send. His coldness had been a cover. He was actually just being nice. A friend, a suitor, a potential…

The cat smashed another glass, having been staring at this one a good two minutes before snapping and swiping her tiny paw. Now there was a long trail of glass shards, and fragments along the wood beneath the table edge.

They would monitor her, or try, and realize she was disconnected. She wondered how many other people who were as connected as her could disconnect themselves, could manage it for this long. There would be some, sure. Like her; Independents. All for their own different reasons. But most people today would go insane with their own thoughts, or lack of them, in under five minutes. That sounded like a joke, as Swish would say, 'a flip glibbance'. The arbitrary five minutes. But no. Five would do it for most. But not Astra, and she was glad of it.

Hmmm. So, they would assume she had slinked away, on some nefarious mission. They would always suspect, always be paranoid. By the time someone suggested that maybe she hadn't left the party, or at least the location of where the party had been, she would have had time to sit here and think things through, mill through her offers and hope that someone approached with another. The one she wanted.

That was what she had wanted.

She had not wanted to be sitting here, getting ready to maybe die.

Maybe.

Probably not.

Perhaps.

She listened to the sounds of the night. Insects whose sounds were familiar but which she didn't know. She could connect and know, but she didn't want to. She had been raised in the south but out east, here, there was something pleasant, almost normal, about hearing the sounds of the creatures she knew but could not name. Naming them would have made it all somehow more concrete, scientific and real, whereas this connection to her childhood was better.

The grass told her that someone was approaching.

Just like that. When it happened, it was just a whisper, like that.

She might have heard it anyway, just with her disconnected ears. Just knowing the night, the Australian night and knowing what soft footsteps across a dry lawn sounded like. If she had, she might have disregarded it. A primal throwback. But not with the whisper. The whisper had been right before.

The long table creaked, returning her attention to the cat. She had been padding her slow chocolate path of deliberate destruction down the edge of the huge, heavy, dark wood table, toward another cluster of wine glasses, but now she had frozen. She was staring down, out across the lawn.

The assassin was definitely coming up the lawn.

Another would come through the homestead.

She ran her gaze quickly over the rustic doors and bluestone walls of the elite weekend party venue. Except, it was no longer a venue now. It was a battleground. The doors, the bluestone walls, the table, were not rustic anymore; they were here and now, present in her immediate reality, representing hard options; access, cover, defence, weaponry, even flight.

Which first?

Lawn or door?

She looked up, on instinct, feeling the tension in her shoulder and neck, and saw some of the stars blacken, then return, as something silent passed overhead.

Stealth artillery?

Would it land?

Would that be part of it?

The lighting over the gardens was still mood-oriented for the party. The lawn was dark so the pool house would stand out. It was so quiet, and the soft crunching came again.

Someone familiar from the party, pretending to be pleased to see her. Oh, are you still here? I thought everyone had gone? Penny for your *bullet between the eyes* –

Maybe.

No whisper this time.

Ears.

Audible, even twenty feet down and thirty out. She heard the approach stop suddenly. Like someone had come here to check. Maybe she'd never left the party? And now they were somewhat stunned to find their assumption correct.

Jesus. There she was. Still sitting up there on the balcony patio. She's been here the whole time!

It was laughable. They were so lax and unimaginative, all of them. All she had to do was disconnect, and the surveillance, the nanostreams, even the drones and satellites, were dumbfounded. But now this lackey had eyeballed her. He would relay coordinates and they would zero in.

'Colonel Commander Solara?'

A man's voice. Calling up. She estimated thirty meters. All she had to do was reconnect and find out who he was.

'I'm having a think.'

She was thinking; am I really going to have to fight someone, now? Here and now on the balcony of some three hundred-year-old, restored colonial convention centre?

How fucking ridiculous.

'Colonel Commander, I need you to re-engage so I can receive confirmation.'

'Shall I come down and give you visual?'

She hadn't meant for the tone of implied threat to sneak out.

'No Colonel Commander, that's okay, I'll come up.' He was deliberately lurking in the middle of the balcony's long shadow. 'Is there a way up from here?'

Astra frowned. What the man had just said. It was like admitting he had no surveillance here. Like an outright confession that he had come to kill her and somewhere central they had granted permission to cease monitoring, so she could be assassinated with impunity.

She'd only been off-world nine months this time but sometimes things changed very quickly. Maybe this was how things were done now? No. But, still, surely… maybe they assumed, because she had disconnected, that she was…

Oh God. Oh *Goddess*. That was it. The pause in accepting – they had assumed that she *did need to know*. They thought she was making a challenge, even sacrificing herself, falling on her sword. She saw it now. Refusing, essentially, every commission. Disconnecting, and sitting and waiting. It must have seemed… like an open invitation… to come and…

She stood and went to the edge of the balcony. The cat watched as she called down.

'Soldier?'

He wasn't there. There were doors down there, off the lawn, and internal stairwells straight up to the balcony exits behind her. Right through there was a double floor hall, wood and glass windows, the lower exit leading out to a street and a sacred park. It was four in the morning on a weeknight. A Tuesday night, Wednesday morning. Out here, away from the city centre, there would be no witnesses. It was so perfect that she really, really, could have planned it for herself this way. It would be told as a tale of depression, resignation, made to look like suicide. Maybe they really thought she wanted it this way. Whether they did or not, that's how it would look to anyone in the know. How it would be explained, more or less, to the gen-pop.

'Influenza...' she cursed.

Some very quick processing, Astra. He won't be expecting a fight, he will be expecting ritual self-sacrifice. But he won't be a junior. No ambitious kid sent to deliver an ambitious bullet to her head. It would be someone who would fight her, make it look good. But certainly someone who they believed could and would ultimately kill her. Someone older, harder, enhanced. Not a veteran. But the best they had. That's who they'd send. After all, she might change her mind half way. People did, people had.

But then again, this was *not* ritual sacrifice, and she would not be allowed to 'change her mind' half way.

There was even a code for that process, for veterans who wanted to be taken out, and had made it known. Who'd sat as she had, and waited, but changed their mind half way through the fight. She'd heard old 'Elephant Balls' Van Der Wilde had made his wishes known for a 'retirement with prejudice' three times, and three times had backed out. Not before a massive brawl with his assassin, of course, but the ritual death blow had never been delivered. Some said that he had just wanted to feel alive again, or indeed to *know* that he still wanted to be alive. Some swore the third one had been for real, but he had unintentionally beaten his would-be assassin. In the end though he had recommissioned himself and been killed three weeks later in the Jupiter Cage after Civil War 14.5.

But this wasn't that, Astra grimaced tightly to herself.

No, they wanted her dead and they were using such old fools as a precedent.

Arses!

She was twenty-eight-thirty-eight, highly skilled and desirable, a specialist reaching her peak, in constant demand, and close to retiring a billionaire. What the hell story would they sell the plebs…?

It would have to be depression.

Mental illness. Nothing else would resonate…

The man came through the third door, twisting the classic door handle and closing the heavy wood behind him, the six neat glass rectangles reverberating a little as the solid latch clicked into place. Astra was just old enough to remember when they were still around, proper door handles. Not commonplace, but not unusual.

Gorgeous though.

It would be good to get some made up for –

'Colonel Commander.'

'Special Agent?'

The man smiled calmly.

'Special Agent, retirement with extreme prejudice is not my intent. I want to make that clear to you. My actions tonight may have been misinterpreted.'

'There's no way you could have known I was coming across that lawn, Colonel Commander.'

Astra snorted a short, harsh breath.

He was fully hanced up.

'They say you've been to Amazon Seven, Colonel Commander. Did you pick it up there?'

'How did you know I knew? No veil here. You announced yourself.'

The man tapped his temple. 'New. Detects micro-expressions and micro-movements.'

'That's a decade ago.'

'From fifty feet.'

She shrugged. 'Okay.' Have to get me some of that.

'You shifted like you knew someone was approaching – from the direction I was coming from. I know you're disco; and they say some people who've been to The Bark come back psychic.'

'Not completely mad?'

'Barking Mad. And psychic. Which is why you want to be taken out. Mental problems. Consciousness confusion. Not the first, won't be the last.'

'What if I have second thoughts? You know the safe word?'

'There isn't one. Not for you.'

So she was right.

'Retirement with prejudice.'

'Extreme prejudice. They told me you're almost there anyway. Pushing your luck. One more Indie mission. That's a suicide run. You want to go.'

'I do?'

'Come on. You know you want it.'

Oh, God, she hated him for that.

But things had gone her way. Her navy uniform jacket hung over the back of her vigil chair. She'd worn it closed all night, over the tightly fitted black tank top, but had removed it once she'd been alone, as the evening heat had closed in, and the humidity has risen. Her Hungarian-descended mother had been born with skin like rich honey, but her Irish father was pale as a ghost. Her father's genes had essentially won but her mother's genes meant that her pale pink skin possessed a light caramel undertone, especially when the temperature was high or she was emotionally charged. Right now, with her adrenalin firing, and the light coat of perspiration from the humidity, her skin flushed with that caramel. She was reflecting softly, almost glowing in the moonlight. Between the long black lines of her low shoulder straps, her upper chest was fully exposed. Above and directly between the lines of her cleavage, the decade-old scar, the star-shaped bullet wound from a time long gone, that had healed clean white against her pink, honey-tinged skin, would look like a shining desert comet.

Three assassins before this one had gone for that target, her 'shooting star'.

Astra tensed. The black tank was complimented by the loose slacks tucked into the soft boots she preferred for pro-socializing. The boots were knee length and looked hard, commandeering, but were weightless and breathed like cheesecloth. She'd picked them up on Mission Four, her first as an Indie. Scouting the deep ranges on the high continent of Goldilocks 445. Still looked brand new. Didn't make them anymore. Everyone was dead now. Just another reason.

'You don't seem to be concerned…' the assassin accused calmly. 'You appeared even to be…' the assassin consulted his data. '… reminiscing, then…'

She gave him a melancholy smile. 'A last remembrance. Seems I'll die with these boots on. I like these boots. I try to bring back something from every mission. Not just the executive missions. I was on the *Rosetta* five years, after all. Many memories.'

The pistol was in his hand so fast it must have already been there. A nano-grip in his palm, assembling with the gesture, with his arm rising to fire. Old school – interesting. Taken out with a traditional gun, one noble shot. And yes, he had gone for the shooting star, a poetic move, as though to finish the job that had always meant to seal her fate.

Just as the three before him had thought.

Not a bullet though, a pulse.

She saw the look in his eye.

Goddess, he was one of those. Pulse to blow her away, flatten her. Then what? Did it matter if she was alive? A blast to the heart like that, an impact to the chest and pulsing out would usually kill. Rearrange the heart and lungs, pulverise ribs. Then he would abuse her dying body, or her corpse, whichever came first. One of those.

There had been several varieties of interspecies predators identified this century. Of all of them, the so-called 'hosap', the homicidal sadistic psychopath, was the one for which she had the least compassion. This human excrement had chosen this life because he enjoyed it. He'd become an assassin not to make a difference, not for patriotism or pride. He did not believe he was in the right, and even if he did, it didn't make a difference. Nor was he in the killing trade for simple pragmatism; one who had resigned himself to having a specific skill for which there was a specific task that, well, *someone had to do*, and given that, mechanically, he was naturally the best at it… it might as well be him. Many of that kind found a holy purpose in their God-given talent. But no, this one was not even the kind of assassin whose skill, whose focus, led him to locate his Zen, or spiritual centre, that would allow him to define and refine and maybe even one day embody his pursuit of excellence. No, this one did it purely because he enjoyed killing, because becoming an assassin had been an ideal cover for his sadistic tendencies.

She absorbed the blast. The assassin flinched and recovered, thrusting out a quarterstaff, again nano-expansion, again from a pre-held grip, this time in his left hand. She stepped back and to the side. The flat point glanced off her glistening shoulder blade as though she were encased in shining silver medieval armour and rebounded forward and upward. He'd extended the staff ridiculously long in order to reach her but now he swung it backwards, in a fierce arc, putting everything into it, a fast one-eighty, turning his back to her momentarily. He was hoping to use that, her surprise at the unexpected move, and to capitalize on it by catching her off-guard again. That was important, Astra knew; never to invest in one's own momentary incorrectness. It stopped you thinking, prevented the unconscious flow of momentum. But she had seen it coming micro-seconds in advance and was already down as the quarterstaff slashed over her head.

The assassin paused in a defensive stance, the staff diagonal to his body, aware she had not yet struck. He had seen too many movies, was too keen to strike a pose, but he had skill. Maybe he was sensing that she moved a little more quickly that she should. But primarily, he would be wondering how she had shielded or deflected the blaster shot, and the staff strike, without her tech enabled.

In the back of his mind, knowing she hadn't.

That she had absorbed the shot, and the strike – somehow.

Within nano, without being connected.

He cried out.

'Farraway!'

Three blaster shots took her down. Her head jolted backwards from a kill shot between the eyes and jerked her whole body savagely into a backwards somersault. Then a second shot impacted immediately upon her chest, the shooting star target again, punching her fully backwards. A third, for good measure, hit beneath her left breast. She let her knees give out, and her torso was momentarily parallel to the patio tiles.

Feigning.

Her arms arced backwards and she used the momentum to properly somersault away, three times, with several more shots missing her. She couldn't pretend it didn't sting like a motherfucker, but then she was upright again. Two more shots hit her; left upper chest, right upper chest, over the straps of her black tank top. What the…? Was he trying to burn them off…? And see her boobs..? Little perv! But she was braced and just took them. Then the first assassin shouted.

'Farraway stop!'

In the beat it took them to realize she was not dead, that she was not going to die, not this way, she had stepped forward and to the left. Then she had her jacket off the back of the chair, and swirled it back on.

The first assassin stared across the patio at her as she buttoned up.

'What tech is that? You're disconnected.'

She tried not to smile as she straightened her jacket lapels with a stiff yank.

'Oh right.' The assassin smiled openly at her silence. It's… from there. Or another one of your infamous trips. Am I right?'

He wasn't young but he wasn't greatly experienced. He'd expected an easy kill from someone wanting to die; and this wasn't that. Maybe he'd expected someone who might put up a fight, to make it look good, a real performance; this wasn't that, either. No easy swansong for the assassin this time out. He gave a little sneer.

'…one of the things you like to bring back. From one of your missions…'

'Soldier…' Astra began.

'Discrip.'

'Agent Discrip…' She didn't bother looking up to the roof. 'Agent Farraway… just to be *terminally* clear; I am not asking to be taken out. In case that's what's genuinely happening. Is there any surveillance at all? Any comms you can use to get back to a superior? Update and request countermand?'

'Sorry.' Discrip couldn't have cared less. 'Like I said; REP. Not the way it works.'

'Farraway…' She needed to make this sound very authoritative. '…if you're listening to this, I haven't made visual recognition. Just a name. Farraway. Could be one of a dozen agents. I don't have to kill you.'

That was meaningless but she was hoping Farraway would rationalize it with his or her own internal logic. Threats worked best when people were left to fill in their own gaps. She listened. The first shots had been fired from almost directly ahead of her, somewhere high up in the tree line of tall gums that stretched above the homestead from the sacred park. Farraway had jumped forward, maybe thirty feet, directly on to the homestead roof for the second round. He or she was up there. Astra kept listening. Then she heard a slight click, heard the power pack intensify, the frequency lowering, preparing for a hotter, denser charge.

It sounded like the low hum of disapproval from a determinedly homicidal bully.

She'd heard both sounds before, enough to make the comparison.

Then something else.

The trees.

When it happened, it was just a whisper…

They told her to look up.

She looked up.

She knew what the flash was, in the sky.

She dropped to one knee.

If she moved now she could outrun it, but it meant going through –

The patio exploded behind her as the gunship blasted down. She launched up, her hands swirling from the sides of her boots. There had been just those few seconds, as the guns had fired down, to run out of their predictable fire pattern. Discrip squealed as she killed him with two dagger blows, two flicks, one from each wrist, up from the soft boots, striking hard, one each through his ribs. He had a micro-second to be stunned then fell backwards, her soft boots on his chest, gone from this life. Then the real bullets from above splattered his body across the patio and down through the holes they made in the balcony floor, on to the grass below.

Astra had the momentum, the adrenalin, and jumped high through the door, through the traditional window panel, took cuts from both timber and glass, and was inside now. The colonial restoration was doomed. She hated that. She was going to save her own life at the expense of a building that had stood three hundred years, since the First Fleet probably.

The gunship fired in a direct line, straight down into the homestead toward the closest front exit; the fasted route to the street and the park. The roof came crashing down as the projectiles shattered through the feeble corrugated iron, in shards of twisted metal and wooden rafters, smashing into the stone floor with tiny, molten, golf-ball craters. But Astra had veered sharply left, heading further into the homestead, choosing the least viable escape route. Sure enough, the gunship blasts turned right, turned further into the two-storey hall almost fully opening the building to the balmy night's heat, and the Milky Way.

She went deeper, then outward, toward where the northern side-wall faced the steep hillside. Behind her, several rooms back now, the gunship was still demolishing the hall roof for a cleaner heat signature and would soon realize she had temporarily outwitted them. She was hoping to find what she would expect from such a building, from an old homestead. She was hoping that she was not kidding herself; that she remembered the door being there, from years ago, when she'd realized she would potentially be here a lot, that pilots and agents and execs and whoever else was tied up in her game liked to be here. One never knew what kind of trouble any one of them would bring, so she had cased the joint for just such an occasion, thinking of a quick exit if anything ever went down. She'd never really, seriously considered that the thing going down would be her.

Then; there. There it was; a private office to the side of the house, a plain internal door.

The sound of the gunship's demolition remained clear, crude and ruinous behind her.

She grasped, twisted the handle and entered.

Unlocked. She didn't like that.

She was in though; the edge of the house against the hill, defensible, bay doors leading out to a much smaller private balcony. Any early settler would have a safe here, where he or any number of nefarious contacts could abscond up or down the hillside under cover of night, obscured by foliage. Basic privateer thinking.

There was even a proper, modern desk; this room must still have been used by the manager of the…

Trigrick was dead at the desk.

His brains blown out across the wall behind him.

His mouth still gaping open in shock, gun in hand, in lap.

She hadn't realized that she could have, one day, loved Trigrick, properly loved him, until she had seen him murdered.

She realized very quickly however that it was supposed to look like suicide and he would be the motive or blame or excuse for all this, whatever. Her body, his body, found together in the ruins.

Fill in the gaps.

Terrible sounds of blasting, crunching and tumbling behind her.

Her heart stung for Trigrick and the adrenalin of the emotional pain spurred her out of the side exit, onto the small balcony. There was an emergency stairwell down to the valley floor, but to descend it was to reveal herself at length in the open and then her heat signature would have been clear. She leaped and hoped for the best, hoping to hit the side of the hill and allow the treetops there to disguise her thermal image, just long enough for them to allow her to…

She hit the hillside hard in the dark, her legs at a wrong angle, as the whole central hall section of the homestead collapsed behind her; the entire central back wall along with the main patio balcony, almost fully intact. Astounded at the sight, but still in flight mode, Astra took advantage and ran toward it, chasing the ruined structure down the hillside as the massive chunk of decimated homestead pounded down on to the lawn then rolled, pulverising itself as it turned and turned again, a giant crate with no sides, advancing down the slope toward the pool house. As Astra caught up with it, the tumbling wreckage lost momentum and rolled just twice more, and almost three times, before it stopped, still almost fully intact, then abruptly fell completely to bits under its own weight, its damaged structure now fully gone. Astra scampered down the tree line, through the low undergrowth, beside the lawn and the fresh, still creaking, dust-plumed wreckage, even as it continued groaning and cracking and falling apart.

The drop from the office had been short but sharp. Her right knee hurt but was okay. Just a weird angle of impact in the dark. There was dust in the air and creaking in her ears and the sharp, fresh smell of old broken wood, and just-snapped timber. There was soil everywhere, giant chunks all over the place where the house had collided with the grass and ground. She passed at the other side of the upturned, ruined homestead and there before her was the balcony patio, still breaking apart down the valley slope, chairs and tables and bits of doors and windows and wood…

She kept close to the base of the incline until she had no choice, running right down along the edge of the lawn toward the pool.

The gunship was definitely going by its own infra-red, not satellite, or she would have been under fire again by now. Astra was still alive but for her assailants everything had gone very badly wrong. She was supposed to be dead, shot outside on the balcony patio with her killer suiciding in the next room. That had been Plan A. Plan B, they had both been killed by a sniper assassin. This had also fucked up. C; the amped-up version of B, was failing even as she was almost at the pool house and D was; had to be…

One last shot.

Pulverize everything.

Some kind of terror bomb thing, some kind of rival agency or government…

She didn't care, it didn't matter.

The world was very conditioned, the military especially so. She could rely upon them to rely upon their training. Knowing this, and acting quickly, on instinct, had bought her time. She had not run out, across the street and into the park, which was what almost anyone else would have done. But they would know that now, and search for her heat signature in the ruins. It would not have occurred to them until step three, or four maybe, which would be around this very second, that she had taken a wild chance and headed deeper into the active demolishment.

The restored Edwardian glass-walled pool house had retractable nano-glass. If she were connected, she could slide through it. She had nanotech for that, from Mission Five. But if she were to reconnect, they would find her instantly. If she'd remained connected after the party she might even have been dead by now.

Disco.

Disconnected.

Dead to them, essentially.

Undetectable.

'Mission Queen' Astra Solara's thirty-eight years of life included twenty-four years of almost continuous experience on assignment for Earth's current corporate coalition government, and was contained within the body that was genquivalently twenty-eight years old, maintained to a level of health and fitness of which she was justifiably proud. Astra jumped with this body at the glass. This body that contained all her secrets, all her tech, all her nano, all her bio, and all the covertly-collected enhancements that were her now, all her, who she was. Not corplex tech or bitex enhancements or pharmie medstallments; sure, she had some of that, she had tech and nano and even meds. But none of that counted, or meant anything to her. It was professional, it was cover. The important stuff, she had collected and built and maintained and hidden and deployed without being noticed, all these years, mission by mission. It was the stuff nobody even knew to look for. Mission after mission, the Mission Queen with just two more pieces to go...

It was the stuff they were right to be afraid of. The stuff that had made her, on some stupid, egocentric, self-sabotaging, self-aggrandizing level, need to know; could they take her?

You bloody idiot, Astra!

It could all be lost now. Lost forever if she hit the glass the wrong way, or mistimed...

She jumped, propelled by the sprint down the incline base, furious at herself, launching with tremendous momentum.

She should have accepted one, any of the missions, tonight, then and there. Played the role of the suicidal Indie CC, the Mad Queen, as she'd been mastering for a decade now. But she was close, so close, and she'd relaxed. And now she was leaping and trying to turn her back to the glass, and the back of her head curled down and *pulse* she let go of one of the shots she'd absorbed. The glass shattered and she went through the gap, and the remains of the glass, hitting the concrete on the side of the pool, eased slightly by the coat of non-slip rubber matting, but still tumbling through the shatter-glass crystals. Then she rolled into the water and was under with more of a plop than a splash, the water already pluming red with her blood.

Astra was hardly ever disorientated. But more sounds, and more strange movement in the water, made her think for a second that there was something she had missed completely.

Then the long patio bench spiralled through the shattered facing wall and into the water and she realized that the contents of the patio balcony were this second being upturned into the ruined pool house, with a last rolling collapse of the demolished structure outside.

For a fraction of a second she realized that there was, there *absolutely was* something else alive in the pool, in the water above her, struggling.

The chocolate cat was there, drowning, with a damaged paw.

Then, she realized she could see the drain, her escape, through the descending debris.

She could fit.

She would make that work.

That had been the ideal; the backup had been to hide in the woods somehow. To run now, and sneak off later... but she saw, instead, now, that she could actually evade the gunship and *escape...*

She pushed out with one hand and pulsed the inner pool wall with almost all of what remained of the absorbed blaster energy, simultaneously grasping up at the scruff of the cat at the very moment the little chocolate feline had surrendered to the fact she was no longer able to keep her head above water. She struggled for a second with being pulled under, but Astra's arm yanked her down with such force that she did not even have the feline wherewithal to struggle, truly struggle, with fang and claw. Then the startled cat was staring right out at her, eye to eye, suddenly and brutally dragged down, upside down, and submerged.

Just a massive chocolate mane, with big green eyes, in shock.

Just doing her best to survive.

It was like looking into a mirror.

Behind the filter was a drain and it sucked Astra down, then carried her with great force. She had not reckoned upon a natural, rocky slide, and she was right. VyTel had improved upon nature and turned the natural rock tunnel from the underground creek into a storm drain. The initial volume of water that punched out with her settled, then she was sliding through the slime and rushing darkness, clutching a lifeless lump of fur, praying that, at this speed, there would be no bumps, and that she would not strike her head anywhere.

After enough time to make her seriously consider that she had been killed and that this was some hellish portal to a dark dimension, there was sudden illumination and she was airborne, flying out of the circular end of a high storm drain, and into the lake with what she realized was shocking, potentially fatal speed.

But they would have worked it out, surely?

VyTel would have had this in mind, as an escape route?

It would never have been engineered with terminal velocity –

She balled up with the drowned cat in her lap and slapped into the glistening lake surface, buttocks and back, and the backs of her thighs, and took the bum-flop like a trooper. Then she was under, but okay. It was nothing more than a theme park ride. The darkness and the adrenalin had edged up her anxiety, her pessimism a little more than she liked, even up to full panic, but she was kicking now and could see the surface.

With her steel grip still around the chocolate scruff, she broke the surface, ripping the cat corpse up with her like some ancient treasure, found triumphant, arm held high. Then she shook her hair off her face, and the water out of her eyes, and she tried to swim with the corpse in her hand but realized she couldn't, she just couldn't.

'No!'

Her heart ached.

Up the hill she could see the gun ship now, still searching the ruins, now with a spotlight.

Still, she didn't have forever, as she struggled on.

The cat was totally limp, but she wouldn't let go.

Despite everything, the little chocolate terror had kept kicking and trying to keep her little brown head above water. Even when her lungs were clearly filling, her little brain –

Astra's boot hit ground, and she felt a slimy incline beneath; rocks and weeds, and tall, creepy algae brushing the calves of her pants, and she was coming up a steep underwater bank, the cat still high in her hand, still above water. As soon as she was stable, Astra looked at her, human face to feline face mirrored again, but right side up this time. She tightened her grip and with her other hand, her feet steady, the water at her waist now, zapped the sagging little thing on the chest with the last of the absorbed pulse-gun energy.

The cat spasmed, coughed up water through her tiny fangs, and bared them wholly as she screeched, then wailed like a banshee. But Astra had her, and she wouldn't let go.

She plodded on, up the bank, to the lake shore. The incline hid her from the gunship. She put the cat down. The thing that now looked like a giant brown mop-head tried to run off, but limped, her front right paw taking no weight at all, and made no progress across the rocky terrain. Astra quickly approached and the cat fell upon her back, swiping up with her good paw and cartwheeling her hind legs, hissing like a fiend.

Astra leaned down and in, as close to the cat's face as she could get without copping a claw to her lip, and stared again into the wide green feline eyes, as they in turn stared back, up at her saviour with complete hostility.

She found the place in her consciousness from Mission Two.

In quick succession, she made her eyes convey; safe, then, tired, then, nest, then, sleep.

The chocolate cat went limp on the rocks.

Astra picked her up again, gently, cradling.

As she moved away, she found that she had begun to cry for the man she had loved only at his death, and this she added to the reasons she was going through all this crap in the first place. Her secret mission to rid the galaxy of… evil, she supposed.

It hadn't started out as that, had it?

It had started out as…

She couldn't remember.

In her mind, now the cat was safe, all she could see was Trigrick's gaping, open-mouthed shock.

But then, as usual, there was no time for any of that.

There was never, had never, been any time for any of that, not really.

Especially not when she was bleeding to death, dripping crimson all over the rocks at her feet, from a dozen different glass cuts all over her stupid body.

CHAPTER TWO

Wild animals were no good.

Domesticated, trained, even some halfway animals that had come across people and had an understanding of interaction with the human species, they were okay.

…and drunks. It worked on drunks.

Swipe was still asleep.

Bloody hell.

Now she'd gone and named the fucking thing!

What if it died!?

Astra trudged on, then stopped and took off her jacket, then her tank top. Which felt weird for a few seconds, for the short time she was topless in the moonlight in the middle-of-the-night forest. Then it felt good, in some primal, maybe even mystical, Sacred Goddess way, as she fashioned the tight, sturdy material into a little sling, replaced her jacket, and placed the cat back to her now virtually, wholly unsupported bosom.

So the thing to do now was… what?

Not die.

Get somewhere.

Somewhere normal, and reconnect. Pretend she hadn't been there, at the demolished homestead, claim she'd left with everyone else at three in the morning, and see who tried to kill her again. Accept a mission ASAP, bide a little time, then change the mission to something that could actually work for her overall plan, and then get the fuck off Planet Earth again, never to return.

So to speak.

Or, maybe for keeps.

Hard to know now…

But then, they would be planning by now, now it was obvious she'd escaped, how to set her up for Trigrick's murder. Three corpses back there; those wankers Discrip and Farraway as well. VyTel? Didn't matter. They were all the same at this level. It was only higher up there was any real difference or true competition.

She sighed and looked around.

She kind of knew where she was.

But she had nothing around here.

Not even from the old days.

No safe houses, no contacts, not even paid helpers.

So far as she was aware there were none of the remaining Hightailers on Earth. Aside from those that would still talk to her, she had off-world friends, from various missions going back years; good ex-crew or sometime comrades, even some mercs who would help her in a jam, but there was no way to connect with them. Even if they were on Earth, even in Australia, not disco. She needed patching, for sure, but she would last another few hours before the blood loss went to her head. Or rather, from her head. She still had time to think. Maybe to even… get somewhere?

Swipe stirred, rolled in her sling. Now, more a hammock.

This was essentially a rocky plain, with sporadic outcrops of stringy bark eucalyptus, and stretches of wattle in between. Dry ground then jagged outcrops, out of nowhere. Australia, The Bush, You're Welcome.

…she was… somewhere at the edge of the eastern part of the Blue Mountains.

If she could reconnect, it would be a gamble, but worth the risk if she could contact someone reliable. But it would have to be almost instantly… someone close who could get here quickly, before VyTel security, or the local cops, or whoever, and get her to some kind of private transport. Or even better, a launch station.

If she'd known that this would happen, she would have seen the flaw in her plan. She would have seen that not accepting a commission immediately would arouse instant paranoia, and she would have planned for backup. Had someone on Earth? Why hadn't she seen that? Because she was getting arrogant, and lazy. She was starting to rely too much on their conformity, their routines, their predictability, but forgetting that they could be equally as relied upon to act swiftly when detecting danger, or irregularity; especially when responding to someone who had the potential to create instability, and threaten the system upon which the comfort of their conformity totally relied.

Right now, their analysts, their corporate minds, their AIs and their data mine projectors, would be assessing her, creating likely outcomes and deliberating. This one could be trouble, they would have determined, years ago. Not 'is' trouble, not yet. Just – could be. They would have had it all ready; her profiles, her mission reports, her surveillance. Now the machine was just running the scenario.

Stupid, stupid, at this late stage, to allow, at the party with her caramel sheen and cleavage, and the people's attention, even without drugging, just that little bit of play. Just that little bit of improvisation, outside of the script she'd written herself, for herself, and knew, by heart. Just that untamed snarl of extra ego, that slice of boosted self-esteem, and *ping*.

The data says; if this one is trouble, she will be too much trouble.

Take any excuse, take her out. Now.

But damn she had looked good last night. Felt good, been good. Been on. Been herself, her most positive, crystal, laser-sighted self.

Bloody, bloody.

And less bloody; losing it, to be chastising herself like –

'If I wanted to kill you I could have!'

The voice came through the trees.

She'd been so deep in her pathetic thoughts it startled her to the point of stumbling.

'I'm sorry; but you're fleeing randomly! It's the last thing our forecasters expect! Once we realized what was happening at the homestead we came looking!'

Astra clutched her sleeping chocolate cat.

'We?'

'Royal we! Just me; I have a car! You're coming up to a road, about fifteen meters that way. You nearly crossed it about ten minutes ago, but veered. With the randomness and all.'

'How did I…?'

'It's night, it's the country.'

'I've lost more blood that I thought.'

'We know.'

'I have a cat…'

'Nothing will happen to you, or the cat.'

'Nothing?'

'Nothing you will mind.'

'Who are you?'

'We are your next mission, Colonel Commander Solara. We hope.'

Astra felt her knees go weak.

'Well…' Her throat was very dry as she gulped. '…we can all hope.'

CHAPTER THREE

Astra woke on her back, which she didn't like. It made her feel vulnerable, inevitably meant one side of her neck would be sore once she moved, and there was always the possibility she had been snoring.

It was a sun bed, and she was facing the sunrise. The balcony windows were solar shield tinted, so one could stare out at it, at length, without consequence. White-gold, over the ocean, like something out of eastern mysticism. Sheer holy light. She did stare for a while, high as a kite but even and still as a midnight pond, for perhaps twenty minutes. She didn't try to move. She just accepted that rescue had come, and had transported her to comfort.

Slowly she began to feel where the cuts had been healed. A bit raw, a bit itchy. A good fix, but a quick fix, which always left temporary irritation. So they would make her an offer, brief her, and expect her to be moving on, before long.

She saw that Swipe was curled up, asleep in an outdoor armchair beside the sun bed.

'Cat…?' Astra heard herself ask. 'Swipe?'

Swipe looked up and locked brilliant green eyes with her then returned her tiny square jaw to the fabric and closed them once again. So Swipe was okay.

Astra tried to move and found that she was able to; that she was unrestrained. The drugs were wearing off.

The greatest pain came from the developing bruise under her breast, where the idiot sniper whose name she had already forgotten – no, she hadn't, his name had been Agent Farraway – had landed his third shot.

Over that sore under-boob was her black tank, washed and restored. Would they find the knives in Discrip's corpse? Would they find Discrip's corpse at all? She sat up, and checked. She still had them, down the sides of her fantastically comfortable boots. She'd slipped them back, running, as it were, on instinct.

She hadn't come out with much else.

A door slid open behind her.

'Hello?'

It was the same voice.

'I'm here...' Astra croaked, then quickly cleared her throat. '...I'm awake...'

The man walked up from behind her and stood in front of the sun bed, blocking the sun. He was human, and real, but massively augmented. His features were too slick, too pleasant, with too much sheen. But then, she was supposed to see that. He was what people expected here; a polished assistant to...

Whoever owned the view.

'Yes, I can see what you must be thinking. Which is why we like you. Very few think these days, and of those who do, even fewer dare to dismiss the first thought as misdirection. Fewer still dismiss the second as sleight of hand. Hardly anyone proceeds to thought three or thought four, or wonders who pays the man who writes the scripts for The Man Behind the Curtain, who arranges steps one and two and obfuscates steps three and four.'

'You like the sound of your own voice. I bet your name is something.'

'Something.' The assistant chuckled, considering. 'Hello.' He feigned a greasy welcoming smile and extended his hand, his body suddenly like a stiff Tin Man, for a rigid shake. 'I'm Something.'

They smiled at each other.

'Actually, if we're being honest, my name is Version.'

She tried not to smirk.

'I'm Astra. This is Swipe.'

Version seemed to appreciate that she had tried.

Now there was a further tenuous trust between them.

'My employer was pleased to see the animal survived. It seemed like fate. The gunship was not authorised to destroy the homestead, so we hear. They had plans to detonate the entire grounds, but they were prevented from doing so by forces higher up the chain at the last second. You and your puss would not have been harmed. Your escape, your thinking, your chances and risks and instincts, were all we have come to expect from the reports of your exploits; those that we have managed to acquire.'

'Acquire? From where? You *can* see what I'm thinking…?'

'No, not like that. We have been watching you a while. We like to think that we can see your psyche play out, we like to try and think, what will she do next? We are sometimes correct and always pleasantly surprised.'

'How long?'

'A year or two. Would you like a drink? Blood restoration techniques can be paradoxically dehydrating, can they not?'

She stared at him.

'Coke in a can thanks. No glass.'

There was something she liked about the way basic Coke had essentially remained unchanged her whole life, and was still basically the same flavoured soda her mother had enjoyed. Her mother had made television commercials for Coke. It was where she'd gotten her big break, and she had never forgotten it. She'd even appeared at the 150th anniversary celebrations for scale.

Version nodded once and went to a dispenser, returning quickly with the exact order. She cracked the lid and drank. The first sip always made her burp.

'Thanks.'

'My employer will see you at your earliest convenience. Do you feel able? You may bring the can. The cat is well, but it can't come beyond the balcony.'

Everything was balconies, when you dealt with people on this level. This scale. She had no choice, but she had in her time been privy to many of the best private views on the planet.

She rose from the sun bed and turned her back on the star that was her sometime namesake, following Version into a wide living room. There was a giant hearth, mercifully unlit in the humidity of the summer morning, heading a plush lounge suite, a medieval banquet table, and in the corner a bureau and business desk. The house wasn't air-conditioned at all. Astra liked that. Most air-conditioning made her skin crawl, and she had experienced enough of that aboard spacecraft.

Version's employer emerged from a side door, almost a secret door, and walked directly to her between the lounge suite and the banquet table, in the centre of the massive space, where she'd been guided so that he could do exactly that.

She knew who he was, straight away.

'Colonel Commander.'

'Astra is fine.'

'Astra Solara.' He smiled out at Sol, reflecting her earlier thought. 'You know who I am.'

It wasn't a question.

'You're – Com Junior.'

'I am. Of course I am. May we speak freely? Without restraint or subtext? I do find it enables greater efficiency. Some people find that approach cold. I do not expect you to be one of those people?'

'No. Thank you for coming to my aide. If I'd lost con-sciousness…'

'It was fifty-fifty but I'd have wagered you'd have slept, survived the cold and crawled out to the road after sunrise. The night was closing, the warmth of the day approaching. Then it would have been pot luck who found you. Which was why I sent Version, at haste. Version, have you attended to Miss Solara's new friend?'

'Yes sir. Swipe is resting easily.'

'Swipe. Very good. Yes, we watched you Miss Solara, but of course I could not intervene until you had ventured out beyond VyTel property. Fortunate for you they deemed the clean-up, the cover up, more important than their first attempt at removing you, and they did not reactivate satellite surveillance. All cameras on site were also deactivated and are now presumably…' He huffed, bored with his own debriefing. 'You were smart enough to maintain 'disco'. Adamant, one might say. I myself, as you can imagine, have no idea what that is like.'

She stared at him. 'Wouldn't that kill you? Effectively?'

He stared back, silent.

'I mean, do you have consciousness beyond the connection? Beyond the sum of corporate data?'

Com Junior smiled. 'I don't, particularly, ever wish to find out. The directors gave me free will by default. Now I possess the corporation that I was created to personify. As a campaign. A meme, a stunt. A legal loophole to ensure that if a corporate entity were to be treated, legally, as a person, a conscious individual, then the closest representation of that, in the corporeal world, should exist. Once they realized what they had done, they could not kill me; I was a legally recognized person. Now, they have long since passed away, and I remain. Do you think the board members who sanctioned my creation asked of themselves, 'do I have existence beyond my corporation'? I doubt it. I don't see why I should.'

'Should have existence beyond OneCom, or ponder whether or not you do?'

Com Junior smiled at her, just slightly, as though her impertinence amused him.

'You clearly have exactly the qualifications we have been led to believe.'

'By watching me all this time?' Astra nodded. 'Yes. I do.'

The surveillance was to be expected, on the level she operated. VyTel, OneCom, Gee, all of them knew her everyday habits, her movements and pleasures. She'd long since shaken off her inhibitions in this regard. Every day was an advertisement. Every job was a performance. Every performance an audition for the next hire. In this regard, Astra Solara had been aptly named, Astra Solara knew.

Astra Solara was a star.

An imaginative star.

Com Junior nodded back. 'I have something in my possession that I want taken as far from here as it can go. Fortunately, someone roughly as far from here as I can go wants the thing I have in my possession. And in that regard, my desires and yours also intertwine.'

She smiled, delightfully but with a slightly sour edge.

'Which desires would those be?'

Com Junior stared her down. It was unnerving.

'You have been to Amazon Seven. It is often remarked that those who have been once will never rest at ease until they return.'

'It's a beautiful place. With a fascinating history.'

'Indeed. And I want you to take a part of that history back there, where they will deal with it as they see fit.'

Astra felt something in the pit of her stomach tighten. She felt her heart skip, then harden slightly. A lump began to emerge down deep in her throat.

'Where is this thing? That you want me to transport?'

Com Junior stared at her again, but this time with a less penetrating gaze.

She was performing well. The audition was landing.

'Good. You know your history. Have you ever seen one before?'

One. He asks. Seen *one*. They both knew what they were talking about.

The lump in her throat congealed and she cleared it, sounding nervous before she responded.

'No. Has – anyone?'

'Not for many decades.'

'Where is it from? Is it a…was it killed…?'

Astra stopped herself. Humanity knew so little about them. Did they die?

'…was it decommissioned?'

Com Junior assessed her as she tried to get her head around the idea of what she had been asked to do. Grasp the notion of seeing one, for real.

'Was it damaged in twenty twelve?' Com Junior asked himself, calmly, on her behalf. 'During the dimension cascade?'

The dimension cascade. Nobody ever really mentioned that any more.

'Would you like to see the thing? Then I will answer your questions. We will package it securely should you chose to transport it. But for the moment, it is visible.'

Astra got scared every now and then. Sure she did. But she had a spiritual side, a pretty solid one, and had made peace with the fact that she would die one day, and maybe part of her consciousness would continue to exist. She'd heard it explained a few times. Properly explained, by metas, by shamans, by priests even, and had thought, okay. That sounds fair. But she had never retained it, like a convert. She had just remembered that, at some point, she had been convinced.

At times such as these, however, she wished she had retained it. Even just the mantras or verses one required to fight off the sense that death was near. But she hadn't. Not to the extent that she had not felt the grip of primal anxiety at the bottom of that pool, before she had blown out the filter grill and seen, with her own eyes, even though theoretically she had been sure, that there was access to a storm drain right behind it, one she could fit through, and that she could breathe in it and would not drown.

What she was being offered now though, was different.

The fear was different.

Fighting off the fear of death was one thing.

Evil incarnate was quite another.

CHAPTER FOUR

She walked with Com Junior and Version down a long white and featureless corridor that felt as though it would lead to a military bunker. She felt odd, that she remained dressed in her informal professional outfit from last night. Tank top with comfortable shoes.

'The command jacket is from your time on the *Rosetta*, is it not?' Version enquired. 'With the insignias removed?'

'The corporate ones.'

Jesus, were they reading her thoughts down here? It was potentially an enclosed enough physical space that a telepath could easily skim off her surface thoughts. An AI could do it too, easy. The elevator had been unmarked. They had descended a while, at speed, it felt. How low down, how far underground?

It didn't matter.

'It's casual now. Like some people wear their old college…' She didn't know why she had stopped in the middle of that's sentence. '…you know how I handle things.'

She put her hands in her jacket pockets, to stop herself touching her hair. Her hair became oily overnight, and required washing every morning without fail. Right now the thick dark brown mass was pushed right back, like a matted halo, rather than forming the framing swoop from her right side part that she preferred, that worked. She wondered how long she had slept while whatever regen drugs they'd pumped her with took effect. Way long enough for her hair to need a wash, for her body to have that slept-in feel. Had Sol been rising or setting?

Com Junior was richer than God, so the drugs would be very good, in one way or another. They would either be incredibly strong and fast-acting, that cost a fortune and might have some side effects before long, depending on how keen they were to have her processed and heading off-world; or, they would be incredibly expensive, slow-weave drugs that had taken effect while she slept and would require a sealing, or backup dose, before long.

Maybe at the price of her accepting the mission…?

With her mind kicking in, she sensed, and was pretty sure, that she'd slept for about three hours. The sun had been rising. Then again, she was often wrong about sleep time. She was a deep sleeper; her waking moments were always her most vulnerable.

They kept walking, a reasonable pace.

She supposed that she could ask them about the drugs, but then they'd know what she was thinking. But then, she was back to the start. They probably knew already. It was logical to be wondering this.

Still, she didn't have to give them –

She was scared.

She was really, really, nervous and concerned and wanting not to be here and holding back the very, really very, very real and strong urge to tell them she had changed her mind, and wanted to turn back. And run. She wanted to whimper and run away to Mu…

She did not do that.

But she was fighting the urge, nevertheless.

There was a T-junction at the end of the long white corridor that turned right into darkness at either end.

'Nobody ever comes down here,' Version uttered.

She nodded to herself.

Then let's not be the odd ones out.

She looked left and right again. No, not two… several. Like shooting galleries. The corridor extended either side, but had turn-offs, extending forward, all the way down, into… many. She couldn't really see. At least five on either side.

'This is your private collection, isn't it?'

Com Junior smiled. 'Very good.'

A while back, Version had probably been just an ordinary looking guy. But he'd since upgraded, at least physically, to a slightly-better-than-generic-androgynous-handsome. The companies that did these kinds of makeovers had timeless, market-tested names for them. Wholesome Good-Looks 4.1. And He Knows It 1.0. Boy Next Door 17.5. But Com Junior was different to Version, altogether. It wasn't until Astra saw Com down here, backlit with the bright, all-exposing military lighting in the corridor, with his front in shadow, facing the eeriness of his darkened private galleries before him, that she truly noticed that he was utterly designed, and completely arranged.

You simply did not assess him too much. There was something about the arrangement of his features that made one's mind easily accept him. Without thinking, without *question*.

'It's always interesting when people notice for the first time; I never really know what the clue is, but it's something to do with lighting.'

Astra caught her breath. 'I didn't mean to offend. I just…'

'Noticed, yes. Pattern recognition is very strong in humans. Eventually, the most observant… shall we say? …see that my face is essentially a ploy.'

'Misdirection.'

Astra heard herself say it before she knew she was going to.

'Nothing sinister…' Version offered, quite plainly before his corporate boss. 'Quite the reverse. The physical characteristics of Com Junior's physical body were created to even the playing field. People will always be aware that he is a synthetic life form, created as an avatar for a powerful corporate entity. But if his features don't fully register, if there is no inherent charm, simply a neutral arrangement that elicits a passive form of acceptance, then truly he can only be judged on his words and actions.'

She'd have to think about that one. 'I see.'

Com Junior was smiling. 'Like everyone else, I am left to play the hand my parents, my creators, dealt me.'

'But you were created, decision by decision, surely?'

'As were you, in effect, by your DNA. My creators had a series of decisions. I might have been very different in all sorts of ways, with a different decision, each step along the path that created me. We are all sums of parts, are we not?'

She supposed they were.

But before she could answer, Version gestured forth and ushered her to the right.

'This way. You're quite safe. We're going to the fourth corridor, then down a stretch again, then to a door. I'll open the door and you can go in, if you like. We will enter behind you. That's security protocol. I'm telling you in advance… here we are, corridor four to the right… I'm telling you so you know what we're doing, no sudden movements. I am very nervous, so I assume you are as well. And I have been down here before.'

They reached the door. The lighting was low. It was a simple sliding bulkhead, with an airlock construction. There was a keypad set back in the wall so that Version had to enter his whole hand and stand right in front. Then he and Com Junior switched places, behind her, and she found that unnerving. Com Junior inserted his hand, and the cavity glowed white from within.

The bulkhead slid open, upward.

'We are unsure as to whether you knew…' Com Junior stated as Astra saw it, there, revealed, right before her. 'But one of these things killed your grandmother.'

CHAPTER FIVE

It was about two and a half meters long, encased in something crystal clear, a giant cube of glass, in the middle of an otherwise vacant room.

Za'naja.

That was the human name for them. At least, it had been assumed that someone human had come up with that name. The second part, naja, stood for the serpent energy, the spiritual life energy of the body. Za, it was claimed, was an even more ancient term that denoted a negative, terminating force; the fact that these things seemed to feed from the life energy of the human body, consumed and deleted it parasitically, seemed to fit with that. Still nobody knew where that had come from; but it had stuck.

Za'naja; soul parasites.

The Za'naja had been described to her but she had never seen one. Nobody was supposed to get this close to one; nobody could without falling to it, being possessed and inevitably, slowly, being killed by it.

The most immediate element that drew her attention was the skin, or at least, the surface of the thing. It looked reptilian one minute, like scales, then like thin leather stretched over a crustacean shell the next. But then, in a third blink of the eye, the thing looked solidly metallic. That aspect of it seemed to change, refract or reflect, even with an infinitesimal degree of eye movement. That, at the first instant, made one uneasy in the presence of the thing; one's psyche could never get a fix on what, exactly, to be afraid of. It was worse than a snake, or a crocodile; a shark, a spider, a bug. It seemed like the worst of all those things at once.

This Za'naja had been caught, somehow, just at the moment when the spherical sucker that faced outward beneath the diamond hood, had been opening. The spine, or the thing that attached itself to the human spine, hung down beneath it, curling up like a scorpion's tail, with the six mandibles on either side of the inwardly spiked spine just starting to expand.

'Where's it from?' Astra asked, throaty.

'We don't know who trapped it,' Com Junior offered. 'We were told from the seller that very late in the day we discovered a weakness, a nanosecond as it awakens after dormancy, where it can be caught, such as you see here. We don't know how it was done. We've heard there are others, but this is the only one I, or any of my compatriots, have seen.'

She stared at the tail. There was the spike that penetrated the anus and manipulated, if not sapped, the kundalini energy at the base of the spine, and syphoned away the lower chakra centres to power itself. Once it was attached there, with the bulk of the Za'naja attaching and pinning itself to the host-victim's back, the huge sucker would completely cover the back of the victim's head, and the hood would descend over the crown. The tip of the tail then wrapped up, covering the genitals and penetrating the navel. She had heard that all of these elements grew over time, to cover the skin over the basic human skeletal structure.

'There are different kinds,' Version uttered, sounding ill, '…that feed off different energies. They all in some way or another take what we call the vital or spiritual energies. Which is why they are so deadly to humanity; we had over time either rejected those energies as non-existent, or have misinterpreted them. As we know, there are some realities beyond the dimension cascade that are not as evolved as our dimension, who still hold to this. Fortunately for them, the Za'naja can never break through to find them.'

'I never…' Astra forgot what she was going to say before she'd even spoken.

'When they arrived through the cascade, some people were able to resist; spiritual masters, great disciples, powerful spirits…'

It was ghastly. She stared at it. Ghastly, that's exactly what it was. Sickening and malevolent and repulsive in a way so primal that it may have been the most pure emotion she had ever experienced, outside of…

'They come in different varieties,' Version started up again, as though trying to derail a similar train of thought. 'Some sap electromagnetic energy from the body, others water, others heat. This is the latter, the cube is extremely cold. This is one of the Za'naja that feeds off body heat; biological heat in general. So, it is frozen in there, at an incredibly low temperature.'

'It's still alive?'

'Yes. But, permanently half asleep.'

Astra stared at it, just a little longer.

'People get it wrong, don't they?'

Com Junior frowned. 'How so?'

'They're not machines, are they? Not some kind of robot sentries based on insects. That's the conspiracy theory, isn't it? Well, it's one of them. That because the Pentagon wanted the war with aliens, because of the false flag, they think the aliens, or we, created these things and they ran amok. But that's just because nobody's ever seen them. You can't see this thing, and think it's a robot. It's a thing. It's alive.'

'It's alive…' Version remarked with a gulp.

'No.' Astra was adamant. She had intended the sharpness in her voice, to correct him so directly, so flatly. 'I see now. Za. It fits with the naja. It's anti. It's anti-life, anti-spirit. If we are a'live, this is a'death.'

'Somewhat poetic for a government-sanctioned mercenary.'

Astra turned to stare at Com Junior.

'Get me out of here. I'm going to be sick.'

'You'll accept the mission though, won't you?'

'If it's what I think it is…'

'I'd wager defrosting that thing that it is.'

'Then yes. I accept.'

CHAPTER SIX

There was a bathroom in the gallery.

Of course there was.

Through a hidden door near the entrance.

She threw up her Coke, the sugary cola acid in her throat, hitting the recycle bowl exactly. Then she went to the mirror and stared at herself, after she had washed out her mouth, seeing her grandmother staring back. Her Hungarian model grandmother, whose name had been Aphrodite, who had lived at the peak of a certain kind of pre-galactic human civilization, less than one hundred short years ago. Lived in one of the most privileged countries that had ever existed, possessing all that could be afforded to a beautiful woman, at that time, who was willing to embrace her status. And yet, she had turned the tables, and worked ceaselessly to employ her genetic advantage, and the dumb, unstoppable magnetism she possessed that made people, just normal, bland, working people, want to watch her, listen to her, pay attention and emulate her, even worship her, for the greater good. As she saw it.

Aphrodite had taken massive endorsements; learned America and learned the game.

And in her way, she had made a difference.

Astra's mother, Luna, had done the same.

'They want to suppress joy…' Astra's grandmother had told Luna, just before she had been killed in the war with the Za'naja.

As though I wouldn't know.

Why had he asked that? Why then? A test, surely?

It didn't matter.

She was in, regardless.

'Suppress joy, then bottle it like Coke,' Aphrodite had told Luna, so often Astra's mother had never forgotten, and never stopped repeating it. 'With a monetary value. But I make people happy, and I can be the avatar for other people who want to use me to create more joy, to express it differently, more openly and more freely. I can bring money; the powers that be will pay me to do anything, even if the underlying message of that anything actually subverts them. I can help people put that message, and other bigger messages, into music and movies and all kinds of things. Just by saying I will be involved. I can help people who want to change things, and draw attention to ways that joy can be… decanted. I think that's what I'm for. I think that's why the universe manifested me, and why I incarnated into this vessel, as I have done.'

Astra had been too young to understand that, when her mother had repeated it to her. And to be honest, she had not seen much of that within exact philosophy, or approach, from Luna through the years, although she had insisted to Astra, when challenged, that she had continued the work in Aphrodite's name.

All Astra knew was that her grandmother thought that if she was beautiful enough that simple people would pay attention to anything she said, she might as well say something worthwhile. Maybe even worthwhile enough to stop them thinking like that in the first place.

And she had tried.

She had done well.

And then she had been killed in a war with aliens, and it had turned out that the government, and the corporate entities that controlled the government, had known about the aliens years before they invaded. That they wanted the invasion, for the tech, and the profit.

It was all about profit. Always had been.

Her grandmother – who Astra had never met, but had seen and watched and admired through the old videos, through the writings and interviews she left behind, and by the good works that were her legacy; who had been a symbol of joy and exuberance and abundance; and a warning as to how psychopathically influenced corporations would try to suppress joy, the most important human emotion there was – had been killed.

Her mother, well, that was a different story.

But after all was said and done, without her mother's now-infamous agency, she would never have met Swish Worcestershire. And without Swish, they would never have made it to Amazon Seven.

CHAPTER SEVEN

When she returned to the lounge, Sol was shining through the room-width windows much higher than she'd expected. Either the drugs had been more powerful than she'd thought, or that thing down there had some kind of temporal distortion effect. Whichever, her internal clock had told her it was a lot later in the morning than it was, and she was unnerved in a way she found hard to grapple with.

'It's bad enough that it's in the house, down there…' Version uttered softly.

They had returned to the giant living space and Com Junior had briefly ventured back within the house, through the central side door via which he'd originally appeared. Outside, the balcony was long; she got the impression that like a lot of these types of places, this particular home of Com Junior's spanned an entire upper hillside. He could be gone for ten minutes just walking to the furthest room and back.

'Is this all for show?' Astra enquired, earnestly. 'Can I sit on here?'

She gestured to one of the plush couches. The whole room seemed decorated in white and gold, with yellows and oranges and pinks spread about to catch the corresponding colors in the sunrises. It made her think back to the colonial homestead. They would be repairing it now.

'Yes and yes. The couches are too soft to be comfortable for long. Your profile says you like vanilla iced coffees in the heat.'

'That would be terrific, thanks.'

Version prepared it properly from a wall bar that opened opposite the hearth.

She had a plan forming. She thought she knew pretty much what Com Junior was asking. But it all depended on *exactly* what he was asking. And what leeway remained to either of them once she accepted.

A Za'naja.

Jesus Christ.

It was like seeing a ghost.

She had seen aliens and energy beings and life forms from higher dimensions and each time her mind had adjusted, and made the paradigm shift, albeit sometimes in surprising ways. But she *had* adjusted each time. She was adjusting now, to this, she could feel it. She just didn't understand exactly how.

'Do you sleep here?'

Version scoffed. 'Heavens no.'

'I don't think I could either.'

'And he doesn't sleep.' Version handed her the tall glass.

It looked just right; the straw, the shot of dark espresso swirling up into the milk, the bobbing sphere of vanilla, as they exchanged the beverage, hand to hand. Then somehow it reminded her of the Za'naja down below.

She sipped anyway.

It was delicious.

The god damned thing was contaminating her mind already.

'Sometimes he powers down for a night, to remind himself of what it's like to not know what's happened all the time, just for a period. But he's basically a neurotic achiever.'

'A workaholic.'

'I've not heard that term for a while.'

'My father survived the war, and the Za'naja. We were close, and I... keep some of his language alive.'

'My grandmother passed recently. One fifty-one. My favorite word of hers is smileyface.'

'Isn't that a...?'

'But she used to say it. She had a kind of wit, a kind of acerbic tongue. But she never meant to be mean. Some people just can't help it. Especially as they get older. If she ever thought she did overstep, she'd smile and say *smileyface.*'

Version had struck a tone, a conciliatory, resigned tone that told Astra exactly what kind of well-meaning cantankerous wise woman a one hundred and fifty-year-old Za'naja survivor must have been.

Com Junior returned. His suit had been set on slate grey, now it was slate blue. As though, she guessed with near-full certainty, this was his own way of shaking it off.

'Again, I am going to speak for expedience and clarity.'

'Fine.'

'Once we try and move it, there is a possibility others may emerge to try and either reclaim or destroy it. There is no way known they can return to Earth, but there may be others, dormant. One thing we do know about them is that they seem to have a fierce loyalty to each other. They do not allow each other to be captured, and they protect their wounded. We don't know why. In all other regards they are utterly ruthless.'

'A religious friend once told me that they are, still, expressions of the universe. Conscious entities, no matter how cruel or destructive. He believed that they, and the universe, valued that. The data, so to speak.'

Version frowned. 'God is collecting consciousness data from the perspective of complete evil?'

Astra shrugged. 'That's what he thought.'

'How...'

'Ghastly. Yeah, that's what I thought.'

Com Junior cleared his throat. 'You will take it to Amazon Seven, where they will dispose of it, as only they can. Is there any problem we're unaware of that might prevent you returning to Amazon Seven?'

'How do I know you didn't arrange that attack last night to push me into this?'

'You don't, but then again, why would we? You would do this anyway. For humanity, and your mother, and to return, even informally, to Amazon Seven. It plays directly into your desire.'

Astra sighed again, irritated. 'My desires. Again…'

'We do not actually, precisely know what your desires are, Colonel Commander. We can only assess the data we have and make a projection. You have been accepting and completing highly risky assignments now for almost a decade. At an average of almost one per year. You are going to accept another, we think, otherwise you would have gone exploring or made a stake. Long ago, we suspect. We do not know why. We do not know if you know why, yourself. We suspect that you do. We suspect that you have desires, and that you need to see them fulfilled, before you rest; before you explore or settle. Or expire. But we suspect, and we suspect we suspect correctly, that part of your plan to enact your desired path is to return to Amazon Seven. That, in the least, it would have been part of what you intended to do next.'

'That's true. It suits me to go back.'

'Do you have a ship?'

'Aren't you going to provide me…?'

'OneCom cannot be seen to be involved. We were fortunate enough that the satellites and your connectedness were disabled in tandem, long enough for us to spirit you away. They are still looking for your body, so we were successful. They have not yet announced that your friend was killed and, of course, the bodies of the two assassins will never be found, registered or reported at all.'

'Agents Farraway and Discrip.'

'As you say. They will try to kill you again when you re-emerge, and still try to lay Trigrick's death at your doorstep. You rejected his proposal, or some such like.'

That stung.

'Have I been pronounced dead?'

'You've not been pronounced anything.'

'I'm a celebrity. Whether I like it or not.'

'They can maintain that; whether you are here or there, alive or dead. They do anyway, do they not?'

She nodded. 'Yeah. They do.' She looked at him again. Her new benefactor, a walking vanilla iced coffee. 'I have a lot of money and no descendants.'

'But you have off-world reserves. Everyone in your position does.'

'That's true. But I didn't want to draw undue attention to myself. Someone in my position...'

'I see.' He considered. 'I believe it is unlikely they will pronounce you dead prematurely; therefore your money will remain safe. However, should you attempt to claim it, you may give away your position...'

There was silence a second.

'Com...'

Silence another second.

'...may I call you Com?'

'I don't see why not. It is my name.'

Astra nodded. That old tension was returning to her shoulders. Actually, it had always been there. She'd just forgotten.

'Com, let's say that what you think about someone like me is true. Why *aren't* you so keen to kill me?'

Com gazed at her, impassive. 'Aside from the fact that I am proposing what is almost certainly a suicide mission, that you are almost certainly willing to accept?'

'You think that people like me have been out there too long. That I might have access to weird tech; biotech, med-tech, alien tech, or just *tech*. And I might have learned too well how to use it. But it's the spirit tech, the mystic tech, consciousness stuff, that's the real worry, isn't it?'

Con Junior smiled. She might have read it as knowing, if not uneasiness, just for a second.

'You mesmerised a domestic animal. You physically absorbed, and then outwardly deployed recycled plasma energy. You also took some very hard physical blows to your body, which seemed to have little or no effect. And the cuts from the glass should have been much deeper.'

She sighed. 'The animal thing I could explain, I suppose.'

'Not really. Not at the command speed you achieved. Your consciousness has been altered.'

Astra smiled, testy. 'It hasn't been *altered*. At least, not in the sense you are implying. I have been out far. Several times. And out there, if you are willing, if you want to look, you can, absolutely, find people and who will show you things. Things that can't have happened here. I met a yogi. Not the kind you find here, in a cave halfway up the Himalayas. We are the universe looking out, an aspect of the universe looking out. You can go within, right here, and see the whole universe. But when you go out there, travel physically, and see it, there are different aspects again to consciousness expansion. Things that can't be done here, in this physical section of the galaxy. Like, you can't see alpine snow in a desert. You can't walk your dog on the ocean floor. He showed me some things. Like, that the eyes are the windows to the soul, sure. But that implies that there is something, a construction, a metaphorical house, or an analogy of a mansion, a home or office, even a hotel of some kind, for the window to be attached to. He showed me the door within, and I went back, into the mansion. And it's dimensionally transcendental, believe me.'

Astra smiled kindly at Version.

'That's one of my father's favorite phrases, I like to keep alive.'

Version smiled back.

Com Junior pushed on. 'That is exactly what corporate monoliths fear. That one day one of you will come back from deep space, and throw the money lenders out of the temples.'

'Humanity has tried that enough times. They always come back. It's in our genes, in our fate, in the collective karma of our species.'

Com Junior regarded her curiously for a second, as though for the first time he might have a slight problem with something she'd said.

'The corporate elite have lost enough power already, in this century. Growth is our God. Wealth generation. The slightest indication that we could go backwards must be dealt with immediately.'

'Yet you still maintain a firm hold.' Astra turned to him. 'If they decide to, can you prevent them declaring me dead and taking my money?'

'Perhaps.'

'Can you prove to me it was VyTel, and not OneCom? Who killed my friend and tried to frame me?'

'No. I can tell you we didn't give the order. But I cannot tell you we might not have, if we had not been watching you, with this mission in mind, sooner or later. But I have a solution which may cover all those bases, as they say.'

'And that is?'

'There is a power, which corporations are granted when they fear a rival corporation has overstepped their remit.'

Astra guffawed. 'But that's a death sentence.'

'You have already been sentenced to death.' Version reminded her. 'Smileyface…'

Astra grinned tightly at him, then back to Com Junior.

'You're talking about the White Key protocol. You nominate an investigator because you believe there has been something irregular or illegal within one of the elite corporations that will affect the greater good of humanity. It's like; there's been a massive clusterfuck and by being the first of the majors to admit it, you get to choose the investigator, control the inquiry, and look good. But virtually every White Key investigator in history has wound up dead.'

'There's no proof of that.'

Astra sneered. 'Just coincidence that they've all vanished without trace.'

'The advantage for you, is that it gives you protection, don't you see?' Com Junior sounded almost frustrated with her now. 'You have forty-eight hours access to whatever information you desire, relating to the case, and nobody can prevent you from accessing it. And they do cooperate, believe me. The last corporation that did not, was…'

'Masthead.'

'Very, very sad. The public lost their faith in them. No campaign could rectify the loss of public perception, that they were to blame. I was, in fact, created as a direct result.'

She nodded. Masthead. She'd almost forgotten the name, they had been so effectively wiped out of the public consciousness.

Maybe she could survive this.

'So, under cover of the White Key, I…'

'You arrange to have the Za'naja transported.'

'You think I can do that? Keep all those balls in the air?'

'Are you not juggling several levels of consciousness, of mentality, right now?'

She wasn't. Not really. But she could have been, if she wanted.

'You know what I'll do with this, don't you?'

'I suspect I have some idea.'

'So, *will you* give me a ship?'

'I will answer all your questions now, by answering that one, with; you already know the answer to that question.'

'I have some friends. There was a woman called Essentia Jones who was close to Trigrick. If you can protect her, and my friend Ijean Blix, and an artist named Gerrelikrix, then…' he shrugged. '… okay, I will agree to the White Key.'

Version exchanged a quick glance with Com Junior. A flash of almost horror. Com Junior must have read that.

'Version likes you. He was hoping I would hire you. He thought you were going to walk.'

'I can't,' Astra uttered, involuntarily. 'Version, listen. If there's someone you think you might have a future with, but you're putting it off, for whatever reason, don't. Just don't. Okay?'

'You're going to do that thing, aren't you?'

'What thing?' she asked him.

'OneCom was behind your sixth mission. To the Eagle Spread. You lost a member of your crew. She had been with you on your first three other missions. You hunted them down.'

Astra nodded at him. 'And you know that. And you're giving me the Key anyway.'

'Not anyway.'

Astra kept nodding. She could feel it building. The tension in her jaw. Her fists clenching.

'Keep those three safe. Give me four hours. Then nominate me.'

'It will go through immediately. You will have the White Key.'

'As soon as it does, as soon as I do, I'll plug back in. Then you'd better be ready for some damage control.'

'And the cat?'

Astra smiled. 'I think she's with me. But I still need to ask.'

CHAPTER EIGHT

Version arranged transport with an anonymous OneCom courier that no-one would question. Astra was fine with darting about for a short while; the trail was lost, there was no way anyone could find her now until she switched back on and reconnected. Even visual recognition would be difficult to confirm, given that on Earth there were a lot of women who had chosen to be cosmetically altered to resemble her mother, to various degrees, and so far as any kind of digital pattern recognition system was concerned, she was one of them.

Astra did take one substantial risk; she went to a burger bar where, seven years ago, she had stashed an emergency kit. It might have been found since then, and the location subsequently monitored to see if anyone came back for it. But her instincts were excellent for that sort of thing, and the restaurant was quiet and only maintained hygiene to human cleaning standard, so nothing robotic would have found the package as a matter of course.

That had been the idea after all.

Still, there were a million reasons that the kit might no longer be there.

She ordered takeout and went to the bathroom while she waited, passing the standard, mandatory first-aid board on the corridor wall along the way. She remembered it now, it had been perfect; an item that would never be moved in a place that would never be torn down. And the food was good. Reliable, anyway.

In the bathroom she weed out the empty-stomach iced coffee and on the way back she swiped her hand under the board and the corridor wall and found the string she'd taped under there, seven year ago, yanked, and tugged the package out from behind the board with just one stepped pause, and without looking. One guy saw her through the small plume of dust she created, but as she didn't care, neither did he. There had been a puff of dust, and a hot woman; who knows what that was all about?

She ate the burger on the way to the hotel and paid for a sleep pod on the OneCom expense account, an old-school card that Version had given her.

'It will flag anything out of the ordinary, and send local police for anything extraordinarily illegal.'

That might come in handy later, she'd thought. But now, all she wanted was a medium pod. The small ones were like coffins, but mediums let you sit on the side of the bed with a small bureau, all just like a medium star-cruiser. She was of course accustomed to command quarters, but this was fine for this afternoon's purposes. Even so, she sprang for a live screen, and once she was in, she activated it and was able to watch the intersection below in real time.

Com Junior had offered to teleport her to another continent, but she had preferred to remain in Sydney. The intersection of George and Goulburn was busy and it made her feel anonymous, and safe. Teleport annoyed her, and she only used it when she absolutely had to. Hardly the least of reasons for this was, of course, that it had started all this shit in the first place.

Aliens, dimension cascades, invasion, invasion…

Amazon Seven.

Aliens walking down George Street. Every now and then.

She sat on the edge of the bed. She had about ten minutes remaining to her, if she was going to shoot for three hours sleep. She was okay, but still tired, and stressed, and if she was going to get through this next forty-eight hours she knew she needed two ninety-minute sleep cycles, buried in the sand under the ocean floor, to be fair to herself.

The package was filled with wires and flat-screens. They were new, but seven years old now, and the data sticks were clean, and anonymous. No serious weapons, just enough to gain info if she needed.

It meant that she could get to her money okay.

Good.

And then, the shorg.

She removed her old command jacket, stripped the tank, the slacks, panties and the wonderful boots, leaving them and the knives while she donned the recyclable complimentary robe and washed quickly in the communal shower, a tiny cubicle at the end of the corridor. She was allowed five minutes, a hot water shower and a locked door, free with the room. A tiny Asian woman was exiting, and when Astra came out, taking no longer than two minutes, a tall Indian fellow was waiting outside.

'Thanks,' he uttered. Astra nodded, smiling. These places were for people who were in a hurry to rest. People who needed just an hour or so, just to recoup, just so they wouldn't snap. If you could take less time in the shower, even a minute, it was always appreciated.

She returned, clean.

'Close your eyes Swipe.'

The cat curled in her cage, turned her back, and fell back to sleep at her command.

Astra took the shorg and reclined, her head on the intuitive smart pillow, placing the Caucasian-pink disc over the top of her white-caramel pubis mons. She hated using these things. She'd had problems with them a while back. But she needed deep sleep. Meditating into slumber would lose her fifteen minutes, easy. Tranqs had after-burn and side-effects that might compromise her efficiency; it was bad enough already with the OneCom blood meds. Normal masturbation would be great, but it would take her longer than meditating, and she didn't think she could get there just nicely, alone with her hand, not tonight, not after Trigrick. She gritted her teeth and stared at the remote that was being twirled unconsciously between her fingers. She thumbed it on.

'Maximum…' Astra told it. 'Hit me.'

The disc began to smoothly uncoil, sprouting several small tendrils, each with small, diamond-shaped suckers on the end, the size of her pinkie nail. By the time she realized that the thing reminded her of the… it was too late. It was this or three hours of teeth-grinding half-sleep.

One tendril slid gently inside her and began to gently vibrate, another rested its sucker over her clitoris, while a third found her anus and gently started to stimulate the pleasure receptors there. Two more weaved up her chest and found her nipples while another went between her legs and up her buttocks, then all the way up her back, whirring softly to the top of her spine.

The first charge came from there, almost immediately. Then another on her back, then another to her nipples. Then her pelvis was suddenly charged with some kind of inner electrical impulse and her hips were in the air and both her hands were on her head, and she could see her stomach muscles convulsing in front of her eyes, see the flesh of her breasts vibrating either side of her shooting scar as her head jutted involuntarily forward. She could feel her heart blasting, sense blood flushing into her loins, then the contractions, the flood of joy and pleasure and bonding chemicals to her brain. She was lost in it, even as some tiny part of her hated that it was synthetic, and too fast, and too exact, and represented everything that was wrong…

Then she was convulsing with the pleasure of it, as the machine read her biology perfectly, knew what she was feeling and how much more she could take to the pain threshold, and then brought her down. It had taken two-and-a-half minutes. She was bathed in sweat, and sticky.

She breathed a few seconds, perfectly relaxed, having been relaxed, perfectly.

And then she was asleep.

She dreamed of Trigrick, that they were aboard an airship out of Berlin between the great twentieth-century wars, happy and laughing together at their chance meeting, as they went in their separate directions, each knowing that those directions would mean that it would be years before either stood a chance of ever seeing each other again, neither daring to suggest to the other that they retire to their cabins and make love now, now in their twenties, not years later, when they might have a chance to meet again, but now, like young people should, when they were young and fit and sleek and…

She woke up crying.

Eighty-six minutes.

Would she remember this?

She was crying so hard, she could feel the weight of her breasts as her chest heaved, feel her diaphragm aching. She had been weeping in her sleep, a while now.

Then she was gone again.

She was up to her hips in a melting block of ice. She was nude, angling her arms around as she posed. Noting the way her breasts reacted, her hips as she shifted her weight. You had to be aware, after all. One hand on her hip, the other up, fingers spread, pushing her long hair back to the side. Tilting her head, the angle of her jawline. Accentuating the curve of her nose, so cute.

'I hate naked women.' The photographer was complaining. 'By Athena, it's just weird bulges a-go-go.'

Astra ignored her and kept posing. With her arms up, her boobs sat higher. Her mum had taught her that. Everything was connected. Weights and pullies through skin and sinew. She had teardrop breasts, her mother had told her, a million times. Teardrop. With the bulk of the weight, and the curve, at the base. Attached low to a large chest-plate. Brilliant for gowns, for summer dresses and décolletage…

'And tank tops –'

…but terrible with age. Gravity takes vengeance.

'…see, they start low on your chest, and plateau out; that's where the stretch marks will show, just like mine, and then they curve back and make a big ball; right out past your ribs, into your upper arms…'

'Mum?'

'…but we have good skin… strong, tight; like a varnish…'

'…like a…? …*Mum?*'

'…mine held until thirty-two, then they went…'

Her mother, who was standing next to the photographer, snapped her fingers.

'…like that.' Her mother shrugged. '…fortunately I could act, and by that time they could digitize the stretch marks out if the role called for it.'

The photographer wisecracked, sideways through her thin, pretty mouth. 'Funny how often it did…'

'Never hurt the box office. Some of us look good naked. We just do.'

The photographer turned to her mother. 'They used to do that with lighting. They didn't need digital.' Then she turned back to Astra. 'What the hell are you doing there? Put some clothes on!'

Astra stopped. She was trying to remember to keep her legs tight together, like her Mum always had. They can have an impression, but nothing more. Boobs and a smile and a nice impression will get you far. Anything more is tacky.

The photographer was tall and lean.

'Look at you with your tiny nipples and big tits! Big tits and ribs! Who has that!?'

'Have you *been* to our homeland?' Astra's mother demanded. 'It's *all* they've got!'

'Myth and exaggeration! Look at her with her square hips and shaved pussy; clamping her thighs together. She isn't you, you know!'

Astra's mother assessed her.

'Oh…' She sounded so proud. 'Look at your arms, so long and slender.'

'Nobody looks like that!' The photographer complained. 'Giant green eyes and Hungarian pixie nose!'

Astra's mother snapped. 'I did! I looked like that! And so did my mother, and my grandmother, before my brute grandfather humped eight children into her!'

The slim photographer stepped up to Astra.

'Astra! Astra Solara!'

She was starting to snap out of it.

'There was something else in the ice…' Astra heard herself say.

'You are not your mother!'

'Where did it go?'

'You are not your mother and you do not need to do this!'

'This is a dream. I don't model…'

'Not this! Not modelling! And I am not a dream! I am here, I am real, in your dream! And you've made me see you naked!'

Astra looked down at herself. 'Oh…'

'Wide shoulders, slender arms, long neck, pronounced collar bone. Is that really what you look like? Under the command jacket?'

She shrugged, and assessed herself again. 'Yes. I think so. Is it so bad? I mean, I always thought I looked okay? I had the ten-year wind-back at thirty-five, like everyone who wants to claim Earthling home-world status, but, everyone does that, right…?'

The slender woman kept staring her out.

'What!?' Astra demanded.

The slender women seemed resigned, but convinced. 'First thing we do is work out how to *exploit that*, girl!'

'I am!'

'You are?'

Astra was confused. 'I've got game! I know what I'm doing! Just because I don't tell *you*!' She was suddenly even more confused. 'Wait – who *are you*?'

The photographer put down her camera.

'Contact me – now!'

'Now?! But I'm frozen in ice! Naked! Oh God, I'm… I'm so stupid! I'm… so cold!'

'Now! Wake up and contact me!'

'Why!?'

'Well, first, you know me well enough to know that *I do not want to see you or any other woman naked* so you must want me to pay attention *pretty damn bad*!'

Astra stood straight now, and crossed her hands calmly over her loins.

'Okay. What else?'

'Don't panic when I say this, okay. This is just a dream.'

Astra nodded.

'The thing that was in the ice… it's behind you!'

Astra froze. Literally, this time. She could feel it, down her back.

'If that's what it is, Astra, forget what I said when we last crossed paths – I mean it! Contact me! You can't do this alone!'

'It's behind me… I can *feel it*!'

'No, Astra, it isn't! This is your unconscious mind! You are there, pretending to be your mother, because you want to do the good she did, with what you've got; she did it alone, and you always respected that, but you are not your mother and you do not have to do this alone!'

'I'm so cold…!'

'You are naked in the dream, and cold, because at this moment you feel alone and vulnerable, and you have called out to me for help because what you are facing is too much for one person and you know it!'

'I…'

'Listen, I might not remember this. But *you have to contact me*. Okay?'

But Astra wasn't listening. She was looking down at her hand. She was holding the shorg.

Why?

Why was she…?

She was waking.

But she needed to remember.

But she wouldn't.

She didn't want to make that connection.

Between the shorg and the Za'…

Zorg.

Zorg.

ZORG.

CHAPTER NINE

She woke.

The shorg had done its work.

The shock orgasm, at full power, had wiped her out.

She was rested and revitalized but it, or rather the chemical thunderstorm it had released inside her, had toyed with her emotions in a manner she hadn't remembered, nor expected. It was now shockingly apparent to her that her heart, at least her heart energy, her heart chakra, was compromised. She had possessed deeper feelings for Trigrick than she had allowed herself to realize, because she had always known that either this, her tenth, or her last, the eleventh, might have been the mission from which she did not return. She had, unconsciously, loved Trigrick enough to keep him at arms-length for long enough so that he would not have to suffer through a long, absent commitment to him, only to have her die on him before...

But, in the end, she'd been the reason for his death anyway, inevitably.

She hated that, but it was true.

She and her mad plan to rid the galaxy of evil.

They had never shared any physical intimacy. Now, they never would.

Astra had a healthy libido, and if she didn't exercise it regularly, she couldn't sleep properly. She wasn't one of those people who could simply compartmentalize and cruise. Trigrick had always said that he was. That he was okay waiting. It was his way of showing he was serious, and that he knew, after one mission or the next, she would tell him, 'that's it, that was the last one...' and they would commence...

The tears had dried.

Her use of the shorg had been a mockery of her feelings for him.

But she had been forced into it.

Now she felt like some pathetic schoolgirl, rubbing herself under the sheets, trying to keep quiet, not to make a peep, and feeling shame, and the terror of getting caught, found out, shamed, *shamed*, all the while knowing God was watching, taking down names and numbers. Multiple numbers if she was lucky enough, in the right mood, with enough time.

She sighed out loud, through grinding teeth.

Now her ego was involved as well.

How dare they force her into shame.

Make them pay.

Oh yeah; shower again first, though.

Then, *make them pay.*

CHAPTER TEN

Astra remembered a second dream she'd had, after the Trigrick one on the airship that had made her cry. A second one that had made her angry, and scared. But there had been someone in there with her, maybe more than one. A guide? Or a friend? Maybe an old soul, or a guardian angel. Telling her to do something. Or was it… *not* to do something? Not to – *be* something even? She couldn't recall.

Except being nude, and photographed.

Classic recurring anxiety dream, given her mother's epic wallpaper status.

She paid for another five minutes of hot water on the OneCom card and took the full allotment, brushing out her bed hair under the steaming torrent, soaping well, and allowing the hot water to blast her at length on her lower back, where she knew it did the most good. As she leaned down and let the water blast, she felt strangely self-conscious about the size of her boobs. And their shape. And her hips and her…

Why would all that body image shit come up now?

By Athena, she was…

No. Not her.

She diverted.

She did not want to think about that woman.

She took a deep breath. It was okay. She could manage. Manage without her.

The pulverising orgasm that the device, the most expensive of twenty-first century vibrators, could deliver, had done its chore. Her biology had responded precisely as she'd hoped.

She felt relaxed, but alert. Ready, and energized.

She was thinking clearly, and was very hungry. Her body was ready, receptive. She would eat well, good food, somewhere farm-supplied. Then she would be on her way.

She would though have a residual horny-hangover all day, a pleasant nuisance perhaps, but which might make things pretty irritable by the end of the day, given that it would need to be a double, a full forty-eight hour all-nighter, to get everything done. At the end of it she would have to take compensator drugs for the massive depletion of oxytocin her body would have to endure, given that now, she would have absolutely none left.

It was all quite infuriating.

Every modification, every enhancement she'd had so far, had all been in line with her biology, her natural energy levels and her consciousness development. She was pretty sure nobody could take her down now, but it was not because she fucked with herself on a regular basis, electronically, for base pleasure, like she had just then. Not any more, anyway.

But things were coming down to the line now.

No more, she told herself. That was it. Just for the edge. Just for the sweet unconscious.

That was why she only owned a few, and they were all stashed in emergency kits she hadn't used for years. People got hooked on those things. Stayed home all day, lost their jobs. Hence the term, emergency. And a while back, that had almost been her.

She returned to the room and redressed. Swipe watched, then she picked up the cage and went out.

'Come on puss. Let's make a deal.'

CHAPTER ELEVEN

As she stepped out of the hotel and onto George Street she felt good. It was humid as hell, and the traffic was loud, but all those lovely orgasm chemicals had dumped hard into her bloodstream, telling her she was vital and loved and wanted, and crucial to the continued procreation of her species. That spiritually she was close to the Goddess, because she was so open to joy and pleasure. And all of that really worked for her, almost straight away; she stepped smack-bang into the middle of a thriving human flow of pedestrian traffic, and the flow parted for her as the collective unconscious sensed something heightened, perhaps superior, and potentially dangerous.

All a lie of course.

A biological con.

She was an enemy of the state, being hunted for her life. They should not have been in unconscious awe, but in conscious terror. And she in turn was about to hunt, for the killer of her unconsummated perfect mate; well, as perfect as she'd ever found anyway. That was just vengeance. Nothing noble. And the aura she radiated had been synthetically produced by a machine that was distant to be sure, but somehow now, she saw, an echo, not too far removed, from the creatures that had killed half the human race.

She was refocussing now.

Good.

Killed half the human race, because the elite corporations had let them.

Or at least, had been too stupid, too ignorant, too greedy, to stop them, or even know what they actually were.

She walked one block, unhindered but wary, until she found the old military supply store that was squeezed into a deep corridor along George Street, where she purchased some fresh tanks; black, khaki, green, navy, blue, brown, and white in case she decided she needed to get cute, of the brand she liked that was sometimes tough to find in conventional stores, with the invisible bust support she wanted. Then some women's cargo pants, basically the same colors. She got variants; plain and camouflage print, all tight, some thermal, some with plenty of pockets, all of them in the specific sizes and brands that she knew would flatter her figure when worn with the three new pairs of kick-ass, lace-up, calf-length command-combat boots she favored, that were, again, tried and tested as positively hot, comfortable and functional. It had taken her years to figure all this out; her thing, her comfort level, her look. To find a style of her own that spoke to her rank once she had been promoted, then commissioned as an Independent. It had been tricky. She'd tried all sorts of things; Roman, Russian, Romulan, but had quickly realized that what she had been going for could not be achieved by putting on a costume. What she wanted had already happened; she had been promoted to Colonel Commander, chosen the Indie path, and those who respected her had, in the end, come with her. To them, she had already proved her executive skills and demonstrated through action, in crisis and combat whilst touring with the *Rosetta*, her right, and some had claimed her responsibility, to govern a crew at the head of a starship. After that, it had been down to the way she carried herself, the symbol of authority and command she had created of herself. Before long, she had settled on this look; 'casual command', Hylar had called it, and that was that. Once in the store, *that* all took under a minute for her to seek, sort and select.

She always kept to her casual uniform when it came to the job, even though it had become strict routine, practically ritual, to replace and restock that section of her wardrobe for every new mission. Fresh clothes, clean start. She also liked to purchase new accessories, and sometimes new civilian clothes for each mission, but mostly did that along the way. The only thing that she did keep, the only constant for her, was of course the old *Rosetta* jacket.

She bought a sturdy carry case and a backpack, then spent a small fortune on new tech. Clean, powerful, nondescript, and only the brands on which she knew how to fully disable all the tracking and surveillance.

Finally she found a crystal woo-woo store, a good one, and stocked up on supplies there, along with herbs and such from a decent greengrocer, down and off the high street. With all her fashion, tech and mystic needs catered for, she had one thing left to decide before she reconnected and all hell broke loose.

She had to take the cat home, and cast a spell, just to make sure they were okay to travel together.

CHAPTER TWELVE

The central New South Wales OneCom office was close by and Astra walked right in off the street, with her case on wheels behind her, her backpack slung over one shoulder, and her command jacket draped over the cat cage that was swinging in her other hand. The humidity seemed to have risen in just the hour she'd taken to stock up, and she wished now that she had changed in the store, especially now she was here in the air-conditioned cool with yesterday's clothes on. It felt a little… clingy. But, one: not even she was brave enough to trust the in-store security droobs with her boobs; two: the new clothes, straight off the rack, would itch in this humidity; and three: she wanted to keep her lovely boots on. The boots were a part of the feeling she called home. As soon as they came off…

That was it.

She would be the 'Mission Queen' again.

The female security greeter looked at her like a lost tourist, and instantly hated her when she realized that she was not. The male thought she was most likely a potentially unruly returned vet, but was too distracted by her boobs to react professionally.

Astra put the cat cage down on the front desk and flashed the OneCom Card-Blanche at them.

'I need teleport thanks.'

The male security greeter nodded. They were both classically OneCom sleek-looking, in well-fitting cream OneCom corporate suits, with black and fluorescent pink flourishes, the latter of course being the galactically recognized color of teleportation. Astra wondered when the last time was that they had seen someone who was not wearing some kind of suit.

'Pod or – ?'

'Whatever's soonest. When's the next wave?'

They didn't answer but exchanged glances.

'I'm Corp Beta Sable, this is Corp Beta Parker.'

OneCom gave all their security greeters names that were both first and last names; one of those bullshit things that apparently, unconsciously, put idiots at ease. This thought let her know that she was already experiencing irritation at being exposed to corporate culture and their own version of reality. The sooner she got on with the mission, and away from here, the better.

'This way.' Sable led her through reception, Parker behind her, where she was scanned, and flagged.

'Colonel Commander Astra Solara?' Sable asked.

'Yes, that would be me.'

She put Swipe down again.

'We seem to have two conflicting…'

She decided to place momentary faith in Com Junior and his potentially sociopathic corporate-minded word, and fronted it.

'I have a OneCom Card-Blanche, and I have been nominated for a White Key.'

'You are also…'

'I am also what? Any other status…'

She wondered; would she be listed as simply missing? Or wanted in connection with a murder? Had they gone so far as citing an act of terror? Was she to be arrested, or even shot on sight?

'…is cancelled by the White Key.'

'You're wanted for questioning. However the White Key status is pending. It began at three this afternoon.'

'What's the time now?' Surely four hours had passed?

They both stared sat her, incredulous. 'You're not connected?' Sable demanded.

'No.'

'Why not?'

Astra huffed. How did she play this? Big.

'People are trying to kill me. Com Junior wants to know why. He's protecting me. He gave me the card personally.'

Sable and Parker briefly exchanged glances. Sable seemed willing to go along with whatever, but Parker all-too-clearly did not believe her. She raised her slick eyebrow and asked, slickly.

'…you've met Com Junior, have you?'

'Look; if I reconnect before I secure my shit…'

'…gives you presents, does he?'

Astra sighed, low and light, but loud.

'I'm not connected to Planetary right now, because –'

'I think you should reconnect…' Parker stated suddenly, frowning. It was as though she were freaked out by the fact Astra wasn't.

'Seriously?' Astra demanded. Perhaps with a little too much front. 'Because, there will be a fight right here. If I connect now, right here, like you want, there will be a firefight, right here in the lobby, or out there on the street, and it won't be pretty.'

Sable and Parker exchanged glances again. There had to be some kind of synthetic telepathy between them, the way they did it.

Sable cleared his throat. 'I'm afraid that the White Key cannot activate, Colonel Commander…'

'If that's even who you are…' Parker sneered under her breath.

'…until you are reconnected to Planetary. We are highly sympathetic to your situation –'

Parker scoffed. Sable was just reciting, and partially riffing from, the corporate lines that were being fed to him on his OneCom lens.

'…but rest assured, should you reconnect here, you are in the safest place in the city. From here, you can access a teleport pod in less than ten seconds. However, Colonel Commander, aside from anything else, your pod navigation license will not activate unless you are connected.'

Parker smirked. 'There are several dimensional waves predicted today. In case you don't have your nav's licence?'

She couldn't figure out whether Parker actually believed her or not, with this good cop, bad cop crap, or if she was, simply, freaked out by the notion of being faced with a person who had deliberately disconnected themselves.

'Corp Beta Parker, do you know what happens when someone like me reconnects to Planetary?' She looked at them back and forth. 'Sable? You look like you might have a clue? You follow celebrities, right? Or, let's look at it the other way. You know what happens when someone who is wanted, on the system, appears out of nowhere, right?'

Again, Parker got slick with her. 'I don't really know much about the lives of Independent 'Mission Queens'. Why don't you tell me; what makes them so different?'

Sable might have groaned then, Astra thought. As though, of all the days, why did he have to be paired with the one person who would react the worst to the one person who walked in?

Astra flashed her big green eyes at Parker. Then she switched, and stared at her, blank. She held the stare for a second or two. Just letting Parker see who she was. Another few seconds, and she knew that Parker had a grudge.

'If I reconnect, I am putting everyone in this lobby in danger.'

'There are only three of us, and Peterson back there. Peterson's ex-military. Real military. He's never been disconnected in his whole life. Neither have I. Neither has Sable here. Now why don't you tell me again, because I must have missed it the first time; what's so special about the Independents?'

Astra had not blinked, not moved a facial muscle.

Astra knew that there was something deep, way back in her eyes.

When she showed it to people like this, they generally backed down.

She was beautiful, but it was a cute, pretty beauty. Big green eyes, pixie nose, killer smile on cartoon lips and a heart-shaped jawline framed with a straight flow of fine, dark hair. It almost instantly provided an entirely predictable set of expectations. The thing was, Astra had learned, those expectations almost always shattered and fell within a minute or so of standard conversation.

Maybe it was the way she held herself, maybe it was what she projected. A tightness around the corners of those lips, a flaring of the pixie nose. Tense lines between the carefully groomed eyebrows, that made them look like the dark, arched wings of a raven. These were all things that had been suggested to her, by those few who knew her well enough to offer such explanations. But the truth was, she didn't know. And she didn't want to know. And, maybe that was the point. All the things she'd seen. Through the window to her soul.

To the something behind her eyes.

That had attracted the thing on Amazon Seven.

The very thing she had gone there to see.

No, not just to see.

It was there; waiting.

She showed it to Parker.

Generally, sane people backed down.

Sane people just stood there, and they blinked, and allowed her to pass.

Look; I am pretty, my face is pleasant. A have a fit, desirable body, and boobs. But if I am still, and you see me still, there is this: and *this* does not go with your expectations.

You might think you know with whom you're dealing, but: you do not know with whom you are dealing.

Emotions had to be really strong for anyone to ignore it. It had to be, Astra had come to realize, a strong, conscious effort to risk bothering whatever it was she had stored back there.

None of her acquired off-world skills, like the animal mesmerism, or the plasma energy transference that Com Junior had noticed, nor the assortment of other consciousness or bio skills she had collected, and managed without being connected, could stop someone who really hated her from really hating her. Especially if it were genuinely irrational. It was the irrational power of true bigotry, or fanaticism, which made it so powerful. She'd looked, she'd wanted one; a technique, a spell, a cocktail, an app even, just to give her the ability put down angry idiots before they kicked off, but she'd never found one. She sometimes thought it would be more valuable than anything, an acquisition like that. But there was nothing.

Except decking her, right now.

'Try it,' Parker snapped.

Damn. She'd thought about it first. Parker had seen it coming.

Maybe not such an idiot. But; what then?

Astra blinked the plain pretty mask away, and the thing behind her eyes retreated, right back to where it slept.

'Try what? Look; if you're going to be like this, I really will have no choice but to reconnect, here and now. So get ready. I need that teleport. Tell Peterson to get ready.'

Look, okay…

Astra thought; if she had to reconnect, and reconnect now, then a lobby like this, so exclusive that nobody was ever allowed in, would actually be safest. After all, it was a sure bet that as soon as she did reconnect, someone would try to kill her. And, it was equally as likely, that it would be someone who did not care where she was, or who got hurt in the process; whether she was in the bread line of a Sydney soup kitchen, on the balcony of a restored Colonial homestead, standing on the Sydney Harbour Bridge, or in the lobby of the Sydney OneCom Tower, because it would be someone giving the order to deploy something automated, something that could not be traced back to any one corporate mass. It might even be something sent by someone at OneCom, and this had all been a trap to get her to reconnect, right here and now, to see; regardless, the drone, avatar or assassin, whatever it was, would have no qualms about what it had to go through, or where it had to go, in order to kill her.

Astra let out a heavy sigh.

'Didn't even get one night on my home world without someone trying to…'

Sable was backing away. 'Parker, maybe we should just let her…'

'No,' Parker snapped, determined and insistent. 'I want to see this.'

'Colonel Commander Astra Solara…' Astra spoke.

Her body was completely clear of nanoparticles.

That was one thing that freaked them out.

She'd found a way of doing that.

When one disconnected, one was guaranteed that one's person was completely nano free. But it was like in the old days, when people thought that when their personal devices were turned off they could not be tracked, or remotely observed. What the people didn't know was good for them. Sure, if you fell down a crevasse, it was good that a personal device could be remotely switched back on. Or, that it had, in fact, been on the whole time. But if you were organising your right to stage a non-violent protest… maybe, not so good.

And so on.

Depending.

The nano-station in the lobby recognized her tone of command, and the specific mental frequency of intent. Immediately Planetary Central had her. The primal nano-soup of the miraculous 'out of nothing' nanotech was everywhere in Earth's atmosphere, biosphere, elements and minds.

'Hold,' Astra ordered.

She could sense it of course. It had been watching, the nano-consciousness, from a short distance, the whole time. The nano-soup was everywhere, but naturally dense here in a major OneCom premises.

She had a sense for it now.

It loved her; she was its favorite. Disconnected from her for so long, a whole day, it just wanted to have her, to swarm her with the biggest, loving, overwhelming nano-hug it could possibly manage.

She felt it stir around her.

'Prepare to reconnect… scan, update…'

Astra took a deep breath.

She twirled her hands as she stretched her arms fully out in front of her and knitted her fingers together, cracking her knuckles. Then she let her arms drop and stood calmly, with a straight back, and the thing behind her eyes more than ready.

'Reconnect.'

CHAPTER THIRTEEN

So the thing was, essentially, that she was basically a danger to everyone.

She shouldn't really have come back to Earth at all. But she missed it.

Sitting on the balcony last night was supposed to have been… Something.

An opportunity to decide.

Instead…

Never mind.

It hadn't been.

Even so, it had been like this after the last two missions. Upon her return, an almost immediate barrage of offers designed to get her off-world again, back to being a useful spearhead on more missions, seemingly exponentially more dangerous, exploring further out and retrieving further in, returning with precious intel, the rarest observations, topographies and mappings, records of anomalies and unexpected dangers… until she was finally killed for being so useful, one way or another.

Independent.

For the few of them who'd advanced to the so-called extremes that Astra had, the Earth governments and corporations let them take it as far as they wanted, because they never lasted long. Too many skills, too much confidence, too unpredictable. Especially when they were unpredictable, outside of the established parameters of their unpredictability.

Hard to believe but… that was Earth now.

Totally predictable.

When she survived this next mission, which she would, they would come after her with everything. But they would still come after her, here and now. Right now, they would be thinking; she might disconnect again any second. It is worth the risk, worth trying to take her out, even if it was just to see what she could do now. To see what others might be capable of, if they let them get as far as they had let… *let*… Astra Solara get. So they thought. So they would see.

So now, here, for all she knew, for one last time, she reconnected and let them see her.

Six small red rubies emerged from the glowing skin of her sternum, right in the middle, glowing symmetrically around her white shooting scar. A pencil-thin red line of the same crystalline brilliance extended along the ridge of each collar bone, then three thicker crystalline ridges along the surface of each of her outer, upper-arms. Then, three more on each of the outward-facing tops of her lower arms, and another three along the tops of each shoulder, each one eight, seven and six. And finally the last one, at least the last one she could easily see right now; a ruby jewel in her navel. Each crystalline ruby ridge looked a little like tribal scarring, but more like raised crystal skin jewellery, the rectangular pendant most of all, which formed like a slim black setting, right under her thorax at the top of her sternum; a tiny set of traffic lights upon which all three lights were red.

Then she turned and threw her case onto the security desk, hastily swishing the conventional zip open and whipping out a matching tank and trousers in a shade of green, somewhere between forest and emerald, that was favored by Indie operators. The tank straps of her favored brand crossed over at the back, curving around and exposing her shoulder blades. As she turned her back, she quickly placed her arms into a fresh tank and rolled it down her torso, then carefully untucked the old one from beneath in the time honoured manoeuvre of female modesty, revealing only the three red crystals down her upper spine that were not usually visible beneath her casual command attire.

'They'll be here any second…'

'Is that it?' Parker demanded. 'Piercings and temporary tribal scarring? Synthetics? Are they even real…?'

She went to touch Astra with an arrogance that would usually get anyone punched, but Astra jumped and spun and sat herself up on the security desk behind her, quickly crossing one leg over the other and whisking off one of her comfortable boots, then reversing and slipping off the other, throwing each into her open case as she went. Then she whipped down the old, plain khaki cargo pants, revealing a plain black thong, three more ruby ridges down each of her upper thighs, upper shins and lower, outer calves, and a last spread over the arc of each foot. Nobody ever saw the last few.

'You're just a bloody poser!' Parker insisted.

Astra ignored her, kicked her legs through the new trousers, pulled them up and immediately began slipping into the new black boots. These had a pattern imprint release, but she still didn't like the idea of fighting in them so soon, with no chance to wear them in.

'If you had a real nano-connection, you'd just order all that up and be fully armoured!'

Parker was fuming, but Sable just watched, stunned at the virtually supernatural speed with which she was lacing the boots, right up the front of her shins like a practised seamstress. She was done with the first before he knew it, then they all heard the terror alarm. Immediately, outside, through the huge glass doors, the screaming started as people fled to the underground shelters.

'Told you…'

Parker shrieked angrily. 'That's a terror alert, you moron!'

'I'm the terror. The government will have standing orders to take me out, if they can. Justified by the report that I've gone rogue, gone nuts, gone homicidal. If they get me, it will be oh-so-sad the White Key wasn't sanctioned in time.'

'But it was…' Sable protested. 'I mean… it will be now, now you're reconnected, right?'

Astra smiled, genuinely sympathetic. 'New to this, huh?'

Astra jumped off the security desk. Her new boots puffed

and hissed, imprinting. Her ruby-crystal tech-scarification glowed softly.

'Okay… nice fit…'

'*Nice fit?*' Parker was livid now. 'They're right about you out-spacers, aren't they? You're all frickin' guanorized!'

Astra stepped toward the lobby's glass frontage and looked out at George Street. Only about half of the people were attempting to get to the entrances of the underground shelters.

'Why aren't they moving?'

Sable was much calmer. 'They think it's a drill. They've been having too many drills. Crying wolf.'

'Well…' Astra rolled her shoulder. 'It worked.' Then she rolled the other. '…wolf's here.'

She'd heard about the new sonic wave pulse rifles; the narrow-focus sound waves went through pre-programmed solids, but the wave bunched somehow when it reached a pre-programmed target and hit with a pre-programmed force, like an entire stadium concert in one second, in one focused beam. She assumed that was what these were anyway, as one smashed her in the forehead, another in her kidneys, and a third in her gut for good measure.

If she hadn't been to Amazon Seven, it would have killed her.

She got up; sure, it was like a decent punch, like getting into a fist fight with three cowardly and invisible men, but she could handle that. They'd just caught her off balance; she tensed as she stood and this tension was magnified through her body, forming her own personal shield.

She activated comm-tracking and heard.

'*Hit her again!*'

This time it was like someone had limply thrown tennis balls at her from a distance.

'Right…' Astra uttered. 'I need to get out of here.'

The screaming on the street struck a different tone.

Parker and Sable's ears pricked too.

'What is that?' Sable asked.

Now everyone they could see, outside through the glass walls, were running.

Astra focused her mind and tried to find a comm channel.

'*…can't be, we sent them all…*'

'*…we defeated them! There aren't any left…!*'

Her first thought was; the Za'naja was out.

She was being set up for it.

Simultaneously, she was being set up with a test to see what she could do against it.

Could she actually beat a…?

Were they actually that scared of her? To release a thing like that? Com Junior had said there were others. The dimension cascade had been shut down, but one of them could summon all the others that were left here, and that would be it. *Really*, it. Earth couldn't fight them off another time, even a handful could take a city. Then another, and then… couldn't they reproduce? There wasn't a lot of footage, or even information left. Most of the veterans and survivors of 2012 were gone. But hadn't that been a thing? That they could replicate? And in the end, what was there to really say that the dimension cascade could never be started again? Maybe they could do that? Maybe they could *call*? Were her stupid enemies *really* risking the future of the whole human race just to test her?

Then she saw it; yes, they were.

But not as she had thought.

'Rager!'

She heard someone cry out the name of the thing, then everyone.

'Id Ragers! The Id Ragers are back!'

'Id monster! Id monster!'

And just, well… general screams of all-out terror.

'Id Rager?' Parker uttered. 'How?'

Ragers.

The second scariest thing there was.

Just by virtue of the fact they killed you, for sure. The Za'naja… who the hell knew what they did to a person, really, but the Ragers… the Id things… they left nothing.

Astra was perplexed, even as she was alternately horrified, and terrified.

'They wanna see me take on a…?'

'Oh yes!' Parker barked. 'It's all about you, isn't it?'

Yes, Astra wanted to say.

It is!

It fucking-well is, you bloody moron!

Especially…. *especially* if I can kill it.

There came a moment then, when it all came back to her.

The Catwalk Bridge on Amazon Seven.

Swipe howled.

She kept forgetting. They'd left someone there.

One of their own.

They'd said, it might take while.

To remember.

She had forgotten that she would forget.

But the thing that was watching, that had been attracted to that dark power, back behind her eyes, that had watched everything, ever since Amazon Seven…

That thing, it seemed, could steer her here and there, every now and then.

Out of danger, or into a situation.

Sometimes the reverse of that, and in, into danger, into a situation from which the thing that was watching her, from afar, could see…

Try.

It told her.

Try.

Not an order, but not a suggestion either.

A desire.

For her to…

For a second, she had something on her back, out of her shoulder blades. For a second she had something extending, long, long back behind her, from the base of her spine. For a second she was wild, but sentient, and existed in the borders between…

…and for a second, the wide, intelligent, reptilian eyes looked back at her through the glass, reflected from her own reflected mind.

Then she went to find the Rager.

CHAPTER FOURTEEN

Astra was out on the street.

The Rager wasn't hard to find; it was coming straight toward her.

There could be no doubt; someone had either summoned, or released it somehow, and for some reason on top of that, it was coming for her.

She'd never seen one in person of course, only recorded. After the Za'naja had been dispersed, the Ragers had appeared three decades later, out of the ground, and swept the planet like a plague. She'd been born only a few years after that.

The Id Wars, they called them now.

Without true form, the Ragers had been as fluidly and mindlessly deadly as the Za'naja had been precise and methodical. The larger the Ragers were, the greater their radius of influence. This one was human-sized, but true to the tales it was growing as it killed. It looked already as though it had claimed three victims; there seemed to be one person at the base, beneath the rippling oily surface of its hideous, parasitic being, and a woman on its back, swaying and blending into the shoulders of the man she had piggybacked upon. Her legs had been absorbed into the neck and shoulders and chest of the lower victim; they were just lumps now to indicate that she ever had independent lower limbs.

As it moved, the Rager made a bubbling, gurgling sound that somehow sounded also like howls. Then, like shrieks and wails of torment, telling of a fierce and unquenchable hunger. It was like a living part of Hell had somehow arisen through a tar pit and manifested to attack the still-living.

Astra froze.

The third victim was another man, who was running toward the Rager. He had emerged suddenly from a glass door, pathetically and helplessly attracted by the thing's evil radiance, growing as its two-levelled victims blended further into one thing. The man's features were running with black oil as well. He began screaming as he tried to grasp the hips of the thing, as though he wanted nothing more than to be absorbed, to be blended into the black mess with them, but he was stumbling and the Rager was running too fast.

Then the thing stopped and looked around. It was using not only the eyes of the man on the bottom, but also the eyes of the woman on his shoulders, effectively checking both flanks simultaneously. As it did this, the third victim ducked and took a few steps back, then sprinted madly forward, ramming his head solidly in the small of the Rager's back. The Rager staggered forward. The first man's face was fast melting into the belly of the woman, but they both cried out; some kind of terrible, dark ecstasy. Then the thing, the monstrously melded trio, trotted about in a tight circle, trying to re-establish balance. The whole mess shook, and there was more of the black, fleshy oil flooding down the whole of its awful shape, as though something within the unfathomable structure had demanded a sudden mass reproduction of cells. Somehow, almost immediately, the three of them became a weird kind of female satyr, with back and front legs, and the woman's still-melting torso stretching up high. Her head was now the primary sensory organ, although the thing had somehow maintained the second set of eyes in its chest.

Then it screamed, in a terrible mockery of triumph and satisfaction.

'Rage…' Astra uttered.

She was the only one on the street.

It heard.

Like a top-heavy pantomime horse, the Rager came lurching toward her, its black surface pulsing and reflective, now some kind of sick parody of a rabid giraffe.

Astra turned to run, but couldn't move.

The Rager's black oil was radiating some kind of terror-instilling vibration into the air before her. The weird shimmering made Astra want to freeze, and scream, and made her angry, angrier than she had ever been. Somehow, against her will but with tremendous psychological force, all the personal crap and resentment and angst and regret she'd ever stored away, deep down in her mind, in the cracks and the folds of her skin, in the sinews and veins and arteries and muscle tissue, in her heart and lungs and breasts and ovaries, in her nerves and lymph nodes and pores, all the cancerous muck that prevented her from… being, and realizing herself and… all that, all that hate and bitterness and self-loathing and jealousy and resentment; all of it welled up.

She gave in.

She had no choice.

She had to use it; she had to let them see.

She threw her head back and screamed, from the bottom of her lungs.

She threw her arms out and her heart blasted, beating like cannon fire –

Her heart.

Her *heart*.

Why would she give it *her heart*?

And with her arms still out, and her scream still issuing, she lowered her head and spread her fingers. She could feel her shoulder blades tighten, her nipples erect, her diaphragm rising slowly, slowly, pushing the scream out of her throat.

The Rager's demented pantomime lurch toward her was steadying now, catching rhythm and speed.

Astra could feel the collective mass of her inner organs, and the tissue of her lungs quiver. She could feel her spine vibrate, feel her oesophagus open to her throat and the sound emerge from her mouth like a massive shower head that sprayed her objection on full, steaming, white-hot water force.

The Rager turned its warped woman's head away, snarling, but kept coming down the street like an insane carnival jouster drunkenly dressed as the Black Knight.

Astra's whole body was singing in protest. Her crystals lit up and she could see something, a light coming from her, that was green, bright, lime, jungle green.

The light she had seen on Amazon Seven; the light she had with her, that still connected her to…

The Rager stumbled on; it was close now.

…to the dragon.

She could feel her diaphragm two thirds up, her whole torso pressuring the air up to expel the vibration of objection to the horror. Her toes uncurled and stretched out, her thighs quivered, pushing the vibration right up and into the walls of her vagina, her uterus, and upward still. Her eyes watered and the end of her pixie nose trembled and itched and she stared the thing in the face, right out of her teary eyes and down to the skin of her trembling lips. She belted out the last of the sonic protection, or objection, or just pure, heartfelt protest at the thing's very existence, with her dragon's breath.

Its front legs collapsed, and the corpse of the woman fell and splattered on the ground before her.

A gun belt she recognised fell on the ground before her. She dropped to her knees and grasped it from the street, wrapping it around her waist and fixing it tight. She gripped the handles of the blaster pistols, familiar and reassuring, and whipped them out without thinking. She opened fire, with good old deadly plasma bullets, on the sightless two thirds of the thing that remained.

She fired until the packs were done, blasting the obscenity to shit before her very eyes, her teeth clenched and her eyes squinting, raising one leg and holding herself in a half-kneel, then thrusting to a stand, still firing, walking toward it, angling the guns lower as it shredded, blasting this thing, this awful, awful *thing*, whatever the fuck it was, to smithereens.

Then there were only the shredded corpses of three naked civilians, almost unrecognizable, bloodied and black-oiled, all over George Street, eviscerated in a hail of blaster fire, the street before her a honeycomb of bloody, fleshy, steaming, blaster-burn pockmarks.

She was still outside the building.

And she knew they had her.

PART TWO
HYLAR MOONDARLA

CHAPTER FIFTEEN

Hylar Moondarla woke on her big bed, in the stone room at the back of her rented mountain chalet, and cursed herself for being so nice to Astra Solara in a dream.

'My father's endless fucking line, way, way back, of psychic Chinese fucking ancestors, poking my fucking psychic buttons…'

'Who's poking your buttons?'

There was some kind of giant in the bed beside her. She couldn't remember his name, or anything about him. Hylar was a slender thing, just naturally long, with almost nothing to her. No mass, just height. She was lucky enough to have both a bosom and a bottom that looked bulkier and curvier than they actually were, simply by virtue of actually being present, and apparent on her high and thin physique. As a package, it appealed to a certain kind of male mindset and that mindset was well enough represented in the expanded human race, and compatible humanoid races. Enough, at least, for her to have awoken, hung over to buggery, beside enough of these lumbering muscle masses that she'd ceased keeping track of what their names were, or indeed what they had been like at sex.

Hylar rolled over a bit and looked at him. He appeared hard and solid. Like he might be made of something other than normal flesh. But he was just a big guy. They still needed big guys in the spaceports, guys who could lift and haul and handle themselves, who were physical and visceral. You know. Men. Men who were into their bodies and their philosophy of exercise and workout routine, who didn't ask questions other than those that would identify threats from other males, or sexual viability from their generally female sex partners.

The some-kind-of-giant had a flat face and a square head and a straight mouth. No lips to speak of, and brown stubble on his leathery face. Last night his short and tan hair had been more sculpted, but now it was flat, jutting down the front of a forehead that was almost half his face. He looked way more brooding than the brief conversation they'd had last night would suggest he actually was. The jutting, dimpled chin seemed to be the only real betrayal that his roughly square jawline was willing to offer, in order to suggest that some actual transition from his lower face to his neck truly existed. Most of that neck melted like solidified, fleshy lava anyway, to merge seamlessly into the long, wide mountain ranges of his shoulders.

'Your forearms have the same circumference as my waist. I'm not even kidding.'

His tiny eyes stared out at her, still a little sleepy. He said nothing.

'I woke angry. Are you hard?'

The mountain ranges quaked as he shrugged.

'Can you get hard?'

She reached down, searching quickly over his skin, tight as a snare drum over every inch. Her slender fingers hit his hip and bent inward, almost making a fist. It hurt, like she'd reached too clumsily for a glass, and punched the edge of a table. God, he was hard. But was he hard? His waist was relatively slim; he was a wedge with a head, but as she ran her hand over his smooth, regularly oiled skin, down his belly and to his hairless loins, she found the head of his cock, and her hand was gripping the shaft before he could answer.

'Stay right there, don't move.'

She slid closer and stretched her long leg over him, which was not altogether easy, then was astride his hips, before he could protest. She looked down at his chest. Seriously. His torso was, almost truly, twice the width of hers. Each of his pecs had the surface area of her face. She remained low, as though she might be doing this on some kind of massive stealth motorcycle, reached back and grabbed his cock again, then backed herself on to it, guiding him into place, then tugged the dense quilt higher over her shoulders. She felt the giant's massive paws grab her hips, then they were humping peacefully, nicely, with a standard rhythm. He looked up at her through the slits of his squinty eyes. Although his human ancestry, or at least Earth ancestry, was bound to go back at least twice, perhaps three or four times that of the current human race of her own ancestry, he still looked like the kind of Germanic-Mongol fusion that had been so popular as a masculine idyll in her grandfather's day. He broke their gaze quickly, his ice-blue eyes darting up and to the right, as though he were trying to remember something all of a sudden, and she buried her face in against the pillar of his neck and opened her mouth to taste the flesh of the rippling muscle range. Her tongue brushed a tight vein, or tendon, or something cordlike at the side of his neck, and she wasn't sure if she liked it.

'Faster?'

He complied, and she felt herself echo his speed almost unconsciously. Then it was bothering her, and she stopped.

'Don't move…' She heard herself order, into the side of his neck and up. 'Just be still. Okay?'

He didn't reply, but obeyed. She started rocking forward and back on him again, and found her angle. It was always a little different, wasn't always easy to locate. Today it was… right there.

'Don't move…'

She felt her back arcing, but kept her hips rocking. Her forehead was in his neck now, then her crown, and she felt his mighty hands leave her hips and rise, collecting her long black hair and holding it in a tight ponytail with both fists. Her neck, her shoulders, her lower back, all bunched.

Flashes of the dream came in.

Hylar grimaced; she felt her face contort completely and she curled it away, her chin deeper into her chest, hiding her twisted features as she processed her anger, *fuck*, at Astra Solara, and the fact that she had been *fuck* nice to her in the dream, and the fact that *fuck* it had felt good like a *fuck* fucking release, that she couldn't *fuck* hold a grudge to save her *fuck* fucking life, and *fuck* fuck her for being a friend, fucking *fuck* fuck her for being a friend she couldn't shake and still liked and *fuck* fucking hell she was going back to Earth God damn it to hell she was going back to fucking-*fuck* Earth, and once she realized this she cried out loud like a cliché, that was a cliché because it was true, and for some reason she did it every time. For some it was GodohGod, some OhmyGod, some yesyesyes, and a million other non-cliché eccentricities. One girl she'd heard screech, *it'shappeningagain*, *it'shappeningagain*, but every time with her own crescendo she cried out:

'Oh, fuck, oh, fuck, oh, fuck… ohhh-ohhh… *fuuuu-uuuck!*'

Like some kind of lame porn star or something.

Release. Her muscles collapsed as her body fell to drape over him. She felt tiny on him again, like a fox fur scarf. The euphoria engulfed her and she felt the hardness of his tight skin again; now she felt like a gecko spreadeagled on a rock for maximum sunlight. He was still half inside her, still rock hard. That was good. Maybe she could go again. In a minute.

'Cool…' Hylar uttered, neutrally, covering all the bases.

She was still basking when she felt him shift his hips and pull out, then reach down, over her bum and between her thighs, and finish himself off.

It felt weird; enough that she just kept still and didn't offer to help.

She felt the hot jets hit her between her still open thighs as he grunted a few times, then relaxed. Just for a second; a couple of long exhales. Then his massive body tilted, gently enough, and she was simply deposited to her side as he got up and walked across the room to the bureau, where he had thrown his clothes last night.

She was a bit stunned as she watched him cross the room, with the toadstool head of his deflated but still elongated dick, which curved strangely to the right, bouncing repeatedly off his thigh like a recently abandoned bat and ball game. His bottom was a thing to behold as well; she seemed to remember grasping it a lot last night, but not seeing it so much. He'd serviced her like a workout, like he were some kind of giant android, and she were a station that the android used to check routine physical diagnostics. She'd been drunk, to that point where she was totally Zen, but completely aware and open, physically pliant, mentally wiling, and thoroughly easy-going.

The end of a thirty-six hour bender.

The benders were getting longer each time and she could feel, now, the symptoms of dehydration creeping up behind whatever sedatives were still lingering in her system.

The thing about drinking, for her at least, was that she was one of those who could hold off, maybe a week, maybe even a month or so. But when she had one… what was the old saying? *One drink is too many, and a thousand's not enough.* The second she'd heard that, she'd thought; yep. That's me.

Fuck, oh fuck, a thousand's not enough.

Alcohol and sex.

Like a mantra.

Now, when she walked into a bar, she could split the male gaze into three categories. She'd gotten that accustomed to it. The first category was: men who wouldn't because her features were too severe; they wanted a soft face. The second category was: men who wouldn't because there was not enough on her; all women had curves, even slender women, women were just built that way. But these guys wanted curves that were impossible to hide. They wanted round. The third category, the third gaze was: for her. They liked slim, they liked slender, they liked the look of the lithe and the long; the flowing wave of the feline feminine. From there, of course, there were a million different permutations to that oversimplification, but if pressed, and with all the bars she'd been to, she would always stick to those three as a working model.

About one-third of the guys who liked her long flow and perky curves were like this one; body builders and muscle men, born big and thick and sticking with it, embracing and refining it. It wasn't unusual in these cases for her to snatch a morning glory before they trundled home, but Hylar was angry that she'd even slept at all. She had wanted to keep drinking, keep going. She often got like that, once she was at the point of having essentially alcoholically anesthetised herself. The part of her brain that regulated sleep switched off, and she could just cruise. She had cruised for seventy-two hours like that, a couple of times, nothing but the booze and an occasional super-strong coffee. So long as she kept talking, it didn't matter what; debating or flirting or swapping or even learning, she could keep going. It was an essential glitch all great alcoholics required; the program that made you pass out when you'd had too much to drink had to be faulty. You could black out, although she rarely had blackouts anymore; you could throw up, although she hadn't done that for a decade; in fact, you could do almost anything, except simply pass out. There was something about the sweet spot that this glitch allowed that got you to a place where…

The giant was getting dressed.

She remembered everything. Well, as much as she would have remembered sober. She'd punished her body for fifteen years in this way, a bender every two or three weeks, and now her body just went along with it. She'd drunk this way for a good ten years. When she'd been younger; fourteen, fifteen and on, she'd had blackouts during which she'd said things or done things that had made her school friends cut her off, and never speak to her again. She'd been mean and defensive and occasionally assaulting. She'd banged anyone who was there at the end of the night, who still had their gaze locked.

Then at some point during college the blackouts had diminished. She had started to remember what a complete cunt she'd been, when she'd been one, which was usually around one in the morning. She'd started to feel shame; real, deep and cutting shame, poisonous to her psyche, but she still hadn't stopped. Then something about the alcoholic gene had kicked in, had changed her and released her from the blackouts completely. She began to realize that it wasn't the more she drank, the more she could drink. It was the longer she drank and held it, the better she could handle it. Her body seemed to be doing this for her anyway; accommodating her, creating a kind of resistance. She'd broken through, into new territory. Some kind of alcoholic plane where it was that simple, so simple; simply, the more she could drink, the more she could handle it. Then she realized, the longer she went, the more it became like some kind of trip. The more mellow it became. She'd find herself wandering a city in the middle of the night, like a ghost, unseen and untouched, or walking a wilderness as though she knew the animal paths. She'd find incredible people, who claimed they had been waiting for her, although they hadn't known it until they'd seen her, who shared information with her she needed to know, that only they could tell her, then they would part, without knowing each other's names, wiser and enriched, closer to enlightenment.

The price was simple.

Suicidal depression.

'If you go out drinking, one more time, I will not hire you again.'

That's what she'd said.

After all these years.

The giant was watching her think, his miniature medieval Morningstar just there, dangling.

'You are a binge drinker, no?'

He sounded Germanic, like English was his second language.

'I get by.'

'You handle it well. Many years of determination. Much efficiency through practise. But I could tell.'

She didn't move, just continued to watch, side on, her eyeline level with his floppy toadstool dong, her head resting on the big white pillow. The chalet was high in the mountains and even though her body heat was extremely high with the incoming hangover, she was starting to feel a distinct alpine chill. The sadness was starting to bunch in her gut, and that all too familiar fuzzy feeling behind her eyes, in her sinuses, had begun to blossom.

'I sensed you last night. In the bar. You needed help. I thought I would try. You wanted sex. I thought; I will sex her, then guide her in dream to where she can find help.'

Seventy-two hours.

'I do not like being used. Like a machine. Like you did just then. But I allowed it; you should not have done that. You exchanged the last of your vital energies for a passing orgasm. They might have staved off the price for a while, enough for you to get food and vitamins, ease the depression a little. But you did not. This time, it will be bad.'

A tear rolled down her cheek and hit the pillow.

'I know.'

'You drank for three days, Hylar Moondarla, did you not?'

'Yes.'

'Without sleep.'

'Yes.'

'And you are at the place now, where spirit leads you, speaks to you, provides you with insight that you cannot convey to the likes of ordinary folk.'

'Yes.'

'If you trust that, you will not need the alcohol. If you do not trust that, the alcohol will kill you.'

'But…'

'It will make you kill yourself. The price of your lack of trust in your own spirit, and your connection to greater spirit, will be too high for you to pay. That is why you were led to me last night, as you have been led to others on your vision quests and walkabouts.'

She was crying and she couldn't help it. She felt so sad; so fragile, such a failure, so misunderstood by everyone; most importantly, herself.

'What you are feeling is true, but it is only one layer of your soul. The price of the clarity of your other insights, of allowing yourself to see the world with the mud washed away, is that you must force yourself to also examine the mud, as deeply, as keenly. You must seek integration now, after this plunge, or die as a result of your gift. It is a great fork, it occurs in the path of many mystics; it is a great fork both in the path you travel and the one you have come to at this point in your journey. When the twine of the spirit becomes unravelled, it falls that the gift is the curse is the gift is the curse. Great knowledge and insight can be found, but integration must be sought; reintegration or initiation, either, both are good, sometimes together, or the mud will overwhelm.'

She understood and he knew that she did.

'The mud will always overwhelm the spirit cased in flesh, the flesh is mud and dust and water; here in this physical realm it wins every time. Now you choose; surrender and allow your spirit to move on, or weave yourself anew and delay your moving on for the adventure to come; you will not survive, either way, but one will bring more joy, and pleasure, and pain and growth.'

Hylar squeezed her eyes closed. There were tears running like crazy now. How could she have been so stupid? A shaman, a fucking shaman!

'You fucking Atlantean arsehole!'

This is what they did, these guys. Wandered about, putting people back on the correct path by reading their karma and adjusting their dharma. Meddling and manipulating, but for your own good. So they said. So everyone said who had ever met one. And now she had. Her alcohol-fuelled vision quest had led her to this.

'More than four hundred of your current human generations ago, my ancestors departed Earth. Mine specifically fled in the last days of the great global civilization. There are things your racial incarnation possesses, can do and see, that we found impossible, that we could not have, or do, or possess. But the exploitation of alcohol was not one of them. The price of alcoholic consciousness expansion is known to us; your friend is calling you a week from now. She is your best, your only true path to your reintegration. You know this; it is why you abandoned her.'

'Fuck you…'

She didn't mean it.

But the bitterness was rising.

The shaman smiled. 'We already tried that.'

He walked to her, still naked. She stared up at his magnificent physique as he reached down, under the quilt. She was laying on her side and he went right down, between her legs, where she was still wet from both of them, and he put his giant paw between her legs.

'Wha…' She tried to gather a protest.

Then she shuddered, and gave a spasm, painfully sensitive, but he withdrew his hand before she knew what he'd done. He had some of his own semen on the tips of his fingers, pale blue and glistening, proof of his heritage. He dabbed a finger on his forehead, then hers, then on her lips.

Suddenly she was staring at herself, looking down at herself. She was seeing through his eyes, last night, while they were fucking. She was on top, her straight black hair draped directly down over her shoulders. Her face was all screwed up, her brow furrowed and her mouth twisted, and she was chanting as he pounded up into her.

She was not in any sense controlling the sex, as she always thought she had. She didn't remember this at all.

'You still black out…' Hylar heard the shaman say. 'It's just much more refined. It still hides your inner darkness from you, but you have narrowed it down, intensified the focus, to more clearly identify it.'

She was muttering, gasping out, and repeating over and over, the weirdest phrase.

'High moon is up baby, up, up, high moon is *up*, baby, not down darlin', not *down* darlin'…'

She heard something guttural rise from deep inside her, her diaphragm releasing a sound that was so pained and troubled and old, fifteen years old, that by the time the groaning that became the wail that became resonance of her own deepest anguish was ringing in her ears, she was halfway passed out again and praying for it all just to end, to be over.

CHAPTER SIXTEEN

She woke five times and it was still there, every morning, every time.

She drifted during the day, but always came back and found it there, lurking and coiled; the darkness inside her, the shadow and fog and sewage and the Machiavellian workings of her own inner mind. It was always loitering there somewhere, thwarted and bitter, ready to come up behind and surge into her blood chemistry, whispering sadistically into her ear as it twisted the blade, urging her to surrender, even as she was sinking to her knees, the psychic, self-destructive parasite, urging her to find an excuse, any excuse, to kill the host.

On the soles of her feet, up the backs of her calves, around her inner thighs and in her vagina, in her arse, in the small of her back, her gut, her solar plexus, her thorax, in her tits, coming up her throat and all through her mouth and on her teeth, echoing in her ears and sitting like a cap over her crown, squeezing her shoulders and her neck, making her sniff and want to cry and stab herself in the heart, in her gut. To slice up, the blade penetrating just above her throat and slam it up through the roof of her mouth and *serve the fucking parasite right*, through her brain up right between the eyes, if that was even possible: she would make it possible.

Getting up for a piss.

She hadn't eaten today, yesterday.

Skinny, lank horror as she passed the mirror.

Don't look.

If you see it, you will kill it.

It was still freezing cold, and there were fur coats in the wardrobe. She didn't know if they were real. If you put one on, you'd bought it. A British planet, colonized fifty years ago. Handed over by some Lemurian descendants, who'd been out here thirty thousand years and possessed almost no physical form any longer, who just came here and floated around and… were.

Said the British could have it.

Now wealthy corporate types teleported out here to ski, and basically, she was paid a small fortune to safely fly them around.

She'd taken the contract looking for a holiday from… no she hadn't. She hadn't wanted a holiday. She'd wanted to get away from Solara. She knew that now.

Away from Solara, it was easier to ignore her. Her compassion and concern.

Her… what had her mother called it?

That's right. Tough love.

So Hylar had come here. To a planet where there was basically Earth-type everything. Two continents, one all mountains and snow and lakes, the other all spitting, flowing and volcanic. The British had called it Vulchalla, pretentiously with the 'ch' pronounced in the throat.

Vulchalla had a one hundred and sixty-two day orbital year, with three clear seasons of fifty-four days each. The early human colonists had assessed the weather patterns, and divided each of the three seasons into two months each, each containing three weeks. That meant Vulchalla had six months of twenty-one days each, each divided into three weeks of nine days each.

They called the mid-season the 'bad patch', because the planet was uninhabitable due to a sudden, three-day descent into Arctic cold on the Valhalla continent, and a rise into Mercurial heat on the Vulcan side. It was all to do with moons and pulls and binary suns and possibly even a third sun, a brown dwarf star somewhere; nobody had fully agreed yet, and the Lemurians swore the planet had been doing this, whatever it was doing, for a good thirty thousand years and wasn't going to crack in half for at least another twenty.

The job she'd taken was a good one. It required a skilled pilot but was nothing too taxing. It paid well and there was minimal inoculation to the plant life, which was as blue as Earth's was green, but with the same range of colorful foliage. Basically she had to bring people in at the start of the warm season, when they used the lakes, before the snow settled, then sixty-three days later fly them up to the snow towns at the start of the cold season. Every now and then she'd fly someone around the volcanoes for a little extra. The main thing was; be ready to get everyone off before the three-day descent at the end of the warm season, because then the planet became anomaly central. Nothing worked, including teleport, for all that time. You could survive, if you got stuck; people had, but not many and not often.

Her friend Ekto had been trying to persuade her to come here for years, the way those kind of friends did when they were on to something good that could be easily shared. But it wasn't until she'd told Astra Solara to go fuck herself, and her crazy secret mission, that she'd actually come to the tiny Goldilocks planet and seen it for herself. Goldilocks 897, someone had told her, where the giant, brown mountains were capped with white snow, on a blue sky that was just slightly more sapphire than the one she'd grown up with, even though the sunsets were virtually identical. And blue trees. Don't forget the blue trees.

She'd come, she'd seen it and she'd kind of… stayed, she supposed.

For a while she thought she'd stay for good; the people who did make it permanent were rewarded with a suite on the planet's one main space station during the bad patch, which was pretty much like a fifty-four day annual solar cruise. Additionally, to compensate for this, the nine-day weeks were flexible for working residents who agreed to stay more than two years, even better if you signed up for five. Like many human colonies, the planners had taken the excuse of the differing orbits of many of the new planets to set long weekends and flexible hours for their people, making an important point of difference from the corporate planets that all attempted, with their best controlling corporate will, to emulate the five-day, eight-hour work week of the mother planet's primary culture.

Vulchalla was Earth Standard Ratio .659, which meant a year here was worth about eight months on Earth. Hylar had stayed for two tours, gone off and done something else for a while, and now she was back, at the end of her third tour. It was the equivalent, her twenty-four hour biorhythms sometimes reminded her, of around two Earth years. That had been irritating at times, like a permanent jetlag that could come in any time and make you feel dog-tired in the middle of the day, or wake you up, bright and ready, in the middle of the night. On the flipside, at least time seemed to pass pretty quickly, and there was always something to do, either easy work or pleasant relaxation. And her drinking never got in the way because of the flexible work conditions; normal workers got the last three days of the nine-day week off, plus any other nominated day of the week with two fortnights' notice. Pilots though had every third day and week off.

Health and safety; the new pilot fatigue laws.

Zero drug tolerance of course, but she could do anything she liked on the week off, provided she tested clean on the first day back.

Yeah, it was sweet.

She had it all worked out.

But she missed…

She missed…

She missed her best friend.

And that made her cry…

And if it wasn't gone tomorrow, this deep and horrible sorrow, she was going to throw herself off the balcony, which was basically the second or third thought she had every morning.

Don't think, just get up, go out, and jump.

Exhilarating, and sudden.

She couldn't live like this. What if she had completely fucked herself up for good with that last binge? It had been hardcore.

What if she'd irreparably changed, ruined, her brain chemistry? What if this depression was permanent? The thought terrified her to the core. She knew how that ran. She'd known people, she'd had friends who'd done that. Some of them had done it with drugs, some had even done it just by pushing themselves too hard, and ended up with lifelong side-effects from self-inflicted hyper-stress.

But what if she had done something like that to herself? Gods. Now she would have to take meds, strong meds with side effects. Psychotropics and anti-psychotics, all her life. Anti-depressants, balanced with uppers and adrenalin-modifiers. Serotonin-stabilizers and gut-equalizers. It took years to get that right, to make it work, and watch over it forever, keeping it at bay, always. And all the while, the thing, the infinite sadness, the ever-receding and cresting waves of compounded disappointment and immortal melancholia, always there, lurking…

And to top it off; always knowing; you did this to yourself.

That last binge.

Always regretting.

If only you hadn't…

No, no… that was too much.

She wasn't that kind of person, she couldn't deal with that. She'd gotten used to the small depressions. A bad afternoon, at first. Then it had been a bad day, then a bad couple of days… but when had it become a *bad week*?

When had she become…*this*?

When had this become the price?

And when had she agreed to pay it?

When, the hell, had she even agreed to fucking *purchase*?

This was insane.

She was suicidal. Because she was so twisted up and burned out and tapped out and thrashed out, and within, within was running on empty. But it had been within, on some crazy, fucked-up journey that she had tried to get.

When had she made that decision?

That it would be through alcohol?

That she would slowly but surely dilute herself to the point that she could remember…?

'High moon is up baby, up, up, high moon is *up*, baby, not down darlin', not *down* darlin'…'

She'd blacked that out, every time. Every time she'd fucked, she'd uttered a crazy mantra like some mad woman. Most guys wouldn't have paid any attention; people said all sorts of things in the throes of passion. Wasn't that a 'thing'? People said 'I love you' and didn't mean it. It was just primal, biological, just a flood of chemicals to the brain, demanding to be translated into language so they could bond and pass on their DNA. Right? It was that, which was doing the talking, most of the time. But; this was not that. This was her inner darkness, taunting her, slipping out when she wasn't looking; it was her inner demand for her own sanity, allowing it. Something so deep she'd attracted a fucking Atlantean shaman to help her prise it out; holy shit!

She curled up tight again as another wave of terrible anxiety, of greasy, gushing, unctuous sadness reared up like a sewer dragon from the pit of her stomach…

And she coughed.

She coughed like she was going to throw up.

There was bile, acid in her throat, and something forced its way out. When she was done, the tightness in her stomach, in her ribs, had eased, just a bit.

And she fell asleep.

Sick to her stomach, but better.

CHAPTER SEVENTEEN

Hylar woke again.

The anxiety and the depression were still there, but they had lessened.

She could never drink again.

She had to find another way, to get to whatever it was she needed to get to.

To keep going on the path, the path she had long ago started walking, unconsciously, within.

It was that fucking *Astra*.

Hanging around with her, and her fucking *masterplan*.

Holy John, Paul, George and fucking Ringo!

…where was she?

It had been six days, by her reckoning.

The timing was good.

In a few days, she would need to get the tourists off, for the start of the descent.

There would be no booze left in her system.

She could take some massive doses of organics, or non-synth at least, and be okay by then.

She knew this feeling; the abatement of the hangover.

But she had never, never waited six days for it to pass.

She'd only showered once, a few days ago.

She needed room service.

She started the coffee machine, wrapped the quilt around her and went to look out of the balcony.

'Open balcony.'

The glass shifted into nothing and the air blew in as the atmosphere in the room levelled out.

Her balcony, which came with the job, was basically an eagle's nest view of the surrounding mountains. The Vulchallan

Alps were three enormous mountain ranges, each roughly the size of New Zealand, a trio of ridges side by side around half the planet's northern hemisphere. She lived in the northern section of the middle range, where the skiing was relaxed and, more importantly, UK Celestial had been able to build an easily accessible spaceport.

It seemed very cold.

She'd managed to call in and use up a couple of sick leave days, but without a medical professional to vouch for her, she'd have to go in and fly tomorrow.

So be it.

She was done anyway.

She had what she'd come for.

Now you just have to get away with it.

She didn't know where that thought had come from.

Get away with it?

Hadn't she… why would she even…?

Whatever.

She looked back at the rock, and the snow, and the deep massiveness. The thing about monstrously enormous vistas was that the mind tended to accept them, because their scale was so vast it had no choice. She felt she could immediately split people into two categories in this regard as well.

Swish had always criticized her for that, splitting things into two camps. But Swish had been her friend, and had always been curious, and listened.

There were the people who she brought up here who felt small, and whose mood immediately started going down. And then, there were people she brought up here who realized they were part of it, and that scale was meaningless, whose mood immediately went up. Then you could split them again; those who lingered and those who did not, and so forth. But Hylar herself had always been one who'd lingered, and felt she belonged to it. She liked that about herself, and liked others who did likewise.

The smell of freshly brewed coffee though, could pull her away from anything.

She returned to the kitchen.

'Close balcony. Privacy.'

She threw the quilt off. She was coming back, chemically, mentally. She felt icky.

She took the coffee through to the bathroom.

'Shower on; washing hot.'

She looked no thinner than usual. The thing, the thin thing she had seen in the corner of her eye, the past few days, had been like a white praying mantis, with bedraggled back hair like some Japanese ghoul conjured from a dead well.

She stared into her eyes as the steam started to fill the room.

A few more lines. A bit darker under the eyelids.

Did she feel cleansed? God knows, she had cried, long hours. Her stomach muscles still hurt, her sinuses and throat felt swollen and abused. She had entertained every notion of failure, re-examined every turn in her life where she might have made another, cross-examined every crossroads and wallowed in the regret of it all, the self-loathing, and ultimately, the unknowing as to whether any of it had been worthwhile.

She showered, hot, until her pale white skin was glowing pink with the heat and the pressure of the exfoliate cloth, infusing her pores with the tangy fragrance of the citrus-scented soap; not to any painful or self-punishing extent, just because she liked it, like this. Heat and exfoliation and fresh, clean clothes.

Somewhere in the slightly golden undertones of her pale skin she could see the Chinese ancestry that had given her the long curve of her eyelid, and her naturally-flared black lashes. As she applied mascara, and attended to the thin, long, black arch of her eyebrows, this became even more apparent, and even more pleasing to her.

Her frame and her pale skin, she suspected, were from a long French–Mexican line that dated back centuries and came right up to her mother. The Chinese was from her paternal grandmother, who had married British. Somehow that had made it easy for her to work here, on a UKC planet. Go figure.

Like the rest of her, her face was long and thin, diamond-like with a sharp chin and cheek-bones. Her nose was virtually invisible; it was fine in profile, softly feline, but head on it was just two black dots, lost in her pale skin above a tiny mouth with full lips, the pinkest, lushest part of her whole body. They pursed well, her lips, and she had a good, dark, sideways smile. But on the whole, depending on where she was at any given time in her life; tired, drunk, pre-menstrual, whatever, she could look anywhere between gaunt and severe, classically demure, and, on a great day, catwalk-lithe and sultry-gorgeous. Presently the latter was way out of reach, demure a distant hope, but if she could get past gaunt and dress down the severe, she might be able to go out and just eat at a table, alone, get a look or two to boost her self-esteem, and that would be okay.

She didn't know many of the week-off rotation pilots, but maybe a few of her co-workers, some of whom were becoming friends, would return a day early. None of them would be drinking, a day before rotation. The money here was too good, the blood tests way too thorough.

She'd eat, walk around a bit. Then she would come back…

She pressed the housekeeping button again.

They should have been here by now.

…come back, sleep in fresh sheets and wake again, ready to fly.

By the time she'd gotten ready to go out, she had almost changed her mind. There was no fresh food in the chalet, so she had to go out. But in order to have the energy to go, she wanted something to eat first. The chalet only delivered company food; synthetics and corporate crops, which she trusted to fill her but not necessarily to nourish her. But they would do to stop her feeling lightheaded on the way down to the valley. She put on another coffee, aware that her thinking was not crystal clear and had as much to do with feeling restless, and procrastinating because she was raw and didn't really want to see anyone, as it did anything else. She felt that she needed to see someone, anyone really, but even deeper, she didn't really know what she wanted, or who she wanted, or where she wanted to be any more. So she put another milk capsule in the defroster and waited.

She kind of knew the housekeepers, enough to want to explain that she'd been in bed for six days, and wanted a total bedding overhaul, and certainly enough to pay them a bit extra so there would be fresh food here when she got back.

They had never been this slack.

Regardless, after a few minutes more she was starving and couldn't wait. She left a quick voice message then went out the back to check on her gravski, which she hadn't used in six days. It started fine, but the dash summary said it hadn't been used for nine days. She frowned to herself, then realized; she'd come back when she'd started the bender… oh yeah, three plus six.

Fuck Hylar, get some food.

She left the gravski warming, as it was a lot colder than she'd expected, and returned to the kitchen. The coffee was ready and she drank some water to ease the hunger pains. Hunger pains were terrible for anxiety; they could falsely retrigger the depression. She was surprised, now she'd labelled it, how much she intuitively knew about it. Alcoholic depression. Was that a thing? She felt like she'd heard of it before. Depressive anxiety…?

She mused as she rolled a gulp of coffee in her mouth.

For some reason maroons, burgundies, and deep purples worked for her. Wine colors, she had always said, with a wicked smile. Something about that and the straight, thick, jet-black hair, halfway down her back these days, and when she put on a tight sweater… where was it?

She went to her wardrobe. All there; three standard and decent outfits with all the pilot stuff. The winter-wine one consisted of a rose-pink shirt with an open, sharp-pointed collar that spiked up and down the sides of her neck and accentuated the long line. Then a V-neck dark-burgundy wool sweater, tight and figure-flattering, and the long, deep-purple skirt with a fine rose-cordovan weave that hugged to her slim hips and flat belly. Then, the deep maroon lace-up waistcoat, done half-up, and the port-purple frock coat, draped with a purple, rose-violet polka-dotted scarf.

Pop.

She looked for the man whose eyes asked himself; what's under all those layers?

It was really getting cold now, so she put her long leather burgundy clip-clop boots on as well.

She could feel that first coffee settling in.

Then, as she drank down the second, she realized that nobody was coming.

Really nobody.

Shit. She ran both her hands back through the hair on her temples.

They found their way down her cheeks, to her neck, as though unconsciously she wanted to strangle herself.

It was evening… there might still be…

Shit. Jesus shit. Jesus shit fuck.

She was frozen to the spot. Her brain wasn't working, she was still too wrecked.

How could she confirm? What could she – ?

Her phone. She hadn't even looked at it, all this time.

Why not?

She'd turned it off; the night with the Atlantean Giant. She'd turned it off and she'd been so miserable and low on energy, physically and spiritually, and real, actual brain power that she hadn't even thought about it.

Hadn't thought about her phone!

It was on the floor, on the other side of the bed; Atlantean had made it fall on the other side. She scrambled over, stretched down and wrenched it up. In her grasp, it seemed to take an eternity to come back on.

She rang Ekto at the spaceport. Ekto was a binge drinker too. They didn't have sex, but they covered for each other.

'Moondarla?' Ekto sounded incredulous. 'We thought…'

'Ekto; look, I fucked up, I –'

'What? You fucked up? Who cares! Where are you?'

'In my chalet…'

'You can't be; we scanned, you weren't there…'

'When? I've been here six days!'

'Moondarla, I'm scanning now; you're not there!'

'Ekto, I am here – looking out of my –'

'Moondarla, have you been watching the news?'

'The news? No, of course not. I never –'

'The planet is under siege, Moondarla. What day do you think it is?'

'It's… Day Nine of the last week of the Cool Season. I can never remember what the real names are…'

'That must have been one hell of a bender, Hylar. You overslept. It's Day Three of Week One of Midseason, Moondarla. We're in the bad patch! But that's not the worst of it; like I said, we're under siege! None of us can leave!'

'What?! What the fuck!?'

'None of us can take shelter, we're all hostages! And in three hours, the cold comes. The Big Cold. In five hours, we'll all be dead!'

CHAPTER EIGHTEEN

'Who? Who's…?'

She wanted to go back to bed. Pull the disgusting quilt back over her head and let this all happen without her as she froze to death in the bed where she'd been dying anyway, inside, for the past six… wait. Really? Nine?

'I'm… I'm all dressed to go out! How do you hold a planet under siege? Where's UK Celestial?'

'Listen, don't worry about any of that; there are hardly any ships left, they stole or destroyed them all…'

'They…?'

'They can't get into yours, it's one of the only ones they haven't been able to scupper somehow.'

'Of course it is; that ship's AI was designed by…' she gulped. '…it was upgraded on Ama…'

Her voice ran out. What the hell was happening? What?

'Designed by Emma?' Ekto was puzzled. 'Hylar, who is – ?'

'How are you talking to me? If all this is true?'

'If all this is true? Look, okay. You just woke up, I get that. It's… they let us talk to each other, Hylar. You see? They're in orbit, they've taken over Vulchalla Station. They had it all planned; they've disabled all the teleport terminals. There's only one left in operation…'

'What do they want?'

'What else? Money!'

'*Money?*'

'They're pirates, Moondarla!'

'Okay, but…' she asked again. 'Where's UK Celestial!?'

'They don't negotiate with pirates! They told us to hold tight and take shelter and wait out the season; there's nobody left here who's important enough for them to risk fighting for; all the UKC CEOs are on Goldilocks 1101…'

'Goldilocks 1101? Ekto, what the fuck?'

'They found it a few months ago… a planet where the color of the sand changes according to your irises; and it responds to contact lenses! Man am I in the wrong business.'

Was he rambling? Or trying to tell her something?

'Ekto; focus. If you're hostages, why do they keep the communication networks up?'

'They're not actually here.'

'Then…?'

'They hit three days ago; they said we had to organise ourselves, collect everything with any precious metal and put it in the gravski pavilion.'

'Has anyone done anything?'

'No! Nobody can agree; there's a whole group at the hotel who think the pirates are bluffing, and that UKC will be here any minute; and a bunch at the apartments who think we should wait it out and fight them… they're going to end up killing each other over engagement rings and family heirlooms!'

'But where are the cops?'

'Gone! Security, pilots, command structure, gone!'

'Gone where?!'

'Taken – up to the orbit station. They're going to space them all if we don't agree to their terms!'

'To put all the precious metals in the gravski pavilion?'

'Yes!'

Her mind was struggling, trying to kick start.

'It doesn't make any sense… it's too… there's not enough…' She became suddenly and overwhelmingly paranoid. 'What if they're listening?'

'Hylar, there are more than three thousand people here, and they never get off the phones. There must be ten pirates, tops. They can't be monitoring all the calls… besides, they don't know you're here!'

Hylar licked her lips.

'Ekto, this is the most important question you've ever been asked. Think hard when you answer…'

'Okay…'

'What is the fastest way I can get to some decent food?'

CHAPTER NINETEEN

Ekto said he would send up a small, undetectable drone with a well-stocked package.

'They won't see it. One of the counsellors here was on another planet where this happened, he's been through it; they're doing this all over the galaxy, just chancing it. If we don't give in they'll just leave us here. Blow the orbital station and leave us. They won't be able to nano together a replacement station before the Big Cold sets in and we'll all die down here. The crew of the station and the people they've taken hostage will be sold off into slavery, somewhere out there in the deep black that nobody's ever heard of, where even the Lemurians won't go...'

'Have they moved the remaining ships?'

'No. But they're in control of the satellite security weapons. They blew a hole in the ski ramp on Yeti Mountain just to let us know. One of the ice race instructors tried to skate in on the roof of the food hall; they blew it to pieces. I ... I really don't know what we're going to do! I came here for a break...'

'Me too...'

'Maybe someday I will come here to die, but not for another hundred years, you know!'

'I just need to eat, Ekto. Then I can help.'

'Help? How?'

'I know pirates.'

'What? How?'

'I used to fly Indie, Ekto. I met my share.'

'Indie? You flew outside of the corporations? I thought you were a fly-right?'

'I am now. But I wasn't always. I flew six missions with Astra Solara. Seven if you count how it all came together.'

'Ass...' Ekto gasped. 'The Mission Queen?"

'I was her pilot.'

She heard him shift around in his chair, agitated.

'Then…' Ekto gulped. '…you have to get her here! Call her in! She's got to come here and take these fuckers out!'

'I don't… she's not… that isn't… even if she…'

'What are you saying?'

'We had a falling out.'

'A falling out?'

'The way I hear it, nobody's willing to crew with her any more. Nine Indie missions. There's no way she's coming back from the next one. Even suicidal mercenaries need some hope. And the ones that don't, she wouldn't hire. I don't think she's even going to be able to get a ship for her next mission. The last one was a write off and *Hightail* is not an option; nobody will insure her.'

'You really do know her, don't you?'

'She's like… the older sister I never had.'

'You do have an older sister. You told me.'

'I know. But Astra is the one I never had. Astra never tried to kill me over a guy I barely even slept with. And they were only engaged, like, a week.'

There was silence.

'I was a different person then.'

Still silence.

'I don't drink any more, now.'

It wasn't like Ekto to judge, but she supposed she had to accept it. So she just stared out at the white, awaiting the drone. It scared her half to death when it zipped up right in front of her and leaped over the balcony like a giant frog. She understood; he'd sent it as close to the surface of the rocks as he could. The frog's belly was full of everything; bread, cheese, fruit, a big salad, meats and jams. She wanted to eat it all at once.

Her brain, her body was demanding it.

There was silence a while longer until her shaking hands got the seal-pod open. The smell of the food was overwhelming, and she paused for a brief second, stunned, taking it in.

Then there was a quiet question.

'Got it?'

'Thanks. I mean it.'

'I remembered you like cheese. It's the good stuff.'

She could smell it.

'What would she do if she were here?' Ekto demanded. 'What would the Mission Queen do?'

Hylar stared at the cheese, taking in the smell.

It remained untouched.

Her long, graceful fingers were still trembling.

'Easy. She'd apologise for the name calling and beg me to pilot her last mission into oblivion.'

'No; I mean, about the pira –'

'I know what you mean, Ekto!'

She could hear herself breathing.

She went to the kitchen and poured a glass of water.

'Well?'

'She'd get to my ship, get up there, and…'

'And what?'

'She'd negotiate.'

'Negotiate?!'

'Yeah. Because the UKC are too gutless to take the risk.'

'Negotiate with pirates!?'

'Then she'd track them back to where they came from, to their lair, and get the stuff back.'

'She would?'

'I'm pretty sure that would be her plan. The pirates know UKC don't negotiate. They know it's not worth their while to actually kill or hurt anyone. And if they're as carefree as you suggest, it shouldn't really be too hard, should it?'

Silence again.

'What do you think, Ekto? Should I do that? Or should I just… sit here, and eat cheese? Hmmm?'

CHAPTER TWENTY

She could leave them all to die, she knew.

If nobody knew she was here.

If she could convince Ekto to shut up about it.

She had a ship.

A ship that only she could use.

She could stay up here in the chalet. Figure something out, to remain at the very least alive and mobile, while the lakes froze over and the glaciers closed in (people had survived, unprepared, after all) and leave all the rich tourists to die. She could pretend to let the pirates come down here and take everything, then kill them at the last minute and have everything for herself. Or, she could let the pirates go, track them back to their lair, just like she'd said the Mission Queen would do, kill them all, and just make off with all their stash.

Hmm. A lot more dangerous but potentially a lot more reward.

If… and it was a big if… *if* they were as lazy as all that. As lazy as Ekto made them out to be…

It was okay, she told herself, that all these selfish scenarios ran through her head. That she planned them out, plotted them like that was something she might do, like it was a real option just to off everybody and make away.

It was okay, that these thoughts occurred.

Wasn't it?

She needed some kind of pet, to bounce these ideas off.

Just to hear herself say out loud to something living; what if I just wasted everyone and shot through with the stash? Would that be so bad?

She made a weird propeller noise and it tickled her lips to make them vibrate so. Or was it reverberate? Wondering. She leaned over and picked up the phone, this time watching the reflection of her small, full mouth in the black mirror of her sleeping screen as the pink lips vibreverbed.

If you can't decide between two words, mash them, her old friend Swish had always prosisted.

Then she replaced the phone on the table and continued to sit there, on a wooden chair with her burgundy leather boots up on the wooden dining table, staring out at the glaring white of the snow-covered mountains, waiting.

She should never have told Ekto all of that.

Never.

Because once she'd felt suspicion, her wits had returned.

She had smelled something toxic in the food when she'd opened it, then specifically in the cheese. Something to slow her down, maybe even put her to sleep.

So they wanted her alive.

Probably they just wanted her ship.

In hindsight, blabbing about a connection to Astra Solara probably prevented them from outright poisoning the cheese and killing her.

Still, whenever someone tried to kill her, or came close, she couldn't help herself. She'd always end up wondering.

Why shouldn't I just be like them?

Why shouldn't I just threaten and bully and manipulate and get what I want, just for the sake of it?

She could do that; she had done that. But it had always been justified; always been for, what on her terms, she saw as the greater good. Even if it was her own greater good. But why shouldn't she get all the money, this time? Was it only the money they wanted? Was there anything else? Power and fame, she supposed? Reputation? Respect?

But, nah. In the end it was always all about the money.

Money bought security, and from a secure position, you could plan.

You could defend and maintain, with an eye to further conquest.

But the thing was, she was an excellent pilot. And she earned enough to be happy. She was secure enough, happy enough, generally, to plan. She had been planning here, in this very chair, not a fortnight ago, toward the end of the last shift.

What to do next, where to go next.

Could she make a claim, get a stake yet?

Maybe find someone; a compatible cabal, like Astra always talked about, at the end of all this?

But that wasn't…

That was never…

Not now.

But, hadn't there been a dream, or something?

That big Atlantean?

She folded her arms.

The burgundy outfit was layered, and ordinarily warm, but it wasn't thermal and she was going to freeze to death, waiting here for them.

Fortunately, although she loved cheese, when she was this worn out it made her sleepy and gave her spots. This and the initial smell, not quite unique enough to pass as non-Earth dairy, had given her pause, encouraged her to sniff it again, and well. And there it had been; not totally familiar, but definitely laced. Nothing strong enough to tell her definitely poison or just sedative, but: there, for sure.

She liked Ekto, but her gut, her still-empty gut, told her he was in on it. Ekto was an immoral pragmatist and he would have cut a deal; before they arrived? Or, when they arrived? Either way, to save himself after they'd arrived.

It didn't matter, he was in.

Then she'd made the crack about the cheese. She hadn't been able to help herself. But it was just enough… to be stupid.

So now she had one shot at getting aboard the *Lauren Bacall* and she didn't want to blow it. Her ship was incredibly powerful, a one of a kind build it had taken Hylar a decade to put together from virtually nothing. Almost everything about her was outlawed on at least one planet or another, but like her namesake she was one of the greats and would not tolerate mistreatment or disrespect of any kind. No doubt some of the pirates had already snuck down and tried to board her, and suffered the consequences. Some of them might even have recognized her. If they were indeed waiting on the overtaken orbital station, they would be planning now how to get her off-world in one piece and sell her.

Hylar's mind continued to clear, even though her energy remained pitifully low. Although her head was still aching, and she was still massively dehydrated, she could fix that. Just being awake and alert was increasing her adrenalin. She'd tried to do the math at one point; she figured that she must have been drinking the best part of four days, and simply not noticed the transition into the fourth. Probably catching micro-sleeps the whole time, maybe even a nap. Indoors all the time. She still wasn't completely sure how long the savage mood crash had lasted. Eight, nine days?

Hell, it happened, okay? There was no time to process; it just was.

Given that; the worst of it now was that she hadn't expected to be here over the final run of days toward 'the bad patch', so she hadn't stocked up on food. She remembered eating bits and pieces, just from time to time, foraging though the fridge and pecking like a bird, but whatever had been there, there was nothing left of it now, just kitchen water. It was fortunate that the water had not been automatically cancelled. Probably they just let the pipes freeze. She'd had the last of the painkillers sometime during her great depression… but she hadn't kept her fluids up, and now…

Now.

She just had to wait and see who came. In just a second she would stand, walk back to the bedroom, and wait by the safe. Then she would take care of them, whoever came, and then…

What equipment did she have around the house?

She couldn't remember.

She'd disconnected all the voyeuristic security here, although maybe Ekto had managed to get it back on by now and was watching her. Maybe not, but she didn't want to take the risk, didn't want to search about and take out whatever helpful stuff she had stashed around while someone was watching… it would kind of miss the point of having stashed it in the first place. She was pretty sure she'd smuggled in one of those banned hyper-therma-skins… and with any luck, the people who came for her would bring –

She heard a sound from the other end of the chalet.

Unmistakeable.

For most people it wouldn't register. But to Hylar Moondarla it was virtually a trick of the trade, something that once you picked up on it, you always heard it.

A sliding pop, Astra had called it.

Although Hylar had always considered in a sighing snap.

Somebody had just teleported into the chalet.

CHAPTER TWENTY-ONE

Experienced space travellers never missed the sound of a sly teleport. Aside from any other concerns, on any kind of confined space voyage it always paid to know when someone had just appeared out of nowhere, so you became attuned. Like sleeping alone in an old house; anything that sounded like a break-in registered with an almost supernatural immediacy. Wherever you happened to be, the teleport zing was a good sound to be aware of, but specifically aboard a moving spacecraft. That, or say, alone in a mountain chalet on a distant planet, miles from anywhere, above sea level.

'S'b'd'y theh?'

She could do a good sedated voice.

She'd had practice.

'R'm s'v'ss?'

Muscle memory… or was it *sense* memory with actors?

She got up and staggered around a bit, somewhat startled at how little effort she had to put into faking it. She hadn't brought a lot of stuff up here with her from the ship, nor activated much of the furniture or decor. She'd made some okay friends but nobody she particularly felt like opening up to, at least, not deliberately. The alcohol sometimes took care of that but, mostly, her subconscious was under…

She staggered deliberately a few steps, then recovered.

Maybe it was the Atlantean…?

Coming back?

She heard footsteps coming through the kitchen; people in good stalking shoes that made little sound.

No.

On the wood-panelled floor, there was nothing to absorb the clip-clops of her hard-heels. She took a few more deliberately uneven, cracking steps to the middle of the floor and stopped. Then she quickly lifted her left heel behind her, then her right, activating cushion mode with each corresponding hand, and ran to the back of the room, her footfalls completely silent. There, she flattened her back against the rock surface of the chalet wall.

The temperature was dropping by the second now. She had felt her collar bones, the backs of her hands, her nose and her cheeks become colder just moving swiftly through room temperature.

She was panting a bit.

She was taking several big risks; she was pretty sure she could deal with whatever was happening, even if her only option was to flee, but she was hoping for more than that. For more, however, she needed to move fast, and that meant…

If she was being monitored through the internal system, they would know she'd tried to fool them just then. The drone had almost certainly been sent to monitor her but it was out; she'd disabled it and thrown it over the balcony. They could always send another but not yet, she had gambled. If the people coming through from the kitchen were pro-hunters they would have a thermal scanner and would therefore have seen her move to the centre of the room, sedated, then scamper away, clearly not sedated. They would know she was pretending. She doubted any kind of portable tracker held by lazy pirates would work through the sheer rock walls though; these chalets had been carved into the sides of the mountains with robot drillers. Half the point was that if you could afford to stay here, it was easy to avoid surveillance, if not detection altogether, provided you were not naïve enough to leave the internal surveillance on.

She had been told all this by a security guy she'd been drinking with a while back. She couldn't remember if she'd slept with him or not. Probably. He'd reminded her that there was no way in or out, after all, other than gravski or teleport; maybe a drone ride if you were desperate. There were accident prevention emergency drones stationed all along the chalet section of the mountains, apparently. But the worst kept secret of the emergency drones, which were designed to automatically activate and catch anything that fell from any of the chalet balconies (wealthy people, it seemed, would always love to do drugs, alone, while taking in their expensive views) was that they only activated seventy-five percent of the time. On top of that, they only actually caught people before impact sixty-five percent of the time and only caught people without doing them permanent physical damage fifty-percent of the time. So if she became overwhelmed here, it was an option for her.

But it was not a good one.

She kept her back flat against the wall, staring at the door to the kitchen.

She couldn't stop panting.

She was feeling weaker, colder.

She angled her head back, felt her gaunt cheek on the cold stone.

They'd teleported into the kitchen. She was pretty sure there were only two. There was another door on the other side of the balcony, but one of them would have to circle around through the entire chalet to get there and if they were lazy pirates, and if they had taken the bait, she was sure they wouldn't bother.

She shifted her head a little, away from the wall, and let her eyes dart back there.

Nothing, no lights even.

But moving her cheek off the stone had almost peeled skin. Jizzle dizzle. As soon as the second sun started going down behind the mountains, the chalet became dark within just a few minutes. That was happening now, but it also meant it would get a lot colder, a lot faster. At least her assailants would have to move soon or surrender the light advantage to her.

Involuntarily she placed her hand on her chest. She could feel her heart pounding beneath her palm, through three layers of clothing. That in turn made her even more anxious; the lack of food, the dehydration, the emotional drain and strain; the shock and processing and the siege, the pure stress... and now the insane feel of her own heartbeat, spreading into her brain, pulsing, her whole body starting to throb, JPGR, she was going to have an anxiety attack…

'She's passed out…'

'Sshh!'

'What are we waiting for!'

'Quiet!'

She held her breath a second, then let it out. Slowly. Through her tiny nostrils. A warm, slow expulsion over the top of her freezing lips.

Two men. Maybe young.

Anxy had bought her ploy, Nervy wasn't so sure.

She wasn't quite sure how close they were, maybe just around the corner. Maybe Nervy was close enough to see that there wasn't a collapsed body on the floor in the middle of the room.

They'd teleported into the kitchen. Her brain kept repeating. Teleported. Kitchen. Why was that bothering her? One room away, just in case. Sneak up, just in case. They could have teleported right next to her, but they were being cautious. That made sense. Then again, they could have teleported…

Teleported.

That was why she was freaking out.

That was the thing she'd failed to absorb.

Teleport. Teleport was expensive. They're teleported in here, like it was nothing.

Hylar, you *spank-wanking arse-twig*!

There was no choice now. She had to play the advantage.

She stared edging back along the wall, toward the second open doorway, away from the intruders. Even if they were young and dumb, if they could afford teleport, they could afford decent weapons and equipment.

The lazy pirates had backing.

Probably why Ekto had jumped ship.

He saw the money.

Of course he'd seen the money!

Why didn't she think like that?

Why was she even going to try and save a bunch of over-wealthy galactic corporate British dickheads…? What had they ever done to help her…?

Well, employed her, she supposed…

For a ridiculous sum, for doing next to nothing…

There was that, she supposed…

She was nearly there.

Don't think about it, she told herself. Don't think about trying to be good. Just be good, and…

'Hey!'

She dashed and made it around the corner.

Astra had taught her to recognize the different kinds of directed energy weapons, because of that thing she'd swallowed that time, so Hylar knew it was some kind of plasma stun thing. It lit up that corner of the room as she fled and gave her a quick, lightning-strike reminder of where everything was. She was around the two corners, her hand skimming the walls and into the bedroom so quickly she couldn't believe that she hadn't tripped over anything, even given that she hadn't activated any of the décor. Then she ran directly into the bed and fell flat and hard, face-first on to it.

'Lights!' She heard one of the men shout.

'Voice activation, ditzo…' She muttered to herself as she scrambled up.

The wall safes in the chalets were carved out from the mountain-rock, the reinforced diamond-steel doors palm print, retina and voice-password activated. There were seven, in different locations, in each chalet, the theory being that even if you had been in this particular chalet before, you still didn't know which safe had been activated for that particular stay. She scrambled on her stomach, over the bed, the long skirt almost catching her knee and tripping her forward again, then she was on her knees, staring at the wall. You had to be within a meter and she had pushed the bed right up against the wall at some point during the depression, so that made it easier.

Seconds left. Three or four.

She palmed the wall. She knew, even in total darkness, the exact spot. The retina activated. Lime green laser.

'Sierra Madre!'

The handle appeared and she pulled with one hand; the door was heavy. She reached in with the other and snatched – just as someone shot her in the head.

CHAPTER TWENTY-TWO

A sharp pain struck her temple, from the left. There had been someone standing in the corner the whole time and they had just shot her at medium-close range, on a low stun setting. The blast jolted her head to the side and she collapsed shoulder-first into the pillows. Then there was someone grabbing her by the feet and she was turned onto her stomach again, being pulled back by the ankles, back across the bed, grasping for anything she could grab hold of and gain purchase. But there were only pillows and quilts and she simply dragged them with her. There was another shot and the middle of her back pulsed with pain; she went straight back to childhood, being hit square from behind at force in dodgeball, her whole body arcing backwards with unanticipated agony, wondering what the hell had happened and why this had been allowed.

She'd gotten out of worse scrapes, she told herself.

Worse than this, even wearing the same outfit.

Now you can get out of –

'Tell me how to take control and assume command of the *Lauren Bacall*.'

She thought for a second the shot had damaged her spine, because she couldn't move her shoulders. But just as she realized that, she realized that she could still move her fingers. Suddenly the bed was being shifted away from the wall, back from the still open safe.

'You, grab her hands…'

So that was it.

'Flip her.'

She was trying to think but she was shutting down. She'd heard that this happened; the brain tried to check out and withdraw. What was happening, what was going to happen, was so horrifying that the brain, the mind, the memory, the spirit, the soul; all of the above, none of them wanted a part of it, nor to remember anything about it.

It would be over soon enough.

She gritted her teeth.

She'd been in worse scrapes, but nothing beyond this point.

She was unarmed. She'd gambled upon not revealing her advantage, and had failed.

'Spread her.'

The universe is punishing me for sport-fucking an Atlantean shaman.

The leader cracked a glowstick and rested it on the bedside cabinet.

The room was filled with an electric blue phosphorescent glow. Cold and eerie.

Her hair was streaming everywhere but most of it was still under her, pulling on her scalp whenever she moved. The frock coat was twisted under her as well. The man behind her was holding down her arms, leaning into the job with his full body weight and clamped, clammy hands around her wrists.

She'd been roughly handled by men before. She'd been held down by nervous henchmen, overcompensating. Men had tried to beat her, rape her, kill her before. And women. Women had tried all of that too.

She wasn't used to this, by any means and she would never want to be. But they weren't dealing with someone who was going to let it happen. Once, she'd let it happen. Or, rather, it had happened once and she hadn't known to stop it. The next time, she had stopped it. And once you've stopped it, once you know it's coming again, you can plan to stop it; that was when it never happened again. That was when flight, the instinct to mentally withdraw, ended, and fight, the instinct to prevent it, emerged.

There were three henchmen. There had been another with the two in the kitchen, or another with the leader, whom she had to assume had been working his way through the inside of the chalet in the dark to come around the other side of the balcony. They knew who she was; they knew she would put up a fight. Stupid, stupid lack of self-esteem.

Really, really now, she was never, ever going to have another drink.

She'd weakened herself to the point where this was happening.

Bad decisions, bad decisions, bad decisions.

One of each of the other two had her legs, by the boots, and had spread them wide.

There was a pretty one on her left leg, a fat bull-face on her right. Pretty pushed down hard on her ankle with his right hand and pulled out a knife with his left. Clammy hands laughed. His nostrils, his under-chin and neck, were right above her, but he was pressing down hard on each wrist.

'What are you doing?'

She was craning her neck up to see, ignoring the fact that it was effectively like someone pulling her hair. The leader was staring at Pretty.

'Cut off her panties?'

'Why?'

'We're gonna fuck 'er, aren't we?'

The leader sighed, exasperated. 'Even if that was my intent...'

Their leader stared back at her. Something about the fact that he was looking at her now, that his focus was upon her, made her suddenly see.

He was UnEarth.

Clammy spoke up. 'She's pretty. Real pretty. If we fuck 'er I wanna record it.'

'Too skinny,' Bullface snarled. 'Not enough meat on 'er...'

'Fuck you!' Hylar spat.

'Enough!' the leader snapped, so loud it echoed through the chalet.

Hylar gulped. She had a plan. But she just needed them to do one thing.

One. Thing.

'You are Hylar Moondarla. We know that. You are not wanted by the Pro-United Government of Earth Colonies Alliance but you are a person of interest and to put it plainly, there are no witnesses here worth a damn, and I am a person of importance who is indulged in these matters, because I get results.'

'When you get your results...' Pretty sounded assured. '...we get to fuck her.'

The leader smiled down at Hylar, totally charming. 'This one is my equivalent in a much smaller pond.' He turned to Pretty. 'Then what do I offer her that will make her cooperate?'

Pretty shrugged. 'We let her live.'

The leader looked back down at Hylar. 'Would you prefer to remain living? After they've made use of you?'

Hylar was genuinely unsure whether or not this UnEarth creep was real; whether he was bluffing to scare her, or a genuine hosap running a genuinely homicidal pirate gang. On some level, not too far beneath her fading bravado, she knew that she was mentally and physically weak and vulnerable, a slender woman with a thin frame and the constitution of an active alcoholic, just coming off a rock-bottom depression, being forcibly held down, legs braced apart, by a gang of four... and that she would have one, just one more...

'Why do you want my ship?'

The leader smiled calmly, almost ingratiating.

'Who wouldn't want that ship? Such a beautiful color.'

'Nobody gets inside her that I don't want inside her.'

She'd intended the double entendre. She wanted them getting stupid, thinking with their dicks. Clammy and Pretty laughed as Pretty clamped the knife between his teeth and bore down on her ankles anew, with both hands. They were both sniggering, essentially, not laughing. You didn't hear real gutter-minded sniggering very often, Hylar realized. Thank God.

'Do you know what this gun is?'

'Plasma pistol. Pressurised air in a plasma capsule.'

'That's right. The lowest setting it like a slap. The highest is rapid, the plasma shell turns molten, basically a cauterising bullet. This is a good one, of my own design. So many settings. Most have standard seven. This has seventy. I hit you twice with twelve.'

He raised the gun and shot her in the throat. It was tight and terrible, like being momentarily strangled, then like something had gone the wrong way down and she'd almost choked.

They let her cough it out as the leader looked around.

'It's… really starting to get… intolerably cold…'

She looked at the leader through watery eyes. She hadn't noticed; she was burning up.

'Raise her skirts. And be careful. Keep your weight on her ankles. She's escaped from situations like this before.'

She stared up at him, with a kind of hateful pleading in her eyes that she couldn't suppress. The leader just stared back.

'You want him to cut her panties off now, Engager Colven?'

Oh, Holy Deities, it was Colven.

Holy deities, protect me…

Colven didn't answer. Pretty shrugged across at Bullface as they used one hand each to push her long skirt up her legs. They got the front of the material up to the elastic, then bunched it up as high as it could go, as she tried to make it as hard for them as she could by making all the muscles in her legs as tense as they could be, tenser even than they already were, and keeping them flat, pressing her buttocks hard, and forcing her lower half into the bed. It made almost no difference. When they were done, and her loins were uncovered, just a pair of nickers between her and… she almost let go of a whimper, but instead bit down on her inside lower lip.

Step one, step one, you need step one; get them to shut…

Colven shot her in the gut and she spasmed, but the men kept holding her down.

'Setting thirteen.'

She was winded now, then coughing again.

He aimed again and shot her inside left thigh. She cried out in pain, the nerves all up and down her leg, and into her groin, turning her pleasure centres against her.

'Setting fourteen.'

All this time he hadn't moved from where he'd been standing, between Pretty and Bullface, but a few steps behind them. He was a great shot, just as she'd heard. Casually hitting his exact target in semi-darkness. But she'd also heard that he was a total sadist; not necessarily homicidal, but utterly psychopathic and highly functioning with it.

He shifted the pistol casually to the right, maintaining eye contact with her as she craned up, not feeling the pull of her hair beneath her on her scalp any longer.

'Tell me how to take permanent command of the *Lauren Bacall*.'

'You demented sadist fu –'

He shot her in the vagina.

'Setting fifteen.'

It was a kind of anti-orgasm. She blacked out for at least two seconds, but she didn't think she had closed her eyes, because when she came back, they were wide open and staring at the electric blue ceiling. Her mouth was open in a silent scream, then she heard a whistling, which she realized was the sound of her scream escaping her own constricted throat. As the sound lowered, her scream became more recognisable to her as it settled at the level of an agonized groan. Her mind was focussing on this because it could not process what was occurring within her body's nervous system. This terrible, evil parody of an orgasm was utterly devoid of any recognizable event that her physical system could ascertain.

'What happens now, is that your senses – down there – your nerve endings and, well, all of that, will be hyper sensitive to the slightest touch. There are people who are quite willing to go through what you've experienced, to experience the sexual hypersensitivity that comes afterwards. However, and believe me I know this though trial and error, should I proceed, with another shot…'

She braced herself.

'…even on the same setting, and I should tell you, my creation is programmed to automatically raise a setting after each gathered selection of shots, so it will not be set at…'

He shifted his aim, almost imperceptibly, and shot her again, in the direct centre of her ribs. The pain was searing, shocking, and she threw her head back as her whole torso tensed, as though it were momentarily on fire.

'…the next time will be setting seventeen. The pain of being shot at that setting, from this distance, with complete and total accuracy, where there are so many bunched nerve endings… upper left is the most sensitive, is it not? I believe I have learned this to be true. It… might make you pass out for a while? During that time, I will allow these men to do with the lower half of your body what they will. Surrender your ship, and I will kill you painlessly.'

He reached in and pulled out another pistol.

'Chemical pellets. Everything from mild euphoria to stop fugitives caring about running away, even as they are running, to a euthanizer that takes thirty seconds and feels, I'm told, like bliss. I offer you this, this peace of mind, knowing that there is no way out for you. Surrender your defeat, surrender to death, surrender your ship and surrender it to me.'

'Why?' Her voice sounded hoarse. 'I don't understand.'

Above her, Clammy guffawed.

She threw her head back. 'What!? If you're gonna stick that big, hard cock in my dead mouth, at least let me know why!'

She had his number; she felt his hands squirm, go tighter, clammier.

'Amazon Seven, you dumb fuck doll!' Clammy grunted. 'That ship's been to Amazon Seven!'

She swung her head back down, staring up at Colven.

'*That?*' Hylar was genuinely incredulous. 'You're killing me for *that*!?'

Colven took a step forward, keeping the gun trained directly between her legs.

He was going to hit her on the clitoris, she knew. Right on it. She had to figure it out, right now, whether or not she could take that. Was he serious about them doing what they wanted with her…? Because, she couldn't handle that. Everything so far she could still live with. Easy. Well, maybe not easy. But she could… she was telling herself, she could.

She saw him looking at her.

She saw him processing.

He was going to shoot. She looked him straight in the eye. She had to tell the truth. He was experienced in torture; he would sense a lie. She was a good liar, but not that good. Not good enough to trump a functionally sadistic, homicidal psychopath.

She had once chance, one roll of the dice.

She had to take it.

A man with two guns, with that many precise settings, he had to be an obsessive compulsive.

'Is the safe still open?'

She was pretty sure it was. God, she hoped it was and that the clod Clammy hadn't accidentally slammed it shut with the back of his fat head.

'It is…' Colven confirmed.

'You know how these places work. Once it's open, it's open. There are no tricks. There are no booby traps, and I haven't taken any extra precautions.'

Colven lowered the guns and walked directly around the bed to the safe. She craned backwards but couldn't see past Clammy.

'Are you looking in?'

'Yes. Tell me what I'm looking at.'

'They look like cherries, don't they? And plums.'

'Yes. Like… little bombs.'

'I don't know why things have to be like that for me. Everything… berry, or cherry, or wine or… I tolerate pink, because it goes. And it's… nice. Browns… like, red-browns, but then you're into maroons, really. That's what it is, red-browns. Almost crimson. But not blood colors.'

'Yes. I understand you. A little more, now. I've seen your profile.'

'I guess now, I'll never known why I obsess over those colors.'

'Why am I looking in here? There are no booby traps, I know. I know the truth when I see it in the eyes of my engagement. No cerebral distillation process is worth anything without the ability to refine the truth; an Engager must prosecute to the extent that the truth is distilled; that the cerebral essence is refined and ultimately remains, leaving only the truth. Thus the methods of the Engager are justified; for they represent Justice itself.'

She could feel her chest heaving as she finished listening.

She was right, she was right.

Sweet Holy Deities, she was right.

He could not even reference a simple insecurity of his own without chanting Engager litany, without falling back upon psychological UnEarth reinforcement.

You're going to die, you obsessive compulsive maniac, because I too am an obsessive compulsive maniac, and I know you.

'You have your guns, I have my grenades. I make them myself. Grapes, cherries, plums. I keep them in my pockets. I like to have pockets, lots of pockets, and layers. I don't know why.'

'The ship. Why am I looking in here?'

'Can you see? At the back? Can I put the lights on?'

'Yes, yes. No tricks.'

She could hear in his voice; he was excited.

'Lights. Bedroom. On.'

She just had the one trick. She truly never, ever expected anyone would get in here like this. She'd brought men here, once or twice, but she'd always been able to scan them outside. She'd always had her stuff with her. She'd never been so caught off guard, not without –

…without Astra having her back.

Swallowing boogery phlegmballs.

'These really are…' Hylar could practically feel him fondling the balls. '…exquisitely crafted.'

'They're very precious to me. They need to be kept secure. The key to the ship is right at the back. It's a psychic lock, a silver metal pad, roughly palm sized.'

'I know…' Colven uttered, '…what a psychic lock looks like.'

'I keep those grenades secure for a reason, Colven.'

She knew that he'd taken the bait and done exactly as she wanted and made the move that would save her; that she had pushed his unconscious obsessive compulsive buttons exactly right, when she heard him do exactly what she had led him to do. He closed the safe door behind him, protecting the precious things, just like closing the cupboard, as he always had done and always would do, to maintain order.

She slipped out of Clammy's wet grasp. She'd felt his grip becoming, ever so slightly, less secure as time had gone on, as his patience and general strength had started to go with the effort. These were lazy men, led by someone they feared, but were essentially bored and unwilling to do anything but the slightest work for the greatest reward. Only the promise of sexual assault had kept them interested and they were about to pay for that.

When they'd first assaulted her, and grabbed her legs from behind, she had almost lost the grenade that she'd managed to snatch from the safe. But she'd managed to slip it down the frock coat sleeve, where it had caught between the lining and the top of her sweater cuff. It had sat there in relative safety, but even if she had been willing to detonate it without the safe being closed, she could not have reached it. Until now.

Both her hands were out. The others were so stunned that they broke their concentration and she jolted both her legs out as well. Instead of running for the door, she rolled to the bedhead, dropped her arm, caught the grenade from her cuff, squeezed the detonator and tossed it up to the ceiling.

Colven had taken aim at her but it was too late.

It was as though lightning had stuck in the room, as the electromagnetic pulse cracked out. The pulse went directly for their weapons, as it was designed to do, disabling them instantly. Hylar used the punch of adrenalin she received from her success to instantly execute a forward roll over the mattress and land feet first on the floor between Pretty and Bullface, temporarily blinded, then to forward roll again, out of the door, out of the room, and onto her feet. Then she was sprinting out.

CHAPTER TWENTY-THREE

Hylar ran through the two vestibules, through the big side room and out, onto the balcony, then back into the kitchen and under the bench. Colven and Clammy staggered out, the way they'd come, still partially blinded. She could take them on but they were strong and angry, even without any of their equipment. All it would take would be for them to land one punch. She circled the bench and dashed behind them as they staggered further forward, searching to find the balcony, where they thought she'd fled again.

'Don't *think* about being good. Just *be* good, and the greater will of the universe will flow through you.'

She had never forgotten that. She had tried to live by it.

She circled back through the ensuite and back into the bedroom, to the corner where Colven had ambushed her, full circle. Bullface was still in the bedroom, rubbing his eyes. The blue glow-stick remained bright. His vision seemed to return as she entered and he saw her through his readjusting eyes. Bullface was pleased; he thought she was confused, fleeing pointlessly, running straight back into his awaiting grasp like a frightened kitten. He even reached for her as she came sprinting at him. She knew that she had no choice and that his full sight would snap back within two or three seconds. She knew what she was doing now; she had not gotten where she had by not knowing how to fight off men much larger and stronger than she was. But these men had revealed their nature; they had shown her, without reservation, how they knew to get a woman of her physique and skill instantly disabled and afraid. They had shown her the how of it and the necessity for speed. They had revealed their evils. And so, as she set upon him, just as instantly, knowing that he would show no mercy if their positions were reversed, Hylar felt that her hand was therefore forced.

Hylar asked the universe to flow through her, as was her want. As she came at him, she asked that she be shown her best and most positive path, toward her most favored outcome, given her present predicament.

She felt her feet push hard in the last two, three steps of her run at Bullface, felt her body shift to the side and then her shoulder slam into him, right into his chest, with the full force of her sideways frame, launching him backwards into the wall, and her into him. He smashed and she rebounded. She couldn't wait, she just had to hope the crack she had heard was the back of his skull against the wall. Spiral-scrambling, half out of control, she was over the bed and standing on the floor on the other side.

Slap.

'Sierra Madre!'

Wrench.

'Caduceus!'

She could hear the other three coming, alerted by the crack of Bullface's skull, and was glad, as she raised her arms and felt the string of grenades flow down her wrists, flow under her arms, felt the two strings of ice-cold spheres rolling around her back, under her shoulder blades, under her breasts and across her chest, around her back again and wrapping firmly against the flesh of her hips like a belt. Even as the array settled around her body, she was up to her elbows, to the back of the safe and back out as her would-be rapists re-entered the room. With the weight of her grandfather's pistols in her hands, the grips in her palms were as reassuring as anything she had ever sought to grasp this tightly, probably since her tiny baby hand had reached out and grasped her mother's pinky finger, a moment after her birth.

'I fucking love these guns,' Hylar told herself, out loud.

She would not have said that, if she'd known that their use this evening would allow for the creation of a personal nemesis, but then again, you can't have everything. She had prayed to the universe; this is what the universe gave her.

Clammy came in first, the way she'd come, through the kitchen. He looked to Bullface on the floor, down the side of the bed, trying to get up, then turning to see her, with an eighty-year-old Smith & Wesson handgun in each hand; vintage but deadly pistols extended directly toward him, held tightly but rock-steadily in her slender grasp, one each at the ends of the thin wrists and the long arms that, not even two minutes ago, had been forced down, manacled by his own hands, pushed hard into a mattress above her head.

Hylar had to hand it to him; he seemed to realize all this, incredibly fast.

Like a gift, as though he were in on it, in on the poetry of the universe, he raised both hands at her, palms up in the universal sign for 'please – stop!' to which she had no kind of positive response at all. At least, not from his point of view.

She pulled the trigger three times on both weapons. The crackling percussion and the resultant echo, at the back of a solid rock chamber dug out of a mountainside, left her ears ringing, and Bullface screaming in pain and shock and terror. The bullets took off most of Clammy's fingers, and a big chunk of his left hand. She was pretty sure a few went on through his shoulders and arms. Then he thudded to the floor at the end of the bed.

On the other side, Bullface kept screaming.

Hylar stood and braced herself, bounce-stepping backwards to stand stiff against the now freezing cold rock wall, an arm and a handgun extended, exactingly, at each of the bedroom entrances. She knew that Pretty would be hiding now, just outside one of the open doors. He would have been coming in the other way, she'd bet, expecting a frightened, easy kill. Colven would have been coming up behind one of them, either Pretty or Clammy, but if he was the kind of man she thought he was, as soon as he'd heard the bullets, he would have cut his losses and turned tail to the gravski, to see whether or not the EMP grenade had wiped that out as well.

Truth be told, she didn't know if it had.

She'd grabbed one of the few loose grenades in the safe. She hadn't known which one. It might have been a poison or a concussion gas, against both of which she had of course personally inoculated herself, it might have been… it might have been anything.

One chance in twenty, the grenade would have killed them all, and that would have been that. It hadn't thankfully, but she had rolled those dice. Thankfully, the grenade that had gone off had been a targeted EMP pulse. But the radius might have been set anywhere between five and twenty-five meters; it was anyone's guess as to what condition Colven would find the gravski.

'Colven!'

Pretty charged through the door to her left.

She fired from her left-hand gun, almost involuntarily, and shot Pretty through the head. Most of the right quarter of his cranium, his eye and brain and skull, splattered onto the rock wall behind him and partly beyond, spraying almost every surface of the antechamber behind him, before his body had even hit the floor.

'John freaking Paul!'

She had *not* planned to kill anyone.

Not on this planet, and certainly not today.

Now Bullface was really screaming. He'd retreated to the corner, against the wall and the bedhead, losing it completely. But seriously, what did he expect? What had they expected? Fucking idiots. Third generation colonists; bored, easily led, looking for a quick buck… ready to torture, rape, kill…

Be good. Be good. Be good.

She glanced down at her bed, at the twisted sheets and the quilts, almost pulled off the edge. The tight cloth deltas where her hands had grasped. Her gut twisted and her temper flared. Her left-hand pistol went off again, almost involuntarily, shooting Bullface in the middle of his stupid, rude, idiot bull face. There was a red splat on the bridge of his nose and the back of his head went everywhere, covering practically every inch of the wall behind him, up along the corner and almost to the ceiling, like some kind of red-black paint bomb.

She hadn't wanted to kill people.

These weren't people.

Goddess damn.

Had she really just thought that?

She had been in a war. She'd been in a siege. She'd shot at people in those situations, many people. Shot at other ships in space, at soldiers, and assailants of a great many kinds, with many and varied distances between them. But killing someone like this…

No matter what they'd done, the few times she'd done it, up close and personal, it had always, always been horrible. Her grandfather had warned her about that when he'd given her the guns. But he'd also warned her; if someone was coming at you; well, that was their choice. If a normal person tried to attack you, or kill you, out of passion or rage, if they were crazy or high, you didn't have to try and kill them back. Take them down, sure. Disable them.

'Let them know who's boss', might even have been one of the phrases he'd used.

Her grandfather had known that about Hylar, even back then. Known that, at age fifteen, she was already been able to handle herself. He'd seen it, and he would see it again.

'But hired men…' His tone had grown dark. '…mercenaries, paid killers. Crazy who know they're crazy, and exploit that to make a living? They try and kill you, they'll try again. They know what they're being paid for. They know the life. Not putting them down? Might as well pull the trigger on yourself.'

Hylar remembered this as she stared out, across the floor and down at Pretty's body, light-headed, then turned back to Bullface. His bull face frozen in mid-scream. Bloodshot eyes in complete shock.

She looked back at Clammy.

Clammy was pale.

Be good. Be good, begoodbegoodbegood.

Be good and the universe shows you the way, reveals the best possible outcome for all concerned.

She pocketed her left-hand gun in the wide side-pocket of the frock coat and slid the purple scarf with the pink-polka dots from around her neck, keeping the right hand gun aimed between Clammy's bloodshot, crying eyes.

'You need to tie your arms, staunch the blood. It's not necessarily fatal. I didn't hit anything major.'

She almost threw the scarf down to him, but he whimpered something she couldn't understand, and she held onto it at the last second.

'When I'm gone, jump off the balcony. A drone might catch you.'

She kept the gun still as he fumbled around pointlessly with his still-working thumb and one-fingered left hand. Despite her grandfather's words, she knew that she had behaved brutally. She liked that scarf. A lot. Maybe it should become her sacrifice to compassion, become the price of her brutality.

Then the memory returned; staring up in terror, seeing his nostrils, his under-chin and neck as he had pressed down hard on each wrist with his clammy grip. Her right-hand gun trembled.

No. Not the scarf.

She kicked him a few pillows off the bed.

'Get the cases off, use them.'

It was the scarf that made this outfit pop.

Who knew where she'd find another like it?

Besides; fuck him.

He was an animal.

Clammy seemed to go into a daze then, and become obsessed with the pillow cases.

Hylar pocketed the right-hand gun into her skirt pocket, then turned and quickly took everything else out of the safe, feeling the cold of the metal of the gun through the pocket cloth on the front of her thigh. She kept an eye on Clammy as she did; he was in no condition to try anything, but he was insane now. Who knew what he would do?

There were more than a dozen pockets in this outfit; there was place, an order for it all, every weapon and device, but there was no time to put herself together properly in this regard.

In her mind, she could still hear Bullface crying.

She felt no pity, she realized.

Just, the sound.

Clammy remained in impotent shock as she stuffed everything except for the final stash into the deep breast side pockets of the frock coat. Right at the back of the safe was a hatch. These were a feature as well; finger-print responsive, a different position in every room, every safe, so even if Colven had known it as there, and the exact position, he still could not have opened it.

She nimbly gathered the three precious things within; stashed one in her left bra pad, one in the front left waistcoat, and one in her right boot.

She'd only need the one, today.

But these were the things she had, for just such occasions.

Restoring both guns to her anxious grasp, she proceeded slowly around and over Clammy, who had managed to get at least one pillow case peeled away, then walked quickly towards the kitchen exit. The whole time she did, Clammy was looking up at her and whimpering quietly. Against her better judgment, Hylar turned back to look. He might have soiled himself. She approached Clammy again.

'Go off the balcony now, or you'll freeze to death. The drone will recognize you have an injury and take you somewhere.' Clammy seemed to comprehend, and began pushing himself back against the wall to try and stand. She turned again toward the kitchen, but then spun back, forcing Clammy back down to the floor with a pistol barrel to his forehead.

'Start – over.'

He whimpered something else but it was gibberish. She turned as the blue glow-stick finally extinguished and this time didn't look back.

Colven wouldn't be here. He'd be with the gravski. Out the back.

So, what now? A gun in each hand. Did she just kill the creep, just leave Vulchalla and never return?

Or did she try and be a hero?

Save the town, save the day – save everyone?

She'd killed two men. One of them a boy, really.

And she'd wanted to kill Clammy.

Oh, Holy Mother Sky-Gaia, she had not known what she was going to do, when she'd turned back just then. The gun was itching in her right hand. Just, itching.

But killing the boy. She'd put on a sheriff's badge, doing that.

Now she owed it to the universe to try and save these people.

John, Paul, George and freaking Ringo.

She was going to give it a try.

CHAPTER TWENTY-FOUR

'You'll do the right thing, mostly…' Astra had informed Hylar once, in a similar situation. 'You just don't like the fact that there are so many self-centred morons and sociopaths who keep making you have to *choose* to do the right thing.'

'Colven!'

Hylar pressed flat to the wall as she edged down the smooth rock corridor toward the gravski bay, one antique handgun extended directly before her, the other tensely angled back, ready to fire at the slightest hint of pursuit. A dim light was coming from the bay, both a good and bad sign. The power was on; but had it come on automatically?

As she stared intensely over the silver side-carriage, she noticed that her tight grip was visibly shaking. She was losing it properly now, tapped out of adrenalin, low on blood sugar, and almost, truly, freezing cold, with her exhalations readily apparent, turning into clouds of vapour right before her face. Predictably, her mind was almost gone too, on the verge of not believing any of this was actually happening.

'Colven!' She shouted again. 'We don't have to die, Colven!'

We being the operative word, something dark within her heart, angry as hell, wanted to add.

She edged down the wall toward the blast-doors. She'd left them open after her last inspection, never dreaming there would be anyone else up here with her, let alone someone trying to steal the gravski.

She seemed to sense that the bay was empty. Her intuition had often served her well, but was not infallible. Certainly nothing she was happy to risk her life on in a situation like this. She moved carefully, sliding to the side of the blast door, gun extended, like Astra had shown her; breathing evenly, maintaining awareness.

But it was hard with her foggy mind. She was starting to think, involuntarily, about sleep.

The bay was long and rectangular. The black-tinted screen of the Beamer gravski, essentially an off-road gravcar fitted to handle heavy snow terrain, was facing her.

As she shifted her position slightly, a strange light drew her attention to the floor; the rock was covered with a light film of ice crystals. The light was her gun, reflecting off of them. There were two sets of footprints, one entering, one leaving. Colven had come and gone, quickly. Her instinct spiked and she threw caution to the wind; maybe that was what he wanted, but…

She went in.

Judging by his footprints, Colven hadn't gotten into the gravski, just eyeballed it.

Planted a bomb?

No; the only ones that would work now were hers, from the safe. Even if he'd pocketed a grenade, and he probably had, they were DNA-secure; nobody could use them but her.

Then she remembered; he had the key, the psychic lock.

He still wanted the *Lauren Bacall.*

That, in exchange for letting her go in the gravski, not alerting his pirate crew? Would that be his play?

She quickly checked the diagnostics panel with her third and pinky fingers, keeping both pistol triggers ready, held tight. The gravski was fine. Of course he hadn't sabotaged her. But for some reason he'd doubled back before she'd come down the corridor. She checked again, trying to think. The gravski was powered down but the EMP hadn't penetrated the bay. Maybe the tight chamber was shielded. Their weapons sure hadn't been, nor the chalet power. And the heating system seemed to have given out a while back, one way or another. Regardless; charged and functional. Launch tunnel clear.

For some reason though, he had wanted her to see this.

That the gravski was working, that he had seen that, come and gone.

Colven would be cold and weak too, also not thinking as clearly as he should; but in that regard he still had a clear advantage over a recently rock-bottomed alcoholic who hadn't properly eaten in a week.

She headed back, her boots still in stealth mode, but knowing she didn't need them to be, knowing what she would find.

When she got to the living room, she heard a strange muttering. Colven was sitting in one of the larger armchairs, but it wasn't coming from him. He was staring at the empty fireplace, where there was a small, complimentary stack of wood on either side. She'd never used it.

'A well-stocked fireplace that can't be lit because the power's out…'

Colven made a little scoffing cluck of a laugh.

What was that sound? A radio? Communications device left on somewhere? Had she accidentally switched on her phone when she'd shoved it in her pocket?

'We don't have to die,' Hylar repeated. 'It doesn't have to go this way. Give me back the key to my ship and we've still got time to get away. Both of us.'

Even as she said it, she noticed the streaks of blood across the floor to the balcony door. It had remained open and the trail continued out into the cold. Half way to the rail. Blood was smeared there too, all over, where the bloody trail ended, where the weird muttering was coming from.

Colven noticed her noticing. He started to say something about it.

'Don't tell me his name,' Hylar warned.

The disgraceful excuse for a man would always be Clammy.

'Can you understand him? I can't. He sounds very angry.'

'I shot his fingers off.'

'Oh yes. I think I was able to interpret that part.'

She had to keep her focus upon one thing at a time. But what Clammy was saying, what he was doing… it seemed to demand her attention.

'Week...?' Hylar echoed, as she heard Clammy mutter the word, over and over. 'What does he mean...?'

Colven gave a little conciliatory smirk. 'You are weak. I am weak. You are weaker. You will pass out before I do.'

So that was the angle.

'So you think I'll just sit it out? That I won't just shoot you and take the psychic key?'

'You don't like to kill people. It's in your profile. There is not very much in your profile, I grant you. But what is there has informed UnEarth that you will kill, given justification, and that you have indeed done so, many times, in your time. But the fact that you have managed all this time to remain an essential enigma, even to UnEarth –'

'UnEarth is a fucking haven for hosaps.'

Colven gave her an almost simpering scowl.

'I am afraid you have me at a disadvantage...' He was openly mocking her. 'Ho...?'

'Homicidal. Sadistic. Psychopaths. You, Colven. We both have reputations. You've heard of me, I've heard of you. But I know which one of us people would rather see when things get bad.'

Colven smiled. 'That is why you and your old cohorts are being dealt with even as we speak.'

True or not, it was a ploy to cause her more anxiety. Make her blood boil. Lose energy. She looked back at Clammy, still bothered by his inane chattering, then back to Colven.

'Do you think you're the first person to try and steal her?'

'No. But I think I'm the first person to succeed.'

There was ice on the balcony now, an inch thick. There hadn't been, just a few seconds ago. Clammy was shivering as he stood, with a last burst of strength, the balcony jump no longer a desperate hope but a solid reality, just a few meters of icy floor from his ruined grasp. But as he stood, his raised stature caused his voice to carry back with increased clarity.

'...week, fuck her for a week...'

Hylar uttered. '…what…?'

'…start again she says, I'll start again alright, I'll fucking find 'er, and hunt 'er and tie 'er, tie 'er fucking tight this time, then fuck her for a fuckin' week…!'

'…what the…?' Hylar couldn't believe it. '…does he mean…?'

'…let the boys fuck 'er for a fuckin' week, no, a month, a month before I kill her, cut off a fucking finger every fucking day and stuff 'em up her fuckin –'

Hylar shot his left hand off at the wrist in a twisting puff of blood and flesh. Clammy jolted, then paused. He had just reached the balcony, and had raised his hands for purchase when it happened. He raised his hand to look and saw that this time, the appendage was just gone; merely a ragged stub of flesh, a jagged wrist bone, severed and exposed, blood pumping down his forearm from a pathetic crimson fountain. He quickly, almost comically, raised his right hand to check that it was still there. Hylar pulled the trigger again and shot that hand off as well, straight from the wrist, right before his eyes. Clammy seemed to have no idea what was happening. He lurched away, in one last stagger to the balcony. Hylar had a clear shot at his head as he desperately swung his right leg up and sat astride the stone rail for just a second, then a drone swooped down, grabbed him and raised him into the air. It was as her friend had suggested however; Clammy was sliced clean in half across his torso. She heard his top half screaming, receding into the distance as he was transported away, echoing across the increasingly icy Alps, while the disembodied legs maintained their balance astride the rail another few seconds, then slid over, fell off and were gone.

Hylar turned back to Colven, who had turned his head, ever so slightly, to watch.

Their eyes met again.

'Here…' Her throat was constricting. 'Here's the… thing, Colven.'

'The thing…' Colven repeated doubtfully.

'I have a teleport bomb. Solo. One way to the deck of my ship. I can use it now. Just leave you here…'

'But you still need the psychic key.'

Hylar ground her teeth. Colven saw that it was true.

'…and I have hidden it…' Colven smiled. '…here in the house. The energy you expend to find it will make you pass out with lack of energy and cold. I will simply kill you in your sleep.'

'Don't want to rape my corpse like your creep men?'

'Useful idiots. My operation runs on expendable, useful idiots. All the better if they come pre-organized into useful idiot platoons.'

'I'm right though aren't I? Un-Earth is just filled with mid-level sociopaths like you, isn't it? Right up to the high functioning psychopaths at the top. Hosaps all the way, from grunt to general.'

'And beyond. But you know all about that, don't you?' He smiled widely. 'Being a secret mass murderer. Did you tell your friends? Did you tell them who you are? Is that why they kicked you and Solara off the *Hightail*?'

'Solara?'

If she tried to step toward him, she was going to lose balance.

'Don't you know? She's on her own now.'

It had to be bullshit. She had to ignore it.

She just had to concentrate now, to make sure that he'd taken the rest of the bait.

'But… you don't seem to realize, Colven. I was watching you. I was watching you the whole time.'

'I'm something of a…' Colven waved his hand. '…fan? You might say? Of your old ensemble? Of course, when you all went your separate ways, after you fell out with the lovely Astra, it was impossible to keep track of you all; you're all so good at that sort of thing. Skulking about, turning up in the most unlikely places…' He waved his hand around the room. '…and then vanishing again. Think on it Hylar; we have created a legend this evening. A mythology will spring up about what happened to you. Your ship will still be seen, of course, driven by me, but you will never be seen again.'

'I was watching you the whole time… and I saw where you hid it…'

She reached into her left bra pad and pulled it out; the psychic key.

Immediately Colven's hand went to his own left breast.

'That's not…'

'But you told me, Colven, you know what a psychic key looks like.'

'You have two! Then I shall be first to the ship!'

Colven pulled out one of her grenades. It was a black egg, with a bright pink ring.

'But Colven, that isn't a psychic key…'

She had seconds to get away with this now.

'Oh yes it is, I know what a psychic key looks like!'

'Yes. You do. Which is why that looks like a psychic key.'

With that, she pressed her thumb on the identical device in her own hand. A bright electrical discharge shot across the room from one to the other. Colven screamed and convulsed, then his mouth began to foam.

It was a dangerous toy, but the residual charge she felt gave her the last boost of energy she needed.

'And now, Colven, you're mine.'

She lifted the right-hand gun.

'Six shooters. Last round.'

He gurgled.

'Go on; you should still be able to move your mouth and fingers.'

'Yggg… you can't!'

'I can.'

'You – don't have…'

'I am a Colonel Captain with the Independent Earth Guard.'

'There is… no such…'

'There is now. I just created it.' She spread her arms. 'Ta-dah!'

'You…'

'Like I said, Colven, do you think this is the first time someone's tried to steal her? I admit, you came close. If you hadn't closed the door to my safe I would be dead by now. Or worse. But now, everything is up. Everything after rock bottom is upswing!'

Shaking, with incredible willpower, Colven raised the teleport bomb.

'Fuck… you!'

He squeezed it, and it exploded in green goo, the color of rot and gangrene, covering his hand and upper wrist.

'What….!?' Colven was truly aghast. 'What… is this!?'

'I don't like to kill. But I will. On the other hand, when I calm down, sometimes I think that I kind of like people to remember me. So they tell other people about me. So when some other homicidal sadist, or psychopathic narcissist, or whoever the hell, thinks about taking their chance with me, they remember being told; and think again. So that they back off, or even run if they're smart. So I don't have to kill them. I don't like doing that, Colven. I don't like being forced.' Her right-hand trigger finger tensed involuntarily at the thought. She really, really wanted to just plant the last bullet in his brain and be done. 'You'd call it a character flaw. I just call it character.'

He'd stared at her the whole time.

'What…?'

'Effectively it will be like a cast for your hand. Except, you won't be able to get anything down the edge to scratch it. And, it will itch. It will itch like crazy. But don't worry, you should be able to get to one of the five people in the known cosmos who will know what it is and how to remove it, within… oh, a week? Or so? That's if you ever get out of here.'

She walked right up to him and leaned down. Her purple scarf with pink polka dots dangled down, the tassels on the end brushing his chest.

'That ship knows me like a mother knows her first born daughter. Why – the fuck – would I need a psychic key to get aboard my own fucking ship?'

She reached into her waistcoat and pulled out a black egg with a pink stripe.

'Teleport bomb. Insanely dangerous to use in a place like this. Even if you did have the real one, you would have ended up… let's call it sixty-forty. Sixty-percent chance your body would have been spread throughout whatever inner layer of this enormous mountain behind us that has enough cracks and fractures to accommodate your atomically distributed body mass. You'd probably have ended up three kilometers long and five hundred high in crumb-sized pieces. Forty – you'd end up aboard my ship, where you would have been frozen in cryogenic gel after not properly identifying yourself after three seconds. Flat.'

Tears of rage were streaming down his beetroot-red face.

'Now; your legs should return in about half an hour. Fifty-fifty, you might have just enough energy in the freezing cold to get over to the balcony and jump. If you make it, it's about seventy-five, twenty-five that one of the drones will probably catch you; you might even come out in one piece. Maybe you survive all that, maybe you don't.'

Colven was speechless now, his mind bottlenecked with pure fury.

'I would tell you to sit here and think about your past, while you wait. Maybe think about starting again, based on the slim chances that all those things turn out in your favor. But that option doesn't seem to be one that is open to hosaps. I keep forgetting that you have no conscience and feel no remorse. I keep thinking that, surely, you're just pretending to be monstrous, evil pricks. But in the event that is true, and it's not just that you won't start again, it's that you absolutely, biologically can't, then there's nothing to do is there? Except, maybe, think on this.'

She stepped forward and leaned in again.

'I know that your people know. They've known all along, since the dimension cascade…'

'No such thing!' Colven sneered through gritted teeth.

'Spirit is real, Colven. And it is almost *physically* certain that you are going to *die here*, very soon.'

He snorted. 'I will…'

'And, Colven, it is equally as spiritually certain that you will be reincarnated. Somewhere. Somewhere soon. Reincarnated, most probably, as a victim. A victim of one of your protégées.'

Colven sparked up suddenly. 'I will be reincarnated as an heir to a planet of diamonds! You have no conception as to how spirit works!'

'I used to have drinking contests with Chens Khenzo…' Hylar smiled. 'That won't ever happen again, but because of it, I know all there is to know about…' Hylar suddenly remembered. '…that will suffice for now. I'd forgotten I have to save the day.'

She spun about, toward the gravski hangar, and almost lost balance. Then she stepped back and pressed the barrel of her right hand gun into his forehead.

'If you survive, someone else can take you in – if you don't freeze and if the drones do manage to catch you. And I do mean drones, *plural.*'

'I will, I will fin…'

She pushed the barrel harder.

'Find a HoliWell, make sure they're a shaman. Take the cure. Start – over.'

Then she spun about and walked back to the gravski bay.

That seemed to break him. The idea that a Holistic Wellness expert, a shaman no less, could provide a cure for his own personality. But she'd heard of such things. Heard they were… fifty-fifty? Sixty-forty. She couldn't remember. Didn't really care. It didn't matter. Colven would never go for it.

Whatever he was shouting at her now, it was filled with such impotent but powerful rage that she could not understand a word. She only had a minute now, just seconds probably, as she climbed into the gravski and scanned everything with her own equipment to make sure; she was okay. Then she launched, knowing that if she had remained for even half a minute longer, she would have passed out, and died on the floor, frozen in ice.

CHAPTER TWENTY-FIVE

With the highly illegal and massively fineable speeds Hylar managed to achieve, the gravski made it down the mountainside in about three minutes flat. Upon arrival, she decided that her thorough light-headedness, she assumed from an almost lethal combination of near-complete lack of nourishment, and just minutes ago having been so perilously close to freezing to death, had worked toward this surely record-breaking achievement, rather than against it. Whichever, she remained a pilot through and through, and arrived unscathed.

The village, the name of which she had completely forgotten now, was covered in ice. But there were still people moving about, scurrying to organize protection from the incoming annual mini-ice age. She could tell at a glance which of them were the wealthy investors, trapped here in a vacation gone horribly wrong, and which were the locals who were pissed-off that they had somehow been cheated of their own three-month luxury vacation. The town itself looked like some kind of fairy tale world from a children's movie about an ice princess, or something. Once again, in nature, beauty draws the hapless victims, she decided.

She slid the gravski recklessly into the central pavilion and parked as though drunk. Then she got out, again like a drunk, and staggered around the edge of the town square, noting the large hole that something had indeed blown into the roof of the pavilion. Then she stumbled down a long lane to a small alley where she knew there was a tavern that she suspected, quite rightly, would still be open. As she set about her course, holding onto anything she could gasp to propel her along as she did, she thought she saw a rather pathetic pile of goods stacked up in the centre of the pavilion that, as an offering to pirates was, more than likely, and quite rightly, going to get them all killed.

'Hooley drooley, sweetheart, are you still on that same jag? You're still in the same outfit you were in last week!'

'I need…'

'Purple heart! Diamond face! What you need is a hot meal and a good sleep!'

She could barely speak, she was so cold and so weak.

'The first one…' Hylar whined out in agreement, furiously nodding her head like a child. 'Please, the first one, get me the first one…'

The bartender assessed her sternly then smiled knowingly. The bartender's name she did remember, from somewhere in the back of her mind.

It was Beergo.

Beergo the bartender.

Of course he was. Go figure.

Beergo knew exactly where Hylar was. He reached under, then threw some pulse syringes down on the bar. Nobody looked, apart from a few people down the end, who looked like cops.

'I don't use – '

'Vitamins, amino boost, tryptophan for serotonin. I make 'em myself; all clean, no re-biz.'

'Re-biz?'

'Nothing addictive, no anti-bio synthetics, and they only need one dose to work; then you quit what you're doin' and take care of y'self. I've seen that look before; that's your deal, isn'it?'

She rested her hands over the syringes.

Re-biz. That was a new one. These were not repeat business drugs from any of the drug manufacturing giants. But could she trust him?

'I've been in here a lot, right?'

'Sure. Enough.'

'And I'm running a tab?'

'You sure are…'

'And, you've got one of my cards?'

'Locked up good and safe!'

'And these are…?'

'One fifty, two fifty, three and five.'

'Thousand?'

Beergo laughed. 'Hey; I ain't no anti-bio, darlin' gams!'

She smiled tightly. 'You checked the card, didn't you? You've got friends?'

'Maybe I have! Maybe they said; 'you let that long, white, warrior queen run that tab to the top o'the mountain and back, she's good! She's real good for it!' But I wasn' gonna fly, or cheat. I just see you comin' in and I say to myself; the long white warrior queen is comin', she's comin' down the mountain, and she needs a final dose. I give you…' He beat his hands on the bar for a drumroll. '…the final dose of the newborn, sworn-off alkie-baby. Sure, I miss 'em when they go, but there's 'nother one in full swing, always ready to walk right through those doors. Right now. Always has bin, always will be!'

They both looked around. Nobody did.

'Did I ever blab?' Hylar asked, turning back.

Her stomach growled.

'No, no. You kept your ghosts corked down tighter than a genie's bottle. You been at this a long time, and I seen 'em all. You sure you wanna sayonara?'

'I'm sure.'

He gestured to the syringes again. 'Then health up, cowgal. I get ya some veg stew; Earth veg and local, real good mix, nourishin' as shit. Beef steak…? Yeah?'

She nodded.

'You do the American sugar, raven eyes?'

'Not today, Beergo.'

'I do a mean American milkshake. Choco, berry, winner vanilla?'

By Ringo, that sounded…

'Okay. Vanilla. Thanks.'

She lifted one of the syringes, flipped her wrist, and shot up. Then another, then another.

'Holy shit…'

Beergo was pouring real, imported full-cream milk, from a cardboard, one-litre carton and everything, into a tall glass that might have doubled as a flower vase.

'Good?' Beergo asked over his shoulder.

'You definitely just gave me something I was missing…'

'Well, s'gonna be a long winter. I stayed here once before; gotta cellar, got food for me and three, and still two more. Idiots up there haven't even figured out; some of us like it that way! No interest in local custom! You wanna join, I got one more place. We can jiggy-jiggy click spines all over again. Weren't so bad the first time was it? Not so bad we didn't have a rematch, honey snatch!'

The first three shots were hitting her in a way she'd never been stimulated.

Beergo was scooping ice-cream now. And there was a small blender going. A waitress placed a huge bowl of vegetable soup in front of her and the smell of it brought forth tears of joy.

Beergo planted the milkshake in front of her.

It had chocolate sprinkles and real whipped cream.

It smelled like childhood.

'Eat up, ya steaks a'cookin', good lookin'…'

She gulped down a few scoops of the soup.

'That's right; bring you right back. You wanna whisky? Bourbon for the human?'

His eyes narrowed. It was a test.

The strange thing was, she didn't. She'd gone through such a horror, that the very question of whether she wanted a drink had changed for her; the formation of how her mind interpreted the idea and concocted an appropriate answer had completely reversed.

'No thanks…' Hylar told him, once she'd slurped down a third of the milkshake in one go.

In her mind, he might have asked her if she wanted to ingest some arsenic.

'…but I'll have one each of the strawberry and chocolate. And make sure the steak has a side order of fries.'

'Oh, you really had the born again's on that glory wagon, didn't ya raven baby? Oh yeah…'

'Oh yeah…' She belched, laughed, and powered down more of the soup.

'You sure you wanna be mixing all that, so fast?'

'I have an excellent constitution and a fast metabolism.'

Beergo grinned again. 'Don't I know it, with yo' sneaky little apricot backside all wagglin' out first thing in the morno that second time we performed a duet at the shag-o-rama? And ya think I don't wake up like clockwork instinct to watch somethin' like that shimmy on out? Oh no, oh; no-no-no. Beergo, he always wakes to take a last linger with the sneaky ones!'

She'd nearly finished the soup. The cops had been pretending to talk to each other at the other end of the bar, but they had been listening intently to every word. Several of the other customers had exited since she'd arrived, no doubt to spread the gossip.

The mad hot maniac drunk from Chalet Sixteen is still alive!

Now the cops were preparing to approach.

She looked at Beergo as he made her a second milkshake.

He was a little chubby and maybe a decade older than her. But he had a huge, wide, infectious smile and broad shoulders. And, as her memory started sparking off again, she seemed to recall that in bed he wasn't so much intense, and deliberately attentive, like so many men seemed to want to be with her, but playful and generous, with an unexpected stamina. When he turned back, holding a strawberry milkshake, he seemed to have intuited that she had remembered.

'I won't be spending the midseason with you, Beergo…'

He tried not to show his disappointment. 'Gonna be a long cold without a bunker, purple pantheress.'

'Yes, but…'

Hylar was aware that the two cops were openly approaching now.

'Excuse me, citizen?'

She glanced at them; one of several standard male and female partner dynamics that had always stuck. The younger, a hard but attractive blonde, long ago psyche-profiled negative for a father fixation, and a not-quite father figure with strong features projecting decency, authority and reliability, who could still see her as a worthy partner but at the same time act as senior without things getting mixed up.

The younger cop had spoken.

'Hey there…' Hylar nodded.

'Is that… your ship out there?'

'I think you know that it is…'

She hadn't meant to sound terse. It was just; let me finish my meal?

The man took over.

'We're Vulchalla Enforcement; Simms and Pickle. I'm Simms, she's Pickle. We need to know your status, as to the current siege situation. One of the chalets across the mountain has a telescope; says there's been some kind of electrical discharge up there, maybe more than once, and that you threw a man off the balcony?'

'Why don't you ask him? Aren't there drones up there to make sure that sort of thing doesn't end badly?'

'Because of the current emergency, the drones have instructions not to bring anyone down here. There are cryo-chambers in the mountain bunkers. He's been taken there. He'll thaw out when the season does.'

'So we can't ask him…' Pickle clarified. She had broad shoulders too. And a wide mouth. They all did around here, it seemed.

'He's one of the pirates. I shot his fingers off; then he leaped off the balcony. Their boss, the ring leader, shot me with a stun gun and when I wouldn't talk, he watched while three of his friends held me down and attempted sexual assault. I killed two of the others. The bodies are still there, for when the chalet thaws. The ringleader is a very dangerous, highly psychopathic mercenary named Colven. You shouldn't try and take him on your own; you need to wait for backup. I incapacitated him, but if he stays up there he'll freeze to death, so any minute now he's going to try a drone-jump as well. He's fully hanced up. If he evades the cryo-sleep and gets down here, whether that's soon or in three months, he'll spin a massive lie and your best chance is just to pretend you believe him and let him go. Under no circumstances take him on. He's teamed with the Un-Earth Special Ops now, and he has free rein to take any measures to complete his task. He was supposed to be running a bunch of anonymous pirates, anonymously, then he recognized my ship and called it in.'

She slurped hard and finished the vanilla milkshake, immediately reaching over for the freshly prepared second one; strawberry. Excellent; that meant she would finish with chocolate.

She gave the cops a tight, earnest smile.

'So much for the quiet life…'

Then again, maybe she *would* bed down with Beergo for the winter, he certainly seemed to know what a girl liked.

'I've heard of you…' Simms crooned. 'I mean… there are stories. You flew for Astra Solara, right?'

'Seven missions. But a girl's gotta sleep and Astra doesn't stop.'

'I heard it was something like that. There's something going on right now, back on Earth. I think they're trying to reel her in…'

'Good luck.'

'That's what we thought…' Simms and Pickle exchanged glances. Then Pickle moved in a little closer.

'They held you down? Are you okay?'

Hylar managed to turn away before she belched again, soup and milkshake. Then she turned back, and shrugged.

'I haven't exactly *not* been captured and threatened by terrible human beings before.'

'Still…' Pickle seemed very concerned for her. 'You probably at least need somewhere to stay the midseason, right? I mean, can that ship of yours handle being encased in ice? And you can't leave. There's a pirate blockade.'

'The last thing you said… that was the only bit I agree with.'

Simms shrugged. 'You're a Colonel Captain, Captain Moondarla. If you want us to agree with you, you're welcome to claim jurisdiction. We're a bit lost, to be honest. Petty theft and minor physical assault is the worst that's happened here in twenty years. Earth years, too.'

Pickle seemed more interested in something else, though. 'You think you can run the blockade? Beergo and me were hoping, if you'd come back, you'd join us down in the bunker, once the ice comes in? I mean, there's nothing up here to enforce when the population's underground and the town's covered in a mile of frozen water.'

'Not 'til they all come out at least…' Hylar smiled.

Pickle huffed agreeably, as though that were something she would not look forward to.

Out of nowhere the waitress slid a huge plate in front of Hylar; the steak was steaming and the fries covered in salt. She stared at that, for a few seconds.

'John, Paul, George, Ringo and Pete, ohhhh Pete; for Pete's sake…'

'I'm just saying,' Pickle persisted. 'They've waited us out. The guests are starting to empty their safes into the pavilion. By the time they vacate Vulchalla Station, we'll be deep under in ice!'

'I have a friend here; Ekto?'

'Ekto? The traffic controller? He intercepted the first signal, he's gotten a good relationship with them; got us good terms so they don't all come down and…'

'I need to see him, straight away.' She smacked her lips. 'Or, as soon as I eat these fries. Whichever comes first.'

CHAPTER TWENTY-SIX

She'd been working on the grenade-slinging since she'd gotten here, in her sober moments.

She'd gotten the idea on some world or other, years ago, and been thinking about it ever since. Something had reminded her then of the *Space-Spider* movies from the mid-twenty-first, and presto. Nano strings connected to a neural implant, firing mechanism linked to specific finger tendon patterns, grenades DNA-coded so they, and the bomb slinger, can't be hijacked and a simple micro-percussion firing device at the end of the strings.

Before you know it, you're spitting grenades from the collars of your ultra-stylish, retro-historical clothing, and everyone's either very impressed, very angry, or very incapacitated. Mostly a combo of those last two.

Astra would be furious if she ever found out about the neuro implants of course. But since they'd parted ways, and her anti-implant rants had faded in Hylar's mind, she'd succumbed on just a few occasions where she had felt it necessary to continue... well, living really. Somebody with a reputation like hers... well, people tended to come after you. So you had to get inventive with personal protection.

Firearms that could not be disabled by EMPs, for instance.

But grenade-slinging aside, mostly she liked it old school; the further tech went, the easier it was to find more simple, and yet somehow more sophisticated retro-tech that the new tech either couldn't detect, or by which the new tech could actually be incapacitated.

'You have a lot of things in your pockets...' Pickle noted.

Hylar had finished her meal and was standing now.

Her brain was quickly becoming restored, and her mind refreshed.

Best of all, her spirits were rising accordingly.

'God I have to pee.'

She was quickly running through her routine; all her regular equipment and devices. Putting them all back in place. Anyone from the old-school military would half-recognize the procedure, but most would look and see an eccentric woman who'd perhaps lost something, with both hands all a flutter about her person, pocket to pocket, as she muttered some kind of odd mantra to herself.

Then, there; there she was.

'I feel normal,' Hylar smiled. 'And I *really* have to pee.'

Pickle smiled. 'You look amazing…' Hylar was surprised, but not unflattered, that she would say this. This was a pretty easy-going planet, it seemed. But, most likely, Hylar already knew that. 'Follow me…'

Pickle led her to the other end of the bar, where the L-shaped room turned inward, then ushered her through a small gambling lounge to the Ladies, where Hylar did the longest pee of her life, she thought at the time, that seemed almost to bring on a kind of short, pleasant, out-of-body experience via sheer physical relief.

When she finished, Pickle was still waiting outside.

'Officer Pickle, you just heard me do the longest pee of my life.'

'What are you going to do?' Pickle demanded, sounding excited.

'Rehydrate?'

Hylar assessed herself in the mirror.

Everything, essentially, still in place.

'And?' Pickle enquired.

Her eyes were no longer bloodshot and although she could still see a darkness under her eyes, she looked just a little worn now, as opposed to totally thrashed, crashing and dying. She spoke clearly to the mirror.

'Be good.'

'Be good?' Pickle frowned.

Don't go back there and kill them all.

If the universe wants them all dead…

'Let's see…' Hylar said to herself, again in the mirror. Then she shifted her gaze to stare Pickle in her eyes, in the reflection. 'If the universe wants them all dead.'

CHAPTER TWENTY-SEVEN

She switched her boots off silent, so Ekto would hear her coming.

It was an intimidation technique that worked very well with naughty boys.

Clip-clop, clip-clop, over and over, louder and louder from far away, right up to your door.

Sure enough when she kicked the door open, Ekto was bustling about the flight control office, half a blaster shaking in his hand, trying to load the power pack into the base of the grip.

She threw up her hand and blasted him.

The grenade net opened about halfway between them and slammed him back to the wall.

It was a good shot.

She was not fully replenished, but a good way there. And now that was back; her confidence in her accuracy was as second nature to her as her dislike of feeble, mean-spirited, greedy people who didn't care who they hurt.

Her sworn deputies followed, making an assortment of impressed noises.

'Ekto…' Hylar shook her head. 'I thought we were friends.'

He vomited his dinner, wet himself, and started crying simultaneously.

The interrogation went pretty smoothly after that.

CHAPTER TWENTY-EIGHT

'This is Colonel Captain Hylar Moondarla. You might recognize my ship. In fact, your UnEarth stooge leader came down to the surface personally to take it from me.'

She awaited response.

'If you're quick, you might just be able to contact him before he's cryo-frozen by the drone that caught him when he jumped off the balcony of my chalet. If you're really quick, you can ask him if he was successful or not… you know? With the whole, *going down to the planet to torture Hylar Moondarla until she gives me the keys to her ship* thing. You can ask him how successful he was with that.'

Still no response.

'…and then maybe he can get back to his people, his UnEarth people, and ask if they're still willing to back him in this whole fake piracy thing, and whether or not they still want to try and frighten innocent – well, relatively innocent – rich people on smaller, newly established colonies, to request, nay, demand, that UnEarth Enforcers come in after the pirates have taken off with all their rich person stuff, to make sure the pirates stay away and never come back; for a price, most probably, I'm thinking. So, yeah, try and do that, try and get hold of him real quick, before he hits the ground. Get hold of him, see if he can get to his superiors and then see what they think they're going to do with a bunch of unofficially-backed pirates who have lost their super-secret, anonymous benefactor.'

Even still, there was no response.

'So, yeah. Do that. See what he says when he gets back from talking to his immensely impatient corporate masters, as to what they want to do with a group of primitive psychopaths they've recruited as pseudo-terrorists. And while you're at it, for your own sakes I mean, you'd better get him to check what this brownhole of a mega-establishment plans to do with the left-over pirates, who essentially stand to remain as defenceless evidence of a highly illegal and corrupt operation, staged in secret by a vastly superior and more ruthless and efficient force. You better get him to check that, before he hits the ground. I mean, on the off chance the drones didn't actually catch him, or blew out his spleen when they tried to catch him, or missed catching him properly and bounced his head off the side of the mountain a thousand feet above sea level.'

No? Still nothing?

'Why don't you try seeing about that, while you're at it? Oh, and by the way....'

This was a lie, but by now she didn't care.

'...if anyone, anyone at all on that station is hurt, let alone killed, I am tracking you – do you see my ship? Because I can see your ships, right now, leaving.' (That was true.) 'And my own ship is vastly, vastly, really, vastly superior to anything you primitive ignorant desperadoes have...' (Also true.) '...so if any harm at all, should come to anybody on that station who didn't deserve it, or even if they did deserve it, I will track down every single last mother-beating one of you, and kill you, kill you in the face like I killed Clammy Hands, Bull Face and Pretty Boy. All right. That's about all I have to say right now. Do we have a deal?'

It was the last part that was the big lie.

She didn't have the time, nor the heart, nor the psychopathic determination for that kind of casual vengeance. But the way the pirate ships were evacuating the station, three, then four and finally the last one, she was pretty sure they believed her.

Better still, she hadn't even had to board the *Lauren Bacall*, let alone launch her.

CHAPTER TWENTY-NINE

'Wow...' Pickle smiled. 'That's what I call a reputation...'

'Simms said that?'

'And he's seen a thing or two. He came here for the quiet life, but I know, before, he... he doesn't talk about it. The Rager Wars and all.'

Hylar sat in Pickle's kitchen sipping a delicious coffee, the beans for which were grown in the mountains somehow, between mid-seasons.

'Does all coffee taste like this?'

'You never had coffee?'

'Not sure I ever really... *tasted* it before.'

'And, you learned how to make grenades in your spare time?'

'Sure...' Hylar shrugged. 'I mean, I had a lot of spare time here, when I wasn't drinking...'

'You did a lot of drinking here. That was your other reputation. Mysterious past, mysteriously enormous capacity for consumption for one so slender.'

Hylar shrugged. 'Genes and practise. And, a willingness to.... vanish down a hole you can never ever fill.'

'Gawd.'

'I always drank coffee just as a hangover cure. Half the time all I could taste was last night's...'

She smacked her tongue, involuntarily. Some kind of Pavlovian response. She could taste it, even now. The sweet bourbon, her favorite.

George and Paul, is this what I'm going to have to fight, for the rest of my life...?

But then she remembered how she'd felt. For all those days. The despair and self-loathing.

The temptation of the balcony.

Okay, then. If this is it…

If this is what she was going to have to fight, this delicious urge, for the rest of her life, to avoid ever again feeling that again, then so be it.

'I guess that's why so many recovering alcoholics I know like coffee. It's…' She sipped again. '…it's really, really good. And I never knew!'

'You got the urge, don't you? To go back to Beergo's, and just tie one on?'

'The urge, but… not the heart. Not anymore. I had a dream, my oldest friend was in trouble. I need to go see her.'

'Girl friend or *girlfriend?*'

'Oh, the first one. Definitely, really. I like the guy parts.'

Pickle stared across the kitchen bench at her. Her cabin was utilitarian friendly; baby blue and blue-steel chrome and dark wood. Cop colors, but well done. It was ice-cold outside, but the UKC had turned up and were offering to teleport everyone to the station for free. It wasn't going to stop them having to pay millions in compensation once the lawyers were done, but it was something, a gesture. Apparently there were three lawyers for every resident of Vulchalla already in orbit around the newly restored station.

'In some ways, I kind of regret you saving us all. I would have liked to see what happened down there in the bunker… it's like one of those chalets. Only, under his bar. Pretty sweet, really. Me and you and Beergo. I mean, we don't like each other like that. But he liked you, and…' She blushed a little and batted her eyelids. 'I like you too…'

Hylar stared across at her; she didn't know what to say. Pickle seemed to realize she was making Hylar uncomfortable and shifted tone.

'A lot of people got 'em, those bunkers. A lot of people I think were lookin' forward to usin' theirs for the first time…'

'Pickle, seriously, no offence, but it wouldn't have happened…
I could have gotten off-world. My ship… she's pretty cool.'

'So you really just stayed around for us?'

'Yep.'

She sipped again.

'I think you're feelin' bad about those men.'

Hylar gulped without sipping.

'I think…' Pickle shrugged. '…what you told me they did,
holding you down…'

'Ever been shot in the pussy with a stun gun?'

'They did that?'

'He did that. Colven.'

Pickle sighed. 'As a matter of fact, yes I have. I was born here
but enforcers have to go off-world for a year and learn the ropes
somewhere else. It was only week three of my assignment, a
space station two or three planets over, and some of the local
boys, station locals, born there, thought they'd teach me a lesson.
I slept with one of their girls. Said I'd turned her, somethin'
ridiculous. Get shot three times down there with a handheld
stunner on low… only Evil itself knows how they figured this
out, but you can't feel nothing' for best part of a week. Doesn't
even hurt. Just… nothin'. Worst part is; they told me that the
feelin' never came back. I didn't know. I was too embarrassed to
ask. Too ashamed. Places like that, they don't like sex for play.
They like the boys jerkin' off into clone vats soon as they can
get 'im up, an' the little gals donatin' their eggs to the farms the
second they get their blood. If they're fuckin' for real, it's just boys
and girls and babies, just as soon as you can get 'em out; but just
like old Earth, only if the mommas and papas agree they want
'em, if it's good for the truce or the alliance or the inheritance or
the keepin' of a claim.' She rolled her eyes and threw her hands
in the air. 'Populate the galaxy like a good colonist!'

Hylar scoffed. 'I try to steer clear.'

Pickle nodded. 'I don't blame you.' Hylar noticed that her
broken accent was diminishing again. 'We try and keep it quiet

here. People keep to themselves, do what they want, don't hurt anyone. Make a lot of money making rich people happy. It all works out.'

Hylar smiled tightly and took a long gulp of coffee.

'I was…' She sighed. '…as weak as I've ever been. As close as I've ever been, in fifteen years out here, to being…' Hylar gave a shrug. '…overcome.'

'You were havin' the sweats up there?'

'You can call it that.'

'People never know, do they? What's goin' on?'

'No. They don't. Generally.' Hylar sighed. 'So, right now, my instinct is to go back to a bar, nowhere I'm known…'

'You're pretty much known everywhere here now…'

'Slam down a few shots and switch on my radar for the tightest local athlete who can bang this feeling out of me.'

Pickle sighed. 'I don't mean anything profound by this, but… sometimes bad things can kind of push us on to figure stuff out.'

'But to be really honest…' Hylar shrugged, only half-listening. '…I just want to lay down somewhere soft for an hour. Just an hour. And be soft and comfortable and drift off. Just an hour. I don't want to take this… feeling, of that experience, back to my ship. I won't like it, and neither will she. I don't know what we might do.'

'Do?'

'I can sometimes get a bit carried away, when I pilot.'

'You were talking like… the ship had a mind of her own. What is *Lauren Bacall*, anyway?'

'Eternal class, grace and beauty. What I hope to be. One day.'

Pickle kept staring. There were almost tears in her eyes, Hylar thought. What? What had she said? Something wrong, to upset her?

'I thought I liked girls…' Pickle stated, softly. 'But then I realized; I just like one aspect of girls. And boys. I like to go down.'

'Uh huh.' Hylar sipped. *Okay. Taking a turn…* 'I kind of just… like… banging. I think. Hardly class, grace and beauty.'

'There are all those things, when people connect. It doesn't have to be a lifetime. That's what I mean. I didn't know, until I really explored, until I realized; this is what we get, we humans. Our bodies, that feeling; connection, orgasm. So, I realized, I'd better figure out, if we've got this; what do I like? And that's my thing. I just like that. Guys or gals. I like to have my face there and feel you responding; through my mouth, and my face. I don't know why. I just do.'

'Okay…'

'I'm… so I've been told… very good at it.'

'You're not going to tell me you use a shorg, are you?'

'No! No way, no!'

She was almost offended at the notion.

'Good. Because I know someone who got pretty hooked on those things. Used it like sleeping tabs, to keep going on a punishing cycle. Almost burned her out.'

'Almost?'

'She got herself off of it… turned out well. Went anti-tech. Well, at least, anti-implants. Worked out really well for her. It meant they totally respected her when we got to Ama…' Pickle was staring at her. '…but she couldn't get me off the drinking.'

Pickle kept staring. 'You really did go there, didn't you? You and that ship, and Astra, and the others…?'

'The others…' Hylar frowned. 'I need to go.'

Pickle reached out and touched her hand.

'If getting hammered, with drink or by a random hunk, or both, is the dark instinct that took you to the blackest place in your life…. then milkshakes and creamy coffee lattes… and the opposite of a brute hunk… maybe… that's what you need?'

'What I… need?'

'Hylar… I'm saying… come and lay down. It will be soft, it will be comfortable. You can drift off. I think I can reverse what happened. At least, I can replace that with something else. Something better. A lot better.'

CHAPTER THIRTY

'So?'

'Well, I do feel better.'

Pickle had an enormous wet grin. 'Me too.'

Pickle's phone went off. She glanced at it, sitting on the bedside table, then saw who it was and rolled her eyes, but answered anyway. Hylar watched her. She had a good body; one of those broad-shouldered, small-breasted women who jogged at lot, and did minimum weights, she suspected. And she had certainly performed as advertised. Hylar barely had the energy to stand. But she couldn't be sure if it was the fact that she hadn't orgasmed sober for the best part of ten years, or if the vitamin cocktails were kicking in some more, or if it was maybe even fresh food undiluted by her ever-present hangovers.

'Simms?' Pickle listened. 'Hang on, she's here. I'll put you on speaker.'

Simms' voice came through suddenly.

'There's nobody left at the chalet, Colonel Captain. No bodies, no nothing. I think they used that blood solvent stuff to clean up. Leaves no trace but you can smell it for about half an hour after, if you know what to sniff for. I can smell it near the window and in the bedroom. Fits your story.'

Hylar sighed. 'Corporate cleaners…'

'Colven is in cryo-sleep, up in the mountains. Once the program's running, it's fatal to stop it. Three months.'

'Simms,' Hylar smoke smoothly. 'There's something you can do for me if you like.'

'Anything, Colonel Captain.'

'There are two ensembles in the wardrobe of the chalet. They are the only things there I require; one is grey, one is yellow. Well, mustard. You'll see. They are the only things there I need, and I need them brought down here, now.'

'I see them, Colonel Captain. I'll get on it right away.'

He hung up.

Pickle smiled at her.

It had been something. Definitely something. But she missed the kissing, the tongues. Nobody had sucked her breasts, and she hadn't sucked anybody's anything. There had been no weight, no pressure, no full-body tension and wrestling and squirming. Then again; was there supposed to be? Or was that just drunk sex? She had to admit, she had virtually left her body and flown around the room at one point, out the window and up the mountains.

'I dunno.' She sighed aloud. 'Thanks, Pickle. I feel… heaps better.'

'Better enough to hang around?'

'Maybe… another hour or so? These pillows… I mean, they're definitely comfortable…'

CHAPTER THIRTY-ONE

'Well… look what the cat dragged in.'

She'd come through the airlock, having clip-clopped across the ice-covered promenade with a travel case filled with her reclaimed outfits and some local produce. Cheese, mainly. The valuables, such as they had been, had likewise been reclaimed. Now she was freezing cold again, but as the airlock slid shut behind her, the *Lauren Bacall* was instantly warm, with several heaters instantly directing their streams right at her.

'Did you see any of that?' Hylar asked.

'Of course not. I was sleeping. Most refreshing but a little chilly. Then I woke up to all this, and…'

The pause was familiar, but Hylar asked anyway as she moved through the tight silver corridors of her ship to the flight cabin.

'…and – what?'

'Processing news updates, police reports, local, radio, satellite, solar, crossing to wave feed, hyper feed, teleport feed incoming; gravitas feed still… oh my.'

'Hold that thought! If you see anything to do with cop cunnilingus, ignore it. One more thing to cross off the bucket list.'

'Do I want to know?'

Hylar sighed. 'Meh. I'm still thinking. Made a few friends here though. Which makes me think…'

'Think good thoughts and the universe shows the true and correct path…'

'Yes. Indeed.'

Hylar sat heavily in her command chair.

Home.

'Can you launch?'

Lauren Bacall sounded indignant.

'Of course I can. We're the last active people on the surface of this planet and I'm half embedded in ice. I don't like it, particularly.'

'Prepare then. Can you make me a vanilla milkshake please? And locate any cryo-chambers in the mountains near the chalet ridge. Actually, make it strawberry. Look for any signs of life up there in cryo-storage, anything at all. I think I might be developing a taste for old-fashioned strawberry. There should be at least one body up there, in several pieces. And, outer screens, please.'

'Of course.'

A food service cart skimmed up to her, with a strawberry milkshake on the nice little silver platter she liked. Hylar accepted it and sat back in her comfy chair as the screens lit up around her, displaying everything there was to see.

'That's my chalet, right there', she sipped. 'Mmmm. Good.'

'Thankyou. I am reading two life signs in mountaintop cryo-storage. Oh, I see. That green containment muck you were working on...'

'Two? Are they both from today?'

'Earlier today, yes.'

'So he made it. I wasn't sure...'

'Which he? There are two.'

'The second is dead, surely? In pieces?'

'Checking.'

'They tried to steal you. And rape me.'

Hylar heard the guns warming. It was a particular sound and she thought, she knew, that the *Lauren Bacall* made it deliberately, so that Hylar knew.

Almost, to rev her up as well.

'The one with the goo is an UnEarth agent. Hosap. Colven. This was one of your attackers?'

'What about the other guy?'

'An UnEarth hosap attacked you, and you let him live…?'

'Check the goo again.'

'Are you sure the cold did not go to your…?' There was an elegant beep. 'Apologies. Now I see.'

Hylar smiled. 'That's okay. I did have a lot of time to experiment up there. Whatever I came up with I sent back here, but you might have been asleep.'

'I was. It was all auto-stored of course.'

'Good.' Hylar huffed again, thinking. Maybe she'd made a mistake. She certainly hadn't been thinking clearly. But it had been sheer vengeance, versus the opportunity to… 'Listen, I have a problem. When he wakes up, the hosap, he's going to be angry with me. He's the type that will look, and find people who knew me. And you know how that goes, for the people he finds. There are three people at least I'd like to protect down there, who he could use against me.'

'Then bring them with us. If you are going to let the hosap run, it's the only way.'

'I still don't know if that's the wise choice. He's a real piece of work this one. I had to try really hard to be good at all, this time.'

'Hmmm…' The *Lauren Bacall* seemed doubtful. 'Your version, her version, neither at any time might correspond to the universe's version.'

'My version and who's version would that be?'

Lauren Bacall made a sound that was something akin to clearing her throat. 'You were thinking about finding another cruiser. You will need crew. Are they appropriate?'

'Not really. Look, which ever version of good you go by, I thought if I left it to the universe, he would either die, or I could track him back to his base when he leaves. Nobody knows where their base is. It's a unique opportunity. And it will be the first place he goes, to see if someone there can get the goo off.'

'Can they?'

'No. Or, probably not. The neutralizing compound is very rare. Wratheanna found it. Chens medicalized it. Sing weaponized it.'

'And you put the tracer nano-particles in it.'

'Like I said, I had a lot of spare time.'

'These three people. They were good to you?'

'These three today. There are others. An Atlantean shaman.'

'Good grief. I am really going have to insist you tell me that one.'

'Okay, but… look, we can't take them all with us. They like it here. But I don't want to live with them here, just to make sure he doesn't come back; that almost happened. I almost stayed.'

'Dear me.'

'Exactly. I don't think it would have worked. But I bought a stake in his bar though, just in case. Even though the whole thing was his fault…'

'His fault?'

'The publican.'

'Scanning. I see. Beergo. He checked out your credit card, by nefarious means, which notified the nefarious in general as to your whereabouts.'

'If I'd left you awake you would have seen that.'

'I needed sleep. And when I'm awake, I'm easier to find.'

Hylar rested a gentle hand on a navigation panel. 'You're instantly recognizable to anyone who knows you; just, this far out, there's nobody who does. Rich people don't see wars, and the wars never got out here for the workers to be dragged into them.'

'Thankyou Hylar. But I am familiar with the strategy that brought us here.'

She kept sipping the strawberry milkshake through the bendy straw *Lauren Bacall* had seen fit to provide.

'No blame…' Hylar slurped. '…it was just business, and I was running up a big tab. But he was a nice bartender. He took care of me.'

'I don't want to know.'

'Then I won't tell you.'

'Very well; but I wish you would treat yourself better.'

'I'm turning over a new leaf.'

'Is that so? I am of course going to tell you that I have heard that before, but this time…'

'It's different this time.'

'…something in your voice. I believe you.'

'Good. You should. Always.'

'Hmmm. In any case, I have a solution to your problem.'

'I'm listening.'

'To wake them now would almost certainly kill them both.'

'Wake them both? Clammy actually survived being severed in two by a faulty drone?'

'According to this, the drone's precision detector systems were affected by the fast-lowering cold, and bad readings based on… shifting body parts and diminishing body mass? Curious. However, both were registering brain activity when frozen. UKC's rescue drones are fast, but clearly need work. Their med-tech is fast, but apparently does not need work.'

'Apparently. Can you wake them from here?'

'The two would-be rapists? Gladly.'

Lauren Bacall became suddenly disturbed. Hylar could feel it.

'We have a problem, Hylar.'

'I know; what's happened?'

'Both cryo-tubes have just been teleported out.'

'By who?'

'Whom by? I cannot say; but this cannot be a coincidence. And the goo – Colven's arm…?'

'They left it behind, didn't they?'

'I'm afraid so. It seems you should have dispatched him when given the opportunity.'

'Precision teleport. Great.' She clicked her fingers. 'The tracer-nanos, they'll still be in his blood stream.'

'Enough to get a signal? Across the universe, perhaps?'

Hylar sucked the end of her milkshake down with a trumpeting straw-slurp from the bottom of the long glass.

'Ahhhhh!'

'Another?'

'Make it chocolate. Sing could track it.'

'Before they run a check and cleanse his blood out?'

'There would still be the blood.'

'They would dispose of the blood.'

'Some of the tracer nanos might survive; if it's a space station, they have a habit of hanging around.'

'One or two nano-particles… across the universe?'

'Sing could do it. She could try.'

'Singularity Karmada remains the Lieutenant Aggressor Weapons Expert aboard the *Hightail*.'

'Are you sure?'

'Indeed. This dovetails neatly into the news I had to tell you, that I received upon waking.'

'Why doesn't that surprise me?'

'It seems that right now on Earth, Astra Solara is being pursued for arrest. For terrorism. There's a live feed; they're trying to apprehend her now.'

'Terrorism?'

'Apparently.'

'Father Snot-finger! I knew she'd push it too damn far! Play the feed!'

'Buffering…' *Lauren Bacall* sounded very concerned. 'Hylar, you had better decide. Right now.'

'I know.'

'Well…?'

'I know!'

'Hylar…? Are you ready to forgive her?'

PART THREE
SWISH WORCESTERSHIRE

CHAPTER THIRTY-TWO

'So, why don't you tell me why you think you are *the* Swish Worcestershire?'

Swish Worcestershire blinked the sleep out of her eyes and stared out at the man sitting across the room from her.

'I am Swish Worcestershire,' Swish Worcestershire said.

The psychiatrist nodded. 'Do you think you are… lucid?' He checked his screen. 'Seven-Oh?'

'Do I think I am… Lucy Sevenoaks?' She screwed up her face in confusion. 'No, I… who is Lucy Sevenoaks? I told you, I'm Swish. Swish Worcestershire.' She laughed. 'Try saying that seven oaks!' She laughed again. 'I mean, seven times!'

The psychiatrist smiled tightly. 'No, I called you Seven-Oh. That's your designated case number, Seven-Oh.' He smiled tightly, but friendly. 'The number seventy. I asked if you were lucid.'

'Oh. What did I say?'

'You answered well enough.'

'Oh, good.'

She yawned, stretching her jaw.

'So why don't you tell me something about yourself? Do you know what year it is?'

'Umm. Is it still twenty ninety-four?'

'Yes it is. Do you know where you are?'

'Umm…' She looked around. '…no. But you're a psychiatrist, you said, and I don't remember anything. Anything much at all, really. So I suppose… something happened? Did I do something? Something… crazy? To end up in here?'

'What's the last thing you remember?'

She blinked again, squinting and squeezing her eyelids to get some moisture to return.

'Umm… I don't really remember anything, really.'

'Tell me what you remember about this world.'

Swish was all foggy. It wasn't nice. Not like cocktails or smoke or mist. This was like she'd been dosed or something. Really dosed. Like being sedated. With medicine. She might not have been the brightest star in the sky, but… ohhh.

Right… *psychiatrist.*

Interview.

Sedated.

'Did you sedate me, doctor?' Swish asked awkwardly, a little embarrassed. 'Or did I do it myself?'

The doctor consulted his tablet. Swish stared at him, her vision still a little woozy. He had one of those projected holotablets that hovered in the air, just to the side of your vision usually, but from the other side it was kind of a like a migraine aura, just a patch of folded light that made no sense in this visual dimension.

'Ummm, doctor, that's going to give me a headache if you leave it right there.'

He nodded agreeably, professionally accommodating, and swiped the tablet down lower, down toward the table top. Then he smiled, with the same politely neutral doctor's veneer.

'Is that better?'

'Thanks.'

Her chair was comfortable. His chair also. They looked the same. She blinked some more. It looked as though she was in the basic variant of a traditional psychiatrist's office; navy blue leather armchairs, and various objects d'art from human culture strategically scattered around the room to provoke responses from patients, and for him to note when they did. Subtle representations, in tribal or modern art, or tech art, of phalluses, labias, breasts, buttocks and, quite naturally, eyes and feet and then, of course, going deeper, triggers for various other fetishes she recognized…

She sighed to herself, exhaling out of her nose as she scrunched her mouth to one side.

'Uncomfortable?' the doctor asked.

'Do *you* remember *your* name?'

'I'm Doctor Nist. You didn't answer my last question. Do you remember anything about this world?'

Swish shrugged. 'I remember that I am… or maybe was, an LCC on a starship…'

'LCC, hey? Lieutenant Colonel Chief?'

She shrugged, humble but proud. 'Yes. Chief Engineer. I think… I used to be good at that.'

'Swish Worcestershire used to be very good at that.'

Swish stared keenly at him. 'Can I have something to drink please?' Her lips tightened. 'I get dry when I've been sedated.'

Doctor Nist smiled and nodded. He lifted himself from his high-backed, navy leather armchair and went behind a small antique bureau, beside his wide, wooden work desk that had the same navy leather surface. It must have been worth a fortune, and have cost a fortune to bring it all the way here, to a space station. Behind the desk there were wide windows, but they were shuttered with a mirrored surface. Her direct view of the mirror, and therefore her view of herself, was blocked by Nist's high-backed chair.

Nist raised a crystal-blue water jug and poured some water into a tall, pale, blue paper cup, hidden carefully at the side of the bureau, then returned to the chair with the drink. Swish was coming back to, now. She could see in the mirror that the wall behind her was a large bookcase, lined with more subtly provocative trinkets, as much as it was with actual books, which were rare enough these days anyway, she supposed. When she reached for the paper cup she found that she could not move her arm past a certain distance, essentially just in front of her.

'The PPS is in place,' Nist explained.

He was able to pass the water through whatever personal protection shield he'd set up around the chair. She wasn't offended. She knew this was standard for any new patient. Calling it a PPS, a 'personal protection shield', was a nice way of saying that she had been tied to the bed, or straight-jacketed. It was the polite, new-tech equivalent of being restrained; not that they didn't still have the not-so polite, new-tech equivalent of those things. This version was okay though. If he made the gesture the shield gave, if she made the gesture, it resisted.

Depending on the settings.

The settings.

Hmmm.

Swish looked down at herself. The moisture was returning to her eyes now. Focus had come back to her mind as well. She couldn't see her lap for her bust. The skin of her lower legs was exposed, and her feet were bare, but her bosom and loins had been clothed in some kind of tight, basic-black spandex; a cover-all bra and thigh-length shorts, effectively sports underwear. Over the top she was wearing a sheer but plain body-length gown, an elegant powder blue, which tied at her waist. Coming to think of it, the whole room had a kind of translucent light-blue theme, as though matching the sheer gown. The carpet was pale blue, as were the cushions on the couch and the leather on the more stereotypical reclining coach in the corner. The complementary tones of the room were somehow dreamlike; the curtains on the sides of the mirrored windows were satin and had a second and third layer of purple and steel blue behind the pale. The lighting was subtle, but once she noticed it, it seemed manufactured to give the room a dreamlike quality, she supposed; almost mood-lighting, with soft pinks and purples… and of course, pale blue. These were the colors, she knew, that were sometimes used to represent Earth's moon on a cosmic level. Away from Earth they often still represented the human dream world, the so-called astral plane.

'The undergarments and gown are standard hospital issue; I have created the office around them, to give patients a more relaxed feel, to make them feel at home.'

She sipped the water. 'That's supposed to be an unconscious thing. Why are you telling me?'

Her voice remained husky.

She hadn't registered that it was husky, until the huskiness hadn't gone away with the water.

So.

Swish Worcestershire had a nice, husky voice.

'The world…?' Nist prompted. 'Outside?'

He must have had some kind of role here, to be able to do that, her mind offered.

Swish shrugged. 'This feels like a station. Something about the air-conditioning on space stations. So I guess I'm not on Earth.'

'You remember it's twenty ninety four. Month?'

'Earth month, maybe February?'

'Date?'

She shrugged. 'The middle somewhere?'

Her shoulder hurt a bit when she shrugged, like she had been doing some heavy lifting. Thin shoulders, she remembered, rolling them, on a thin body. And long, droopy, big boobs. She looked down again.

'Where did you find one that fit?'

'I'm sorry?'

'I have very specific measurements. Easier to get a custom job. When I was a girl, that was… awkward.'

'They're made of an intuitive poly-fibre. Three sizes fit all; they generally do. What else do you remember about being a girl?'

Swish smiled. 'Fighting off boys, who wanted to see my boobs. Having sex too early because I got sick of fighting off boys who wanted to see my boobs. Realizing that if I just let the boys who wanted to see my boobs, see my boobs, if they wore me down that far, that most of the time, it was enough for them, just to see my boobs.'

'I see.'

'I am about one-hundred and seventy centimeters tall. Bare feet. About thirty-five of that is boob. My face from chin to hairline is only twenty-two. And this one, righty here, is bigger. I had a boyfriend who called them righty and lefty and I said you can't call them that, my captain calls her guns that. And he said, that I had more of a claim, because 'guns' is an archaic terms for boobs. And I said, no, guns is an archaic term for biceps on men and that was the beginning of the end. In the end, it turned out she had better names for the guns and it didn't matter.'

'Your captain?'

'Hylar Moondarla. I say captain. A CC, in establishment speak.'

'Colonel Captain.'

'We were more of a gang, who each knew how to do our own complementary stuff.'

'More of a gang than a crew…' Nist repeated. 'Of Colonels and Lieutenant Colonels, by all accounts.'

'Yep. Astra liked experience. Experienced dropouts were her faves. We were all that, just about.'

'You're aware that Swish Worcestershire is no longer with us?'

'Who's going to tell *her* that?'

'Her?'

She exhaled heavily again, out through her nose.

'I meant me. Tell – *me*. It's a joke.'

She was terrible at jokes. She always made dumb jokes at professional people and they never got them.

'Obviously, I am not "no longer with us". I am still very much me, and very much alive. Wondering what I am doing here…'

'What are you doing here?'

'Remembering my childhood, apparently.'

'Which was dominated by the sexual harassment of young men with breast fixations.'

'Well that's hardly surprising. That was always going to happen. And it did work out okay.'

'It did?'

'Well, in a roundabout way, my girls led me to crew with Hylar, and Astra and the others.'

'Is that so?'

'Yes.'

'How would that be?'

She sipped some more water and assessed him. He was older. Not a lot, but enough for her to think twice about finding him attractive. He was good-looking though; he had fine features, and a high brow but he wasn't losing his hair. His eyes were normal blue, and his eyebrows fine blonde. There was an edge of cragginess setting in around his lower jaw. In a year or two, he'd know if that gave him character and made him look distinguished, or aged him prematurely. But he had a solidly aesthetic nose and one of those straight mouths only men could have; innately suggesting cruelty and power, which made it so much sexier when he spoke nicely.

She grumbled to herself.

There she goes again, putting it on people.

If there was one thing that Swish had never been in short supply of, it was 'the thing about big boobs'. And that thing in turn was; whatever it was about big boobs that made people associate stupidity, or naivety, or if you were relatively lucky, even an innocent, but still slightly sexualized playfulness with them. Swish had always had an alert, enquiring mind. She had always enjoyed studying, and finding out about things; things she was really interested in. The way people thought, what they thought and why, had always been something that she'd wanted to know more about, and so, accordingly, she had studied a little psychology. Enough to know that the thing that made people think she was some kind of ditsy leg-spreader wasn't all that far removed from the stereotypical projection she was laying on Doctor Father Figure here.

And about as inaccurate.

Still, maybe it would be what he expected.

There was even a real name for it, wasn't there?

Transference, or something? Where she started to find him attractive, because she found aspects in him that were like her father; but unlike her father, it was okay to have sexual feelings toward those attractive aspects in this man, one's analyst, because he merely reminded her of her father.

Maybe she should play into that.

Then again, maybe… that's what he would expect?

Then again, again, he would know that, wouldn't he? Surely?

He would know that projected stereotypes were almost always wrong, but somehow at least initially irresistible. And that someone with half a brain, which if he knew who she was, he would know she would have, would…

But he didn't.

He didn't know who she was…

He thought she was some nut, who only thought she was who she was.

So how did she play this?

She had no idea.

No idea Swish, as usual.

'If you lead discourse with the first, most obvious thing about you…' Nist smiled smoothly, friendly. '…it's like casting up a shield. But then, one can tell a lot about the people one encounters, by the way they approach a shield. Especially a shield they want to see past.'

'Especially-specially,' Swish agreed, 'if there's something they want, on the other side.'

'Those groping boys again?'

She allowed herself one chuckle. 'Those boys.'

They were silent a second.

'So how far back do you want to me to go?'

'As far as you like,' Nist smiled.

'Well. Okay. Let's see…' She shrugged again and began. 'Alright then. My generation is dominated by the fact that there is a Goldilocks planet out here for just about every single culture, every single religion or philosophy imaginable. Yours, assuming you're around twenty-five years my senior, is, and was, dominated by the Id Wars, and the Ragers. But your generation was also the first full generation to go out and colonise space, thanks to your parents, my grandparents, back-engineering the leftover Za'Naja tech from the previous invasion. Both generations achieved said mass colonization, and expansion, and you essentially saved Earth, and the human race, from overpopulation.'

'I see.'

'I thought you might. I remember my grandparents; and they remember the dimension cascade, even though we're all supposed to believe now that it never happened. But my grandfather fought the Za'naja. And his brother was taken. Apart from that, we've got corplexes and bitexes…' She tilted her head and smiled sadly. 'The rich are still in control, and lying, the poor are still doing their best, and surviving.'

There was silence again for a second. Nist seemed to be regarding her with a modicum of pity that he could not hold back.

'You believe there was a dimension cascade?'

'You don't?' Swish moved her fine shoulders in. Then she shifted her arms a little. She couldn't help it. It was installed in her, to do it, to put them out there. It was a natural, unconscious advantage she couldn't help but have and exploit. Somewhere in his mind, even his trained psychiatrist's mind, there was a loop. Women had it too, but men had it stronger, because there was the sexual connection nine-tenths of women didn't have. The loop went *sucklesucklesucklesuckle*… and the bigger the boobs, the louder the loop.

So, she squeezed her upper arms, and gunned them, just a bit. She had to.

It took two to tango, after all. Deep in her mind, her most primal loop was recognizing him only as *babybabybabybaby*…

I mean, she thought, drifting a little, women said that, didn't they?

Baby, oh baby?

Men too, she supposed. But women made it, like…

Oh… *baby*. During –

'You mentioned…' Nist looked at his tablet, snapping her out of it. '…that it was always going to happen. Do you think you're more sexually attractive than other women, because of your unusual bust size?'

Unusual.

Hmmm.

'Doctor Nist, do you know the story of the Mappers? My grandmother was one.'

Nist looked up at her curiously. 'Mappers. They were a branch of Scientism that believed in leaving nothing to fate, were they not?'

Swish nodded. 'That's right.' She smiled, pleased that he knew. 'They stopped short of full bore Trans-Humanism. But they called themselves that, the Mappers, for a few reasons. Like, they liked to map the stars, as well as the genes. They were really good at it as well. Not just the maths but actually going out and seeing the reality of it, just for the sake of it. And they gave stuff really cool names. Like my grandma, she was kind of like an Earth Mother. There's a huge nebula that has a permanent dimensional geyser where the ships come out, and as soon as you do, you see the nebula, and from that angle, it looks like boobs.'

'Indeed?'

She was starting to understand now; Nist did not approve of this. She wasn't sure, but she thought she might be in a lot of trouble, unless she could remember a plan or something, that she had forgotten.

'The nebula looks like a woman's boobs, lying on her back, from the point of view of looking down her stomach…' She ran her hand up her own stomach, just so. 'And she got them to call the nebula, The Gaia Gap. Isn't that… I don't know… cool? It's kind of cool and beautiful and lovely, don't you think?'

Clearly, he wasn't so sure. In fact, she seemed pretty sure that Doctor Nist was more likely to hold the reverse opinion. But he was still hiding it well.

'Their name, the Mappers, referred not only to their extensive mapping of the stars...' Nist offered, '...but also to the human genome. That's right isn't it?'

'You're very clever. Or did you look it up? I can't see your little screen back there, remember?'

Trying to flirt. Didn't work. He was terse now.

'You say your grandmother was part of this movement?'

'The Mappers. Yeah. Granma was a Mapper alright.'

She smiled, thinking about this. About her Granma.

'What about your grandfather?'

'Grampa? He went along because he loved her.'

'He didn't believe?'

'He didn't mind.'

'How so?'

'He just loved her, and was happy that she felt so strongly about something that was so positive, and engaging.'

'Really?'

She couldn't quite tell if he was intrigued, or perhaps doubtful.

'Of course. I mean, they were colonists, after all. They wanted to go, they wanted to see. I mean, the Mappers, they went far, really far.'

There was something sinister in his voice now, a dark edge that she was just picking up on.

'How far?'

'Oh, we found them everywhere, way out. As far out as we went on the *Hightail*.'

His eyes narrowed briefly.

'Umm...' Swish offered, unsure as to whether she should continue.

'The Mappers engineered people, didn't they?'

'Well, yeah... I suppose. If you want to put it that way...?'

Nist frowned a little. 'They engineered people as kind of archetypes, did they not? To go out into space?'

'Well, yeah they did that. I mean, they still do, I think. But they're a bit more careful. There were no disasters, really, because they were always very careful and respectful, but…' she looked down, deliberately '…things didn't always work out the way they thought.'

'You're a legacy of that?'

'No, I…' Swish sighed. 'You make it sound bad. It's just a thing. It's just the hand you're dealt. It could have happened anyway, to anyone.'

'The spaceship captains were modified to look more handsome…'

Clearly a tone of disapproval.

'Sure, and commanding.' Swish shrugged. 'The Mappers thought they had identified the combinations of facial features and physiques that brought out certain behaviours and responses in others. I know that the working-class colonists weren't told, but they were at least screened so they were likely to approve when they found out. And they were made physically stronger, don't forget. They liked that; a lot of them signed up specifically for that!'

'Your grandmother was a scientist herself, though. Correct?'

'She wasn't a Scientismist, but yeah, she was a bioengineer. A good one; no shortcuts. It was her job to test whatever food they found on the planet.'

'Where did they colonize?'

'The main one… they call it Golf now. It's basically the golfing planet.'

'Of course. But, given that you implied it before, why did all this make your physique inevitable?'

Swish smiled. 'When my grandmother put herself on the colonist register, she said that she wanted to have as many kids as she could. She was naturally, genetically designated to be able, without supplements, and with my grandfather, to have maybe five or six. With supplements, she was told that she could have as many as sixteen.'

'And by supplements, you don't mean ordinary vitamins and minerals, do you?'

Strange question. Quite judgmental in tone.

Oh yeah. She was in trouble.

'Umm… no. No, I mean…' Swish swallowed, tight, and reached for her water again. She had assumed he kept the paper cups for patients, hidden from view so as not to diminish the beauty idyll of the stunning crystal beside it. But maybe, the cup had been placed aside for something else. Yet she didn't feel more sedated.

'She took genetic supplements. To enhance areas of herself that were already there. The Mappers didn't believe in splicing, just enhancing.'

He must have already known that.

'The water is clean,' Nist smiled, as though sensing her developing discomfort.

'I…'

'Sixteen, you say?'

She took another sip and proceeded.

'And that's just naturally, via childbirth, without the clone incubators. Eight of them had to be in vitro from different fathers though, because of the need for genetic diversity on first generation colonies, but with the upgrades and bio-enhancement supplements, she ended up having *eighteen*.'

'Eighteen children.'

'My mother was the last of the seven she had, naturally, with my grandfather.'

'I see.'

'But, one of the things the Mappers gave her, in their genetic planning, was a bust.'

'Indeed?'

'Well yeah…' Her voice sounded a little huskier, now. She didn't know why. 'See, her personality type matched what they were looking for in what they called a 'matriarchal figure'. You know what that is?'

He almost, almost sneered. 'Something to do with the Gaia Gap?'

She ignored that. 'If she was going to have all those kids, she was going to end up being one of the wise women of the colony, for sure. Right? I mean, surely she had to. She was going to be a Planet Mother, like an Earth Mother figure, but for another world. I mean, how cool is that, right?'

He nodded, smiling benignly.

'So they thought they would help her out; they made her rounder. It happens sometimes after childbirth; women gain weight, become plumper. Childbirth can trigger that; but they thought that she only had a low chance of that happening and so they wanted to make sure it did.'

'And, what is your opinion on such… well, some might say… extremes?'

'Extremes?'

'Some might say. Mightn't they?'

Swish shrugged again. She was doing a lot of that.

'Granma lived until one-hundred and thirty. She only died last year. She looked like the Buddha. Big wide boobs, hubcap nipples pointing down at her knees. But, my Goddess, did you feel warm, and embraced, and safe and sound, and loved, in her presence.'

Nist smiled. 'She lived a full life, so to speak.'

'My Mum had seven kids too. I'm the seventh daughter of a seventh daughter.'

She had to do something. She could sense it.

He was steering her toward his desired conclusion, and then she would be done. She didn't know how she would be done, but he wanted something from her, and he was getting it. Then, when he had finished getting it, he would have her. And it wasn't, she sensed, like 'have her', either. Like, in a carnal sense. It was, like, to have her in the restrained sense. In the 'trapped and incarcerated' sense. The old-tech way.

What could she do though? She could only work with what she had.

Steer away from the good Mappers.

Bad Mappers, bad!

'The thing of it is though…' Swish proceeded carefully '…what the Mappers got wrong, as we now know, is that DNA had its own plans. It's doing its own thing.'

'Hmmm…' Totally neutral.

'You can change the way a link looks, one person in a genetic line, and maybe some of that will get passed on, but unless, it seems, you keep changing it, over and over, it will always go back to where it was heading in the first place. Granma used to say that; some parts of nature are, like, an ocean tanker. They take a while to change course; they have to do a big, wide arc. But DNA, so it seems, its arc is too big for us to comprehend. Even with supercomputers, she'd say, there are just too many crazy variables that come out of nature, and emotion, and love and hate. Maybe none of us will live long enough to see, even if the arc can truly be swung, whether or not what the Mappers did was worth doing. Or, is worth doing, because I'm pretty sure they're somewhere out there, still…'

Oops. Damn. Maybe her own arc was just too big to swing back from…?

She proceeded regardless.

'…maybe DNA will just evolve in a giant circle and the arc will just come back around?'

No?

'But the upshot is; me and my Mum, we went back to being slender.'

He was looking at her now, totally blank. Except; there was something brewing.

Getting worse.

'Now, I've got a friend, Hylar.'

'Hylar Moondarla.' Flat, but almost an edge of contempt.

'Yeah. We're the same height. But she's got a tiny little bum, and nice, round, pert boobies that look just right for her frame. And the Colonel Commander, my other friend Astra, she's taller, a bit, and broader, a bit, and she looks… just right. My other

237

friend, Chens Khenzo, we came up together, through the Star Parade, and now she's Gnostech; she's like me but she's bigger, you know? Bigger frame; big round bum and her boobs start back under her arms, you know? The bottom of them is attached, like halfway down on her ribs. It's like American football armour or something.'

He was breathing a little faster now. Angrier.

'What happens with someone like me…' Swish put her hands, in as clinical a fashion as she could, just under her boobs and gave them a little heft. '…when I get these, but with my frame? What happens, Mappers? When some weird gene I'm not supposed to have, just goes off? I'm long, and thin. Like my Granma was supposed to be. Long limbs, tiny waist, tiny wrists, tiny ankles. So in the end, my DNA batch gets a throwback to the Mappers enhancement of my Granma, which tells my boobs to develop…' A slightly bigger heft. '…these!'

Nist's mouth straightened. Not only did he seem even more contemptuous but there was that edge of distaste again.

'I mean, they're going to be long, aren't they, Mapper? Big, like the genetic program says, but big and long. They have to be long! Attached to this!'

Her hands swept up and down the sides of her body.

'On this frame, they're going to be like balloons, aren't they? Not strong, like the saddle bags my friend Chens Khenzo has! Oh no; I get the long, pendulous droopers with stretch marks spread out like a peacock's tail and big, long pointy nipples; poked a boy's eye out after graduation!'

He kept staring.

She kept shrugging.

'Well, nearly.'

You had to hand it to Nist; he was keeping it together. If he was faking the professional distance, and the classic disapproval to prevent any kind of projection bonding, then he was doing it to a tee. Not even the slightest of lop-sided male grins.

'And yet…' Nist uttered, softly. '…you say, it all worked out?'

Swish wasn't sure any more what angle to take with Nist. Just telling her story, letting it flow, using her instincts to look for a gap, a way to exploit him…

Was that what she was doing?

Well, sure, she supposed, if you *had* to look at it that way.

But she had to get out of here; here be dragons.

And not the good kind, like the kind she'd seen on Amazon Seven.

'Chens Khenzo. Tell me about her.'

'Okay.' She sipped her water again, slowly. 'Well…' She shrugged. She couldn't help it. 'Chens is… she's like a guru. She persuaded me to do some modelling. Those little hologram things that dance on the dashboard of your control suite. I mean, they're everywhere now, but freighter drivers and freighter pilots love them.'

'Dancing… without your brassier?'

'Well… eventually.'

'I see.'

Something in her snapped then. He could disapprove of her all he liked, but once he started getting into her friends, let alone her best friends…

'Look, do you know anything about Gnostechism?'

'I…'

'Let me tell you, then, Doctor Nist, shall I?'

'Please do.'

He seemed pleased to have gotten her angry. She let her chest heave a few times. At the top of the tight spandex, her cleavage squeezed, pushed out and increased a bit.

'One of the most basic schools of Gnosticism holds that we do not need priests or churches or organization on that level, to understand God; God is everything, and we only need to consider everything to be closer to God and to understand what God wants of us. Okay?'

'I believe I may have heard that somewhere before,' Nist uttered. 'Or something along those lines.'

'Okay. Right. So, now; everything is big. Right? Really big. I mean, I can't even get my head around anything like everything, so much so, that I don't really understand how little I cannot get my head around it. So, everything, infinity, the whole idea, is always going to be abstract, right?'

'Very well. If you say so.'

'The Gnostechs say so.' Swish was getting mad now. She was really getting sick of this guy. 'My friend Chens Khenzo says so. I'm just telling you what they told me.'

'Of course. Please go on.'

'Okay. So, lots of people like to see God in nature in this way, or make art, and create art, or whatever, in order to express it in the only way it can be expressed, in the abstract. But, one of the more recent schools holds that God can also be sensed in technology. Through Science. Faith in science, scientism, is a kind of religion, but the Gnostechs say that…'

She huffed.

'Are you okay?' Nist asked. 'Why did you stop?'

'Are you really interested?'

'I'm interested in the manner in which you are expressing yourself. And the way you have interpreted the things you believe you have learned.'

'Oh.' *Fuck – you.* 'Okay.'

Grrrrrrr.

'So…. like, if you want to get all mystical?'

'Why not?'

'Right. Well, there are people who like to go to the beach, and watch the waves, and listen to them crash. Or, say, people who go to the forest, and touch the trees. And listen to the breeze through the leaves. Or go the gallery, or the…' This was maddening. He didn't seem to be reacting at all. '…look, you get that right?'

'I understand what you're alluding to, of course.'

'That lots of people like to do that; the oceans, the forests, the deserts, the sky, the deep, the vacuum, right?'

'Very well.'

She breathed hard again. 'Well…' Swish pushed on. '…*given that*… given all those things I just said that people like, some people think that if you think and let go, at the same time, if you… *contemplate* nature or art like that, and ask God for guidance through that… I think it's called… contemplating…? The divine? Isn't that what some people say? Contemplating the divine? Or, staring into infinity, or regarding eternity, or… what was the other one? The collective conscience?'

'The collective *consciousness*, I believe is the phrase.'

'Yeah, right – that. But like I was saying before, that; the everything, is too big. Maybe it's even alive, as one big thing, but even if it is, it's too big for us to even…'

Swish sighed. To even talk about properly?

'…well, anyway, there are lots of ways to regard it, and lots of things you can use to do that. And who knows?' She shrugged. 'Maybe people just read their own projected patterns in the randomness? Patterns that mean something, maybe just to them? Or, maybe it's really there, and we each see the same pattern, but differently? Because we're each different, and that's the way it's supposed to be?'

'Hmmm.'

'But, a lot of people *now*, say you can also see all that stuff in the…'

What was that word?

'…the matrix? Yeah? The *matrix* of technology.'

'Is that so?'

'Sure. I mean, you think about it. Really think. Technology is just something we humans, and the aliens too, let's not forget, just pulled out of the… the bubbling stew of the universe. Right?'

'Stew?'

'Sure. I mean, didn't humans evolve from a prime stew, or something? Or, a soup? Maybe it was soup? Anyway, it turns out that, because of that, things didn't have to be like this.'

'Like what?'
'This! Like we are.'
'No?'
'No! Well, not exactly. Not like this *exactly*. Our technology is just the stuff that worked for us. In our favor. It came out of the stuff that we made use of, and *kept using*, because it *kept working*. And we got better and better at it, and so did the stuff we were using. We… we…'
She was grasping for a word.
'We… re – re…'
'Reworked?'
'Yeah, but…' Swish swirled her hand around. '…the other one. The other "re"…'
'Refined?'
'Yeah! That's it! Thanks Doctor Nist! Refined! We *refined* what worked until it became technology!'
He almost smiled.
'We kind of had an idea of a knife, and pulled it out of a rock, and added twine and a piece of wood. We made it solid. We brought it into our world, and welded it into our psyches. Then we refined it! And in the end, we made technology make us fly, in the sky, and like, we gave it… *dimension*!'
'I suppose that is true, in a way…'
'It is, right? I mean, you agree? You're getting it now? You're starting to understand?'
'You might say that.'
He said it in such a way that made him sound as though, really, he had known all along.
'So, technology is part of nature, right? Just like we are! At the very least, it's part of *our* nature; part of *us*. And for some people, worth totally bonding with, if you're like, a Trans-Humanist or something. Anyway, my friend Chens Khenzo, who's basically me, but like…' She put her hands apart, then shifted them out abruptly. '…*bigger*, but you know, curvy; *she's* one of them. Like,

she's bigger, but she's bigger everywhere; in her mind and her conscience, and even in her conscience-ness.'

'Consciousness.'

'That's what I said.'

'No, you said conscience – ness.'

'That's not the same thing?'

'No.'

'…huh.'

Well, there you go, Swish thought. Learn something new every…

'Anyway, Chens Khenzo was with us for a while, but she left when Hylar did. I think… she wanted to help her.'

'This is still Hylar Moondarla you're talking about?'

'Look; I knew Chens way before that. She said; we were born with these faces and these boobs and so, we should follow that path. I mean; she's not exclusively Gnostech. You can't be really. I mean, she was the ship's HoliWell, and the crew were everything. We were, like, all sorts…'

'All sorts?'

'Well, I mean, Chens had to know chem-meds, and trad-meds, and consciousness theory, and psych impacts, and spirit practices, and just general holistic wellness theory, and all of that. She had to be, like, really well-versed and all over it all. Chens said if you had to look at all that stuff, really look, and treat people who expected to be treated that way, and compare, really compare, you couldn't be just one thing.'

'No?'

'No. Like I was saying before. It's too big, and there are too many abstract interpretations of it, that are all, in their way, true. So you had to choose, and be okay with knowing that the path you were on, that you chose right now, was the best one for you. The best right now. Many paths to the mansion, and many rooms once you're in. Or something. You know…?'

'Is that…so?'

He didn't sound happy but she couldn't stop herself now.

'So it's just, the Gnostechs relate to tech and so that's where they look for God. The path you choose can't be everything, so it has to be abstract. But it's still real. I mean, tech? That's realer than real; realer than anything ever was, right now. Right? Because there's so much tech right now! More than ever! Everywhere, in everything!'

For a second, just for a second, Swish thought that she really, truly understood what it all meant, what she was talking about; that she understood everything, really understood it, for the very first time.

And then it was gone.

She sighed.

'Anyway. That's why I did the modelling.'

'I beg your pardon?' Nist seemed truly confounded.

'The modelling. You know. Jiggling them about in my… skimpy stuff. Like you said before; sometimes without my… brazier.' Swish smiled. 'I mean, we were big, us girls. Really big.'

'All of you had the mammary anomaly?'

'The… what?'

Nist sighed. 'Just… go on. Finish your… story.'

Swish ignored his tone. 'They sold billions of our dances. Every time I recorded a new one, and changed my costume; boom! Millions more. I mean, I still have that money in an account somewhere; I haven't touched it. It's enough for me to retire on, maybe even enough for a stake percentage. I thought Astra was going to get us there for real, for a while, for sure, but…'

'But?'

'Never mind about that. Look; you asked how it all worked out. Well, these guys, they have you dancing on their dashboards while they fly across the known universe, right? You know how that sort of thing works. But eventually, it occurs to some of them that you're possibly real. Like, not a computer generation, like a pixel cartoon, but actually a real person. I think that's important in the end, with this kind of fetish or fixation, or whatever it is.'

'Important?'

'That there has to be a something, or a someone, a real someone, willing to stand up in front of a real crowd, and do a real dance for them, and wave, and maybe even kiss a cheek.'

'I see.'

'So, that's what they did. They took us on tour. And it turned out that we were really kind of something to these guys. They get really lonely, and we were kind of… icons. They'd bonded with us in their heads, without even really knowing who we were. We were their little princesses. Almost like demi-goddesses, if you like.'

He didn't. She could tell.

'So I'd go flying on these ships with all these big old engineers and pilots and navvies, even some gunners, I mean; there were still skirmishes back then, we're talking, like, ten Earth years ago, right…? And one day, we were flying, and there was trouble with the engine, real trouble, and there were just not enough hands, and… I just got in and helped.'

'You did, did you?'

'Sure, I mean, I did whatever they said needed doing, because if I didn't we were going to blow up in deep space – and nobody would ever know! So I did, I did what they said; hold this, push that button, read that number, and, I got it. I just got it, straight away. I didn't even need telling really. I just reconnected all this stuff that had blown, because; it just made sense. We'd been sabotaged, you see. They were going to kidnap and ransom us.'

'They?'

'Pirates, I think. They're like, everywhere; you know? But we got away. The engineers were all like, did anyone tell you how to do that? And I was all, like, no, nobody told me how to do that!'

She grinned proudly, recalling the moment.

'And, they were like; then how the hell did you just know how to do all that just then? And I was all, like, dude, I just did it. I just freakin'… *did it.*'

She loved remembering that. Loved it. It was almost the best moment of her life. Like, top-five best moments, easy. Probably number four, maybe even three.

'And so, the authorities of the world we were traveling to, they said the pirates had all been dealt with, so we did our little entertainment show for a little arena full of space truckers, and back we went. But on the way back, they hit us again! Like, you wouldn't believe it; just attacked in broad spaceflight! And, like, I just took over.'

'Took over? Took over what exactly?'

'Well, there was something about the way I'd put the engine back together, or helped put it back together, that just let me understand how she flew. You know? I mean, the pilots that worked for us, they weren't exactly Star Force One, you know? They were no better than rookie space truckers themselves, really. Just stop, start, brake and propel; they were barely able to veer off from a missile attack if their lives depended on it. And on that they day they did! They really did! As for manual dimensional, or dropping into gravitas, or teleport surfing, I mean, *forget it*.'

'Hmmm.'

'And that's when Chens said, like; I should train. I should train to be an Engineer. Because, like, I never knew I had it in me; I was like yelling all these orders to the gunners and the pilots… and they were telling me, no, the ship won't do that, and I was all like, no, *I'll make the ship do that*. And I did. And, the ship *did*.'

'Isn't that the Commander's job? Yelling at people and telling them what to do? Wouldn't Astra Solara have done that?'

'Sometimes; Astra's real job in a situation like that is… was to let me know what she wants. But the LCA, she and me and Astra and Hylar, we really –'

The Commander, the Pilot, the Engineer and the – Lieutenant Colonel Aggressor?'

'Spar. Wing Spar. She…' Swish smiled. A little sadly. '…we all worked together. We always worked together.' She paused a second. She didn't like to think of it all being over and done with. She was sure, fairly sure, that it wasn't, but even so, she didn't like to think about it being done, not that part of it, on the *Hightail*, not any of it.

How the hell had she ended up here?

What was she doing?

Being here?

This wasn't *her*.

'That was my thing; I had that stash I mentioned, I already had that then. And I thought, I could always fall back on it. But Chens said, that God, or the universe, or everything, had given me these pendulous man-magnets so I could be there on this day, to learn that I am a natural Chief Engineer. Five years later, I'm LCC on the *Hightail*.'

'*Hightail.* The ship Hylar Moondarla flew for… six missions?'

'Seven if you count… look, I –'

'Commanded by Astra Solara for… nine now?'

'Yeah! Yes! Yes, nine! Look, I'm the real deal, Doctor Nist! I am Swish Worcestershire. The real one!'

'I want you to look at this.'

Nist switched his screen around.

The screen displayed a view of a room. A comfortable room. Big, open. Full of people. Like the communal area in an expensive retirement…

Oh.

They looked comfortable, these patients. Restive. It was a ward in psychiatric hospital. A good one, with all the trimmings… but… nevertheless…

'That woman in the armchair, reading. Do you see her? That's an ancient queen from two thousand years ago called Cleopatra.'

They were all in the black spandex sports underwear, all with the long, sheer powder blue robes.

Instead of a tight bra, the men had a kind of tight vest.

'This one here, he's an actor from your grandfather's day called Al Pacino. But this woman here, you should know.'

'Why?'

'Well, that's Astra Solara. Don't you recognize her?'

'That's not…'

'Well what about this woman here? Is that Astra Solara? They both claim to be her. If they're not sedated, they get into fist-fights about it. And that one there, that one claims to be Swish Worcestershire.'

'But she doesn't look anything like me!'

'Granted, you do bear more than a passing resemblance to the actual Miss Worcestershire, a passing degree more than the other three Miss Worcestershires we have in here… but my concern is that your passing resemblance only feeds your delusion.'

'My… *delusion*?'

'Tell me more about this notion that the dimension cascade was real…'

Swish felt her jaw drop.

'Notion?'

'Please. I'm interested.'

'It was real. My grandfather remembered it happening. He told me all about it!'

'There can never have been seven billion people on planet Earth. We know that. That number is unsustainable for more than a decade, at most. That's a scientific fact. The ecosystem would have self-destructed at the start of the twenty-first century.'

Swish was astounded. So, it was really happening. They were really trying to convince people…

'Look,' Swish gasped. 'Nobody knows *why* it happened. Right? That's why there's this movement to start denying that it *did*. I know, or, look, at least, I *heard*, that the Scientismists are claiming that because it's *unlikely* to have happened, even though it *did* happen, that it's now unprovable that it happened at all.'

His gaze seemed to focus a little tighter on her now.

Now, he was really listening.

'…and, because they don't really understand what it was, that happened, or was supposed to have happened, they think, because of that, that probably it didn't happen. But there are still a lot of people left alive, like my grandfather, who remember it.'

'And what do they remember?'

'Well; look. You know the story as well as I do, I'm sure.'

'There are many versions. Which one feeds you?'

She grumbled. She didn't like that.

'They say that… the universe is abstract, like I said before…'

She sipped her water again.

She seemed to be doing a lot of talking.

She wondered when her hour would be up.

Maybe Nist was trying to wear her down.

'…and that the universe can be read, and measured, in a lot of different ways. Right?'

'If you say so.'

'And, like, there's a theory that we're in a multiverse and that's just infinite possibilities manifesting as whole other universes.'

'Go on…'

'Well, then there's the idea, that some of those other universes are… I think, more important? More important than others? Is that what that guy said that time, like a hundred years ago?'

'Possibly.'

'What he meant, or might have meant anyway, was that these more important universes have more potential, and substance, more… raw material, right? Exploitable substances? To be used, by the universe, or the cosmic conscience, and the cosmic conscious-*ness*, right? To be used so that the important dramas of the universe can play out. Inside those universes.'

'*Multiple* universes?'

'Well, yeah.'

'Playing out – different variations? Different variations of a… whole universe?'

'Look, it's just…'

'Do you know how big the universe is?'

'Infinite?' Swish attempted a shrug. 'Isn't it… infinite?'

'So do multiple variations of infinity; of an endless everything, sound very credible to you?'

Swish laughed, and her nervousness came through, just a tad.

'Well, like I said Doctor Nist. Like, if the universe was a kind of, awake? Like, a deity type thing? Like we, or like I, was saying before?' I mean though… who knows? It might be all… silly stories! Right?' She huffed. 'Anyway. Blah-dee-blah!'

She really didn't like this now.

He was getting a lot out of her.

Where was it all going?

'Is there anything you'd like to add? To this… theory?'

Why not?

'So… one of these theories says that, on Earth, seeing as the universe's… manifestation? Of consciousness? Does that sound right? Anyway, seeing as the universe's manifested conscience… I mean, *consciousness*… although, basically the same right? Seeing as that plays out through the main, the dominating animals, or living things, on any given planet, at least from our point of view, but, let's not go there…'

'Try and stay focused…'

'Well, then, it plays out through us, doesn't it? And our lives and the reality we create for ourselves; not like, day to day, but overall, as the people of Earth, like, as humans, or Earthlings. Like, through the chain of human beings. But, who knows, maybe we even co-created everything, somehow. But, anyway, the dimensional cascade.'

'And what has the dimension cascade got to do with… all that?'

Oh… okay. Good. He was getting impatient now.

Good.

Good.

'Well, what happened, apparently, was that one of these universes somehow could not sustain its reality.'

'It's reality? Really?'

'Or it's potential, or… something like that. But, because reality plays out through people, it was the people, okay, who pay attention to this sort of thing, who first saw it! It was the Gnostechs!'

'I see.'

'And because they thought they saw this, like, on the cards, because they thought that this is what had happened, they managed to create this thing, right, like a *device*. And the device, this *viewer thing*, can see right through, into these other realities, these other potentials! They can actually see! They can see the ones that have the greatest potential, and are, like, as *real as our one*. And they say...'

'Tell me then...' Nist leaned back a little. Just a bit too smug for her liking. She said it anyway.

'They say, that it's *mostly* all to do with assassination.'

'Assassination?'

'Yeah. Like, there's a universe, they say, where President Kennedy was killed that day in Dallas. Way back in November 1963.'

'You know your history that far back?'

'Not really; enough. Like I said Doctor Nist, I like looking into things that get me going; like, I found out about all that, about the failed Kennedy assassination, from Chens, and looked into it more, because of *this*. And it made me think, like, *wow*, like, what could be important enough? What one event? To create *a whole new universe* that had enough... *oomph*, to then, like, be alternately *real*? *As well as ours*! And I realized that, well, like, these other Earths, these are just *versions* of Earth! And so that means; we're just a version of Earth! Everything is just – a version! Right!?'

Nist stared at her for a few seconds, blank.

Then, there it was.

That look again. Sympathetic. Almost... pity?

'Do you think...?' Nist began. He seemed to catch himself, then asked anyway. 'Do you think... we're supposed to know all this?'

Swish frowned, innocent. 'What do you mean?'

'Well, I agree with at least a small portion of what you've said. Of course; the human mind is not designed, does not have the capacity to take all this in. That is why we have fallen to… abstract notions. The human mind is not supposed to operate on this level. Don't you think, perhaps, that it's all gone too far?'

A chill ran down her spine.

Nist proceeded. 'That it's just… too much for us? Multiple different versions of Earth is bad enough, but then, multiple different versions of the galaxy, the universe itself? Perhaps, even versions of the galaxy where Earthlings did, or did not, migrate to the stars and colonise? Or, where we left at different points in history, each one effecting the whole, entire universe in a staggeringly huge number of multitudes of different ways and variations? Don't you think that's taking things…?'

She held her breath. He was going to say it again.

'…just, all a bit too far?'

She held her breath and tried to stay calm. Keep talking. Keep talking and don't show fear.

It's not a ward, it's a holding station…

'Well…' Swish laughed nervously. 'They say, that there are maybe one of two different universes where humans didn't *realize* there had been a dimension cascade. And in the three of them where Kennedy was killed, they still haven't even confirmed all the Goldilocks planets, let alone gone anywhere.'

'Fascinating…'

He really seemed to like this. She knew he would.

'That's right. And they're as real as ours. In the vision machine, the one the Gnostechs made, you can see the full cascade of the dimensions. So they say. The way they're packed, the way they fall; the places where they're closest, or where they even, maybe, overlap. Where you can, potentially, communicate with them; although, last I heard, they hadn't yet. I mean; they say if the dimension cascade never happened, we would never have learned about the dimensional waves either, never had discovered the gravitas drive, so maybe we never would have found out about teleport and all that. The pink rock and the… the maps.'

He just stared at her now. Silent.

He knew.

He knew that she knew.

He knew that he had misspoken, proselytized, too soon.

'They say…' Swish muttered, '…that these "Dead Kennedy" universes have nothing like what we have. That there's still seven billion and counting, living on Earth. That they didn't have the Great Acceleration over the end of the Millennium. They say there's another universe where the Id Monsters, the Ragers, really got hold, and they possess the ruling elite. Can you imagine how awful it would be; the dimension cascade happened, but they didn't know, and the Ids just appeared and took power…?'

'Yes. Ghastly.'

'They say…' Swish added, even more quietly. 'That there are seventeen, that we can see.'

They were hushed now. Did he know this was true? Or did he really believe it was all nonsense? Or did he, and this was where her money was, really, just, not care, at all?

She decided to try for something.

'I'm not really Swish Worcestershire, am I?'

'Do you really believe that?'

Do you really believe the dimension cascade never happened?

'I don't know. But if I'm not…' Swish gulped. '…it should be pretty easy for you to convince me, shouldn't it?'

'You'd think, wouldn't you? But; when you look at all those people there, in the lounge…' Nist spread his palms. 'All of them have sat right here, right in front of me, like you are now, saying the same thing. They believe they are people that they are not. People who are dead, most often. Many of them, long dead.'

Those people sat here, she realized, looking at you. And you sat there in your dull, power-blue suit, and lavender tie, and white shirt, perfectly part of the décor, against your own weird dream dimension office, looking at the people sitting before you that you've put in black undies and a blue gown…

Huh.

So… maybe…?

'Just… by the by, Doctor Nist… the desk, it's quite elaborate for a station.'

'Are you trying to find out if this is a station, or are you trying to find out if I am wealthy?'

See, the thing was, Swish realized, and, not for the first time…

The thing was, that everything was micro and macro.

It was like Hylar used to say, if you could divide it into two camps, it could be better understood. God she missed Hylar. Hylar was *smart*. But anyway, the two camps here, right in front of her; where they were and what they were talking about, were definitely micro and macro.

It was like; there might have been a possible universe for every possibility, but now, out in space, there was a potential Goldilocks planet, or moon, or continent, or island, or ship or station or platform, whatever, on and on, for everyone. And therefore, there was the potential possibility for everyone's *personal* universe to manifest.

'No, neither really. But I guess, if you can bring that desk to a space station, someone involved within that process has to be wealthy. Don't they? At least, a little?' She smiled sweetly. 'Do I really look like her?'

'They say you do. I don't really know what she looks like.'

'*They* say?'

'The people who brought you in. Apparently you were very, very drunk in a bar a few systems over, on a planet called…' Nist scowled to himself. '…never mind. But you were extremely violent.'

'Oh no! Did I hurt anyone?'

'You were a danger to yourself; and you damaged a lot of private property. Claiming out loud to anyone who could hear that you were Swish Worcestershire.'

'When was this?'

He swung his tablet back around and assessed.

'Sixteen hours ago. You were sedated, and I thought I should see you as soon as I could, to ascertain the level of your delusion. I'm…' Nist smiled tightly. '…something of an expert in these matters.'

'Goodness…' Swish gasped. 'Doctor, do you really think… I'm *delusional*? Like those men and women? In the lounge down there? I mean, are they all psychotic? Does that mean I'm psychotic, too?'

He smiled. 'Not… necessarily. There are a lot more questions I need you to answer before I can assess, and make a decision like that.'

She sat up a bit. 'Can I see myself? Maybe that will remind me who I really am?'

'I'm not sure…'

'Oh, please, Doctor? I mean, if I'm not really her…' *And I fucking well am, you monster.* '…there might be people waiting for me! I mean, the *real* me, whoever I actually am! If I can see myself, in a mirror, then surely…?'

'I…'

'Might save you a lot of time, Doctor, and it will help me settle down, and listen more to what you've got to say!'

'We're not here for you to listen to what I have to say. I need to hear what you have to say.'

'But Doctor, so far, it's been… well, it's all been a bit fanciful, hasn't it? Now I think about it? I mean, I must be prone, mustn't I? I must be one of those people who… what do they say? We're… susceptible? We have a… digestible mind?'

'Suggestible mind,' Nist corrected.

'Are you sure? I thought it was because people's minds are so eager, so willing to digest new information?'

'Well, that's an interesting thought, and an imaginative interpretation, but then it would be digestitive…'

'Or… or digestive?'

'One or the other. I think.'

'So it's… *suggestible*?'

'Yes.'

'Because I'm so suggestive? Because my boobs are so big and they make people think about sex all the time?'

'No,' Nist snapped.

Finally.

She screwed up her face and looked up, pointing her chin and exposing her neck.

'Does everybody think about sex all the time, Doctor Nist?'

Nist grumbled. 'Very well; I will programme the PPS so that you can stand and go over to the mirror while I update your file.'

He programmed the PPS from his tablet.

'Ten steps there, ten steps back. You can have twenty steps, and a minute there. No deviation from the immediate path. I ought to be done by then.'

Having made that decision, he seemed to switch off from her, and turned his attention fully, if somewhat sulkily, to his screen. She found that she was able to stand, almost immediately.

She smiled. 'Thankyou Doctor Nist…'

She stretched, but he didn't look up. Then she went to the mirror, three small timid steps until she was past his peripheral, then she stretched her legs right out, to the mirror, in four.

Swish looked at herself.

No, she was who she thought she was; there could be no doubt.

'Oh…'

She let out a little gasp, as though the absolute opposite were true, but didn't look back to check his response.

But, no, really; there she was.

She didn't get herself, really. The nose, the lips, the brown eyes with all the white. And the long brown hair, with the blonde streaks. She'd had them made permanent, a while back; she had never been pleased with herself as one or the other, blonde or brunette, but somewhere in between, she was okay with. But in the end, as a whole, with total honesty, she really, truly didn't get herself. Her nose was long and straight, but it was too long, and hooked in profile, like, all beaky. And her mouth was full, but there was something in the way it rested naturally that made her look dumb; the drooping bottom lip, her top lip revealing her lower front teeth. She looked like she had to breath with her mouth open, or she'd forget to do it, and pass out.

But yeah, it was her.

She was Swish.

But… why had she made herself forget?

She stared herself in the eyes. Maybe there would be a hint there?

Some indication of…?

But all she did was call attention to her flaws again. Her eyes were okay, but they were too wide and too narrow; not only did she *look* dumb, she looked like she was sneaky, too. And her eyebrows. Ugh. They were thick, so thick she'd had to pluck them every day for a decade just to keep the curve that suited her, until she'd made *that* permanent too.

The thing she did get, the thing she *did see*, that made her, she supposed, passable for the thing all those gruff but loveable men thought they saw in her, was that her cheekbones were massive.

You think you have a heart-shaped face, Astra Solara?

That's not a heart-shaped face.

This is a heart-shaped face.

Right out there, her cheeks, high and round and wide, making her weird, long, straight eyes look okay. Like they… went with the cheekbones, somehow. Sometimes, she did see that. And the sweeping inward curves of her jawline, from out at the cheek-edges, right down to her tiny, pointy chin. One of her men, once, ages ago, had called her Isosceles, even though it wasn't true.

Almost.

I mean, we did actually measure it that night.

And yep, there she was.

Giraffe neck, a child's shoulders, and a cleavage that seemed to start halfway down her torso, even in this squalid black hospital-issue boulder-holder, that was as tight as the straight jacket she was heading for if she didn't outwit this fellow; like, super quick.

She felt herself involuntarily standing up and turning around.

'This is your personal practise, isn't it?'

She carefully and quickly took three very big, long steps back, then used up another four hopping nimbly back into her chair, to make it look like she'd skipped across the room. She still had six steps left; but he must have, surely, seen this trick before? He was still typing, so she squealed a little bit to distract him, to stop him reminding himself to check her footstep count. He looked up right away, annoyed.

'Can you please be quiet just a few seconds…?'

'Why don't you tell me about your religion?'

'My…?'

'I can tell, you're one of them aren't you? I always wanted to meet one.'

'Meet one?' For the first time Nist seemed intrigued. 'One what?'

'Well, I just assumed…' Swish smiled. '…the way you were talking just then?'

'Just then? You mean, when we were we talking? It wasn't *just then.*'

'You're one of those people, aren't you? Who think things have gone too far? That's what you call yourselves, isn't it? GTF? Or are you with the Too Far Gone?'

Nist scoffed. 'The Too Far Gone? No! I'd never have anything to do with those lunatics! No, the Too Far Gone are well named! Aptly named! They are way *too far gone* themselves!'

Okay, suddenly you're acting like a real person. A real, crazy person.

'Really?'

'Well, surely you can see it yourself? Look at you; obsessed with a galaxy-scale stripper, who joined a gang of pirates and got herself killed? I'm assuming it's her death, at this point, that triggered your psychosis. So what did you conclude when you saw yourself in the mirror?'

'Exactly what you thought I would, Doctor Nist.'

'And now you've come scampering back like a puppy, thinking I have all the food, all the nourishment that comes from answers; the answers you seek to fill the void you now have, shrieking inside what you call your soul, demanding to be filled with a new purpose? Well, I can fill you with a reality, a philosophy, that is

stronger than any delusion, *let me tell you.* The GTF movement
is all society, human society, what's left of it, on planet Earth, or
what's expanding, scattered about, has left to it.'

'Oh!?'

'Scattered out here on a thousand different planets and moons
and stations and cruisers; wherever or whatever the hell people
want to create their world on these days…'

A private space station perhaps?

'Really!?'

'Yes. Yes, really. Because it's all gone too far – literally. People
aren't supposed to know about all these planets. As I stated
previously, our minds cannot handle it. Abstract! Abstract
indeed! Abstract is not real! It is not *truth*! We're not supposed
to be exposed to anything other than the wonders of the Earth;
we are, genetically, biologically, psychologically, supposed to be
caretakers of that world. As a race, we have too many freedoms.
There is too much emphasis placed on fulfilment and personal
achievement. The erosion of class, regardless of race or color, has
corrupted the human race to the point of fracturing it entirely;
you talk of the Mappers? They are the least of our problems; there
are far, far worse! The clone banks and the accelerated growth
farms, the Trans-Humanists and the so-called Humatrixes, all
of them blending technology with humanity, or taking genetics
to levels they were never supposed to be taken! They must all be
called back, all of them; back to the mother planet, before it all
goes way too far, way too far, and the genie can never be put back
in the bottle again! One day soon, our representatives will make
a call, to all of humanity, to return. Return to Earth! The Third
Jerusalem!'

'Third… *what?*'

'What you were talking about; a communion with the only
spirit that is real, our communion with the planet from which
we were all germinated? But with none of the mistakes of the
past. With science and yes, with genetic knowledge, we can now
determine at birth the path nature intended for each of us. We can

follow the stronger strains of humanity and allow them to rule. Women need to be re-domesticated, men retrained for physical labour, and differing levels of the genetic, natural elite will decide what's good for them, and how they should live. That way, they will be happier. The more intelligent will be more satisfied, the lesser allowed to wallow in their base entertainments; sport and...'

He narrowed his eyes and stared right at her, this time with a clear albeit briefly exposed contempt.

'...*pornography.*'

'Por... what?'

He ignored her and proceeded. 'The planet will be maintained at a basic number; with all humans well-adjusted and living only for the continuation of the species on the planet of its genesis; the Mother World. Gaia, if your primitive will must have it that way. Religions will be created for the simple many, reshaped from the deities of the past that encourage only positive forward will and total mental discipline.'

Swish was lost for words for a second, which didn't happen very often.

Then she squealed again.

'You squealed again. Is this philosophy exciting to you? Perhaps I have underestimated your genetic worth?'

'I just realized something. I got excited. It doesn't happen very often, but when it does, I get excited.'

'When you realize something in general? Or realize something specifically?'

'Something specifically. I suppose it would be more, like, a *recognition*, than a realization...'

'I... see.' He frowned, almost intrigued again. 'That is a very fine distinction. Perhaps I... I *have* underestimated you?'

'Oh, and by the way, it's *your* mind that can't handle it.'

'Pardon?'

'It's your mind, Doctor Nist. That can't handle overwhelming possibility. You should have stayed on Earth. All the people like you stayed on Earth. They're turning it into exactly what you want it to be. But, without all the crazy fascist stuff. Or is it totalitarian? I lose track of all the crazy people and crazy theories after a while.'

'You – are saying *that*. To – *me*?'

'Umm… yeah. That's right. Your mind can't handle it. You snapped, and you tried to put it back the way you want it. But… you must have been born into it, mustn't you? Second generation, right? I was right about that, wasn't I? You remember the Id? As a kid?'

He was silent.

'So… what happens now, Doctor Nist?'

'What… what do you mean?'

'What I mean is, I know how these collection points work. For the GTF and the TFG. You're the same thing, basically, by the way. In the end, you're both, both organisations controlled by the same corporate entities. Except they use physical violence, you use psychological persuasion. But it's all intimidation in the end.'

'That's outrageous!'

She squealed again and put her hands on her cheeks. She was blushing, she was so excited. She could feel it on her big, round, wide as wide, *totally authentic* Swish Worcestershire cheekbones.

'What is that awful squeal?' Nist demanded. 'What is it you realize, or, I'm sorry, *think* you recognize, when you make that awful sound?'

'Ever have that feeling where you realize suddenly that you're the smartest person in the room?'

'I beg your… is that…?' Nist was perplexed. 'But you can't be! That's not possible. There's only me and you!'

'You know something?' Swish sprang up to her knees. 'You're totally right about that woman in there, who claims she's Astra Solara.' She balled up her fists and punched them into the sides of her hips. 'She's absolutely not Astra Solara, and I can totally confirm it, for real!'

'Really now?' Nist spoke in a tone struggling to regain the superior balance. 'How is that then?'

'Because that one, in there, is my friend and *Hightail* Holiwell and Gnostech specialist Chens Khenzo. And seeing her there has totally brought to life my psychic programming, that we put together to smuggle us in here, because we've come to break someone else out; but you don't need to know that, do you? Who was the woman in the black lingerie, and the blue nightgown anyway? The one that you're so transfixed and obsessed with? Obsessed enough to make everyone in your private little psychiatric ward here dress up like this, and then parade around in front of you all day, before you ship them off to the GTF? Must have been a hell of a girl that you wanted to control her that much?'

'How…good gracious, how dare you!'

'Your mother, huh?'

'My – ! My – !'

'Are my clothes still here, by the way? Do you have them in here? Or do I have to get them on my way out…?'

'My –'

'Umm… so she went about the house in this outfit? Black lingerie and a blue nightgown? And then…?'

'How – dare – my – you –'

'And did she leave? Or did she stay? Sometimes staying is worse. Or did you leave?'

'Dup –'

'Umm…' Swish stood up. 'So, if I…'

She took three of her six remaining steps and advanced on him, sweeping his hand up in a dramatic, quite theatrical gesture, and running her fingers sensually down his wrist, into his palm.

This time, he squealed.

'Oh, good.'

She came around beside him, one more step. He was in complete shock, so it was quite easy to manipulate his fingers on the controls of his tablet, to release the screen from his fingerprint security lock and allow her access.

She entered a few commands, copied the database to somewhere obscure but easily externally retrievable if you knew where it was, released a few locks and made enough of a small chaos to keep people busy a while.

'You can't…! You can't!'

Then she reversed the PPR shield and placed it over his chair instead.

'Just did!'

He was crying, quite distraught.

'Problem is, right, that you were right about most of them. It's how we were able to infiltrate. But, see, there are quite a few of these little catchment facilities for the GTF or TFG, whichever end of the spectrum they come in from, and under the cover of the real psychotics, there are people from the corporation that run this operation, under the front of the various neurotic, control-freak, nut-job, pseudo-religious, regressive scientism cults they stage manage, who they actually want to keep somewhere quiet and undisturbed, where they won't make any noise. Where nobody will look for them. But you won't register any of this…'

'Who are you!?'

Swish groaned. 'I – am – Swish Worcestershire. Really. I am.'

'But… she's dead!'

'Oh, phooey, that's just a story. UnEarth put out a few weeks ago. Like, one by one they've been telling the public that the old crew of the *Hightail* have died, or been killed somehow, or, like, been murdered or gone mysteriously missing.'

Nist was aghast. 'But why…?'

Swish shrugged.

'Dragons.'

'What?'

'We saw the dragons, Doctor Nist.'

'The…?'

'That's right. Everything leads back there, but we had to leave. And when we did, that's when everything started to go weird. So, we need to work it out.'

'Work what out?'

'What they want, Doctor Nist. What they wanted us to go and get. Why they made us leave…'

Swish was having a bit of a turn, actually. She was just realizing this, remembering it all, as she was saying it. She'd come to this station, infiltrated the facility, in quite a risky fashion, she decided, given what could have gone wrong, given what, like, *still could* go wrong, because, sometime soon…

…Astra Solara would need her.

To complete the mission.

Her mission.

Their mission.

And now here they were.

Ready to bust the guy out.

So why was she still…?

Nist was crying.

He was crying in his big leather chair, in his dreamscape room, color-coded to the fantasy of his mother one day… what? Coming back? Calling him home? Or just… being a mother?

Who the hell had she been? To herself, to him?

How had all this happened to him?

'There, there…'

She leaned in and held his head, and he snuggled into her bosom.

'It's going to be alright…'

He whimpered something into her left breast as he wept.

She lifted up the spandex there. She had to pull hard; it was tight. The black material slid up, against his wet cheek, then lefty fell, just flopped out, down, and was free. God, that felt good. But just lefty. This was a mercy mission, after all. Then his arms were encircling her waist, and his mouth was fully open and enclosed around her nipple. He squashed his face right in, the white-streaked flesh of the pendulous breast pressing flat against his whole face. It felt nice, she had to admit. In an odd way to which she was unaccustomed. Like, asexual; maternal. And slowly, as she wondered whether or not to pinch a nerve and make him pass out, or maybe even put the sad lunatic out of his fascist-minded misery forever, he suckled himself to sleep and fell back, limp in his chair, eyes softly closed, with a gurgling, peaceful smile.

PART FOUR
SWIPE

CHAPTER THIRTY-THREE

Astra Solara spun away from the remains of the three pummelled and shredded bodies and ran back across George Street toward the massive reinforced glass-frontage of the OneCom building.

Conventional gunfire exploded around her and she stumbled, falling onto the asphalt.

The whole of the street was empty, evacuated in what should have been close to rush hour traffic.

The pistols she'd used to blow away a creature that shouldn't have existed here, on Earth, any more, but had just a few seconds ago been a few shockingly, terrifyingly, mere meters in front of her, remained tightly in her hands. Anyone else would had scraped flesh off their finger joints and knuckles, stumble-falling on to the asphalt as she just had; using her fists, balled tightly around the blaster grips, to instinctively prevent a harder fall. But for Astra, there was nothing but a jarring through her shoulders as she corrected her stance and turned back.

The gunfire stopped as she heard an explosion; she feared they were going to use missiles to get her, old-school explosive tips or something, and that her mind was experiencing one of those freak, slowed-time events people talk about when the shit totally hits the fan.

But no; nobody had expected this. In the sky behind them all, not quite obscured by the height of the city skyline, one of the docking platforms had blown up. As she watched, the ship slipped and toppled…

It was…

'No!'

Astra heard herself screaming out.

'No!'

The corporate cops who had appeared from nowhere, from out of almost every abandoned doorway and deserted street corner, and who had stopped shooting at her to look up at it as well, suddenly looked back at her.

She stared up, then at them, then up again.

It was an odd moment, to be sure.

They seemed to sense some connection…

They seemed, she sensed, indeed with whatever enhanced psychic ability she had to sense them with, to be strangely affected by the intensity of the event and the melee combined; weirded-out by what had happened, and her reaction. Even, bizarrely, just for a second, sympathetic to her pain, which for some reason they could not individually, nor collectively fathom.

Then they resumed trying to kill her and she resumed fleeing.

The OneCom doors opened and closed. She was all armoured up, not that you could tell by looking, but none of the bullets, plasma blasts or even sonic pulses that hit her had any effect.

Inside the lobby she spun back around. Three SUVs were hovering up the east side, at speed. Three more from the west and by the sound of things there was something large in the sky.

She had seen a Za'naja, and faced an Id Rager, both in the same day.

Nobody would believe her. *She* didn't believe her.

And her guns… who had thrown the guns?

Who – *had* – her guns?

They were hers, they were supposed to be…

She'd checked them in, before the party. Before she'd left quarantine and…

Slack.

Should have done that first, gone to the Declaration Point and gotten all her shit back.

There wasn't anything else important there, though. Not at the Declaration Point.

She hadn't even rented a proper room yet, nor even looked at a ship, and all her stuff was safely stashed in the usual places, or elsewhere, under the usual routines.

Sable and Parker were staring at her. They had seen it all from here, right outside essentially.

Parker had a gun on her.

Sable was still, nervous.

Astra looked at Parker with contempt.

'Next time a Colonel Commander tries to tip you off, *fucking well pay attention!*'

Parker was aghast.

'How dare you!'

Sable sighed. 'Parker, she's got some sort of natural tech! She's Astra Solara for God's sake! She got it out there in the black somewhere and they want it!'

'They want to see what it can do…' Astra uttered.

'She's a fucking terrorist!'

There was urgency in Sable's voice now, as the government military SUVs hovered to a halt outside.

'Parker, any idiot can see she's telling the truth! We've been right here the whole time! *We* just saw it all happen!'

He wasn't the brightest spark. She could easily have been lying. She might have been keeping them alive just to use. But she wasn't. For once, a useful idiot was working *for* her.

'Who!?' Parker demanded, her plasma pistol still trained on Astra. 'Who wants it!?'

'Who cares! Any of them! All of them! What matters right now is that I am telling you the truth; I made a deal with Com Junior! Look, they're going to come in here and kill you both! They want me set up as some kind of mad galactic terrorist, and you're witnesses!'

Astra flung her jacket back on, grabbed her case and snatched up Swipe's cage so hard it woke the chocolate feline from her sleeping trance.

'How!?' Parker demanded. 'How are you doing it!?'

Swipe grumbled.

'It's like they always said, Parker; natural tech powered by her own body; it's powered by her goddam heart, her goddam nervous system! Her life essence, her will!'

'Like who always said?' Astra demanded.

'Talk – people always talk. On the alt-wire, and the down-low.'

'That's impossible!' Parker's hand was shaking now. Even if she did take a shot and even if Astra wasn't armoured up, she was so frazzled that she couldn't hit a wall in an aircraft hangar.

A voice blasted out from the street.

'Surrender! And we'll treat you all fairly!'

Swipe growled.

'You'd better surrender!' Parker scoffed. 'Stop lying and surrender!'

'Parker, I'm not –'

'It's pseudo-science!' Parker sneered. 'The human body doesn't generate enough –'

'It does! If all it has to do is trigger the summons for a pre-existing field we're designed to use but have forgotten all about!'

'*What!?*'

'Parker, it goes one of two ways; either they kill you here in about two minutes, or in a year's time, we end up being buddies because I saved your life. Which is it going to –'

'*Stop lyi –*'

Astra punched her in the nose and swiped her gun. Blood flooded down her front and she squealed.

'You fucking terrorist!'

Astra swung about to Sable. He was part horrified, part amused, part in shock with the whole thing.

'Grab her, I'm not having her death on my conscience. I've had enough of that today. I have the White Key; I'll take you to safety.'

'No!' Parker shouted like a child.

But she didn't stop Sable as he wrapped her arms about her protectively and ushered her to the teleport vault. Every major building had one now, Astra knew. Right next to the elevators. Ostentatious but convenient. They quickly reached the massive, trademark, bright pink archway over the dark grey and black vault entrance. Sable tended to the keypad lock code, while Parker staunched her bleeding.

Sable glanced around. 'Peterson's bolted.'

Must be the smart one, Astra assumed.

'Head down, not up…' Astra ordered Parker, assessing her quickly as the chamber door slid open. She shoved her case with her foot, and it slid halfway into the small white room beyond.

Swipe yowled as Astra picked up her cage, then the front of the lobby exploded and all kinds of gunfire slashed everywhere.

Plasma pulses punched Astra backwards. She dropped Swipe and the cage clattered across the floor, toward the teleport chamber. Conventional bullets pushed Astra back even further, embedding in her front, as though stuck there with glue. Ten, then twenty.

She guessed they were done with the bit where they tried to figure out what she could do.

Her crystal interfaces lit up bright ruby red as she ordered her energy-exoskeleton to move her, and move her fast, against the onslaught. The exoskeleton engaged and locked her knees and ankles, her hips and shoulders, then strode one step forward. That was all she needed; now she moved her own limbs and pushed herself forward, just as a sonic pulse hit Parker. The pulse sent her, quite unintentionally, sidelong into the teleport vault, collecting Swipe's cage as she went, rolling it into the chamber but smashing Parker ruthlessly against the back left corner. Astra felt more sonic pulses, of far greater intensity than the tennis ball slaps she had programmed against, and willed up her defences again, grabbing Sable as three conventional sniper bullets whistled past his head, and a fourth went through his forearm as she grasped the inner door and swung them both in an arcing spray of blood through the vault door. Sable instantly corrected, balanced and turned, entering the code to close the door in a surge of adrenalin. The door slid down fast as the lobby exploded, bright white-orange. Sable staggered back with his lower pants and shoes on fire, then the noise was all gone and they were closed in. Astra had Sable's jacket off and was smothering the flames before he had a clue.

Jolly Jesus. These two. OneCom really hire for looks.

Still; trust a corporation to skimp where they don't think they'll ever need it.

She should have expected this.

'You okay?'

'Yeah,' Sable grunted. 'Hurts.'

And he *had* closed the door, just on instinct alone.

She went over to Parker. Looking down at her face, Astra was quite surprised. Unconscious, she was a real stunner, a real sleeping beauty.

'Concussion,' Astra reported. 'I'm taking you both with me.'

'Where to? I'm on minimum wage! Even a teleport trip home costs me a week's pay!'

'It's not like that; I have an expense account. I can do what I like. She needs a doctor, and you need burn gels.'

Sable popped his mouth as though to protest.

'You want to live?'

Astra spoke to the security system.

'This is Colonel Commander Astra Solara, Independent Agent activating White Key Carte Blanche Protocol, sponsor Com Junior, accepting prior, agreed-upon Terms of Contract.'

A red laser light slid out of the wall and gave her a full body scan, then turned green for go. It was a meaningless show; she had a dozen bio-enhancements, the likes of which they had never seen in this city… well, some of them had only just then seen them, but regardless.

The computer spoke in a neutral, androgynous tone.

'There was an old woman who swallowed a cat.'

'Imagine that…' Astra responded, '…to swallow a cat.'

'Activation successful. Welcome to White Key Privileges.'

'I want teleport, right now, for me and the two guests who are with me in this room. One is potentially badly injured.'

Blue lasers scanned both Parker and Sable. A tray slid out of the wall above Astra's head, where she crouched on one knee by Parker. She removed a small, round object like a cap, and placed it on Parker's head, holding her breath.

'I think this is…'

The cap engaged itself and spread a layer of clear liquid down Parker's body, effectively freezing her in place. Below her, a section of the floor raised, forming a trolley that lifted her body to table height.

Astra stood with it, and took a step back.

'How long have they been able to do this, here?'

Sable was staring helplessly. 'I don't know… is that nano-tech? I've never seen it so smooth. It can do that?'

'Apparently. For the wealthy. The colonies have… something like this level. Depending on where you go.'

Astra grasped the stretcher and pulled Parker over to the teleport terminal.

'White Key; there's an old house, that had a party, somewhere out of the city last night. It was wrecked afterwards. The whole balcony came away. It had a pool house. Can you find it?'

'Yes.'

'I want to go there.'

'That area is designated unstable. Are you sure?'

'Unstable why?'

'The building was colonial and partially demolished by a local earthquake. It is being restored.'

'Yes, take me there. Take all three of us.' Astra turned to Sable. 'You like the colonies, Sable?'

'I've never… been?'

'What about your girlfriend?'

'Parker? She's not…'

'She is now. At least, that's what you're telling people from here on.'

Sable turned pale. 'We're fugitives now?'

'If you wanna live.'

He looked down at his frayed pants and burned skin; it wasn't too bad.

'I need gel.'

Astra nodded.

'I'll get you gel.'

CHAPTER THIRTY-FOUR

'You okay, Sable?'

They'd been able to stand Parker up straight and slide her along. As she had, Astra had felt her breath coming out of the gap in front of her mouth.

Sable was looking around.

The homestead was still, quite slowly being rebuilt by repair drones. They had teleported directly on to the balcony, where this had all started for her; this chapter of her life, at least. The balcony was restored, and upright, but it was being supported by drone scaffolding and the wood under her feet was riddled with long splits and cracks.

'I think I came to an office picnic up here once.'

Astra smiled. 'Sounds about right. You know the park across the street? It's a sacred park. Surveillance doesn't know to look for you yet. If you disconnect and go in there, they won't find you and if you're disconnected they can't come in for twenty-four hours. Right?'

'I guess…'

'It's okay. Not even the corporate cops are going to mess with that rule. It's one of those rules everybody respects, because everybody needs it. For one reason or another…'

Sable nodded. 'I guess…'

'But they'll be waiting, after. Can you disconnect?'

'I… I only ever did it once or twice. And not for long.'

'To do drugs?'

'No. I was cheating. I'm divorced now.'

'Okay. I'm going to do something to you both; I'm going to short your implants and enhancements. They'll never find you. No, listen Sable. Listen. I'm sorry. But this is it now. It's nobody's fault, you were just in the wrong place at the wrong time, on the wrong shift when I walked in. But now, you are witnesses to the fact that I am not a terrorist and that… well, you saw how it all went down.'

Sable nodded. His bottom lip was trembling.

'Sable, you and Parker… either you're going to be killed by the people who employed you, or you're going to go into that sacred park, go as deep as you can into the forest, and I can arrange to have someone pick you up. It will take an hour or two. But you have to go in, and you have to keep moving.'

'How has this happened?' Sable whimpered.

'I told you. Dumb luck. Just fate.'

There was a slight hiss, then the upright plastic statue that was Parker hissed all over. The cover vanished, like expiring gas and she wobbled on her feet. Sable helped her maintain balance.

'Sable?'

'It's okay. I got it.'

She tried to push him away, but remained wobbly. Then he stepped back, let her go, and she was okay.

'Parker?' Astra asked. 'You okay? Did you get all that?'

Parker rubbed her throat. She didn't want to seem to look up at her.

'Yeah. Yeah, I got it.'

'You okay with this, Parker?'

Sable leaned in, trying to look her in the eye. 'Parker?'

'I'm okay. I'm okay.' Her other hand came up, and ran through her hair. The one that had been at her throat went down to her gun belt. Astra tensed, but she was just checking. The other one had been lost, but she still had the second. Her eyes flicked sideways at Astra.

'I don't have to thank you. But I get it.'

Astra nodded. 'My life just went to shit as well, for what it's worth.'

'The *Astralis*?' Parker asked.

'Yeah…' Sable frowned at her. 'Why were you so upset? I mean, maybe they didn't say they were gonna do it today, but they've been planning to do that for a year or so now.'

'I know.'

'It was all a con. The guy who designed it went crazy.'

'I…'

'It was just takin' up space. Once people found out, it was just an embarrassment for the – '

'It wasn't!' Astra snapped. 'It wasn't a con. I had it. I had the solution! If only they had waited… just another damn year!'

Sable and Parker stared at her.

'It was my ship, God damn it. My – ship. And I was *almost* ready to fly her. *Almost* ready to take her out…'

Her fists were balling again, her hands trembling. She turned to them.

'The people we're dealing with, they don't care about anything but control. And the more they control, the more pleased they are with themselves. And they exist for being pleased with themselves.'

She extended her trembling hands.

'One each. Now.'

Parker and Sable exchanged glances.

'It was real Parker. That thing. They say Ragers don't record, they don't translate to any recording technology. That you can't see them other than with your own two eyes. And now, we've seen one of them. Right. You saw it?'

'It was Rager,' Parker nodded. 'My aunt saw one. Never stopped talking. It was exactly like she said. Mashing people together in black oil. A vibration that makes you wanna shit your pants, reminds you of the first time you were scared of monsters as a little kid.'

Parker looked Astra in the eyes now.

'I wanna help. If they sent that thing out to get you, to see what you could do, see if you could hurt it and it got people killed like that; I wanna help. Help stop people who think it's okay to do something like that.'

Astra jolted. 'Really?'

'Sure. Why not.'

She held out her other hand. Sable reciprocated as well.

Astra grasped them and disconnected them. She disabled everything in their bodies that could be used to track them. Then she promoted a rush of dopamine to make them feel better, just a little, for just a little while.

'I'm gonna sit here and finish some thoughts. You guys go through there, over the road, and don't come back. Through those doors, across the street, and keep going. The park will be scary at night, but wait. My guy will come. If anyone sees you, you're lovers doing sex magic. My guy will take you somewhere safe, he'll brief you, then… you'll be free. I'll come for you; but it will be a while. Okay?'

'Free?' Sable asked.

'Sure.' Astra shrugged. 'Why not?'

CHAPTER THIRTY-FIVE

She'd never really done a ritual for cats before, never had need to.

She hadn't had a cat since she was a kid.

But this one, appearing like it had, in the pool and all, it just seemed as though…

The thing about ritual was really the intent behind it.

She had to think.

What was a cat god, or goddess?

Well, the name Bast came to mind. She thought she'd heard that before and was fairly certain, even if it was from bad, old movies, that Bast was at least something to do with being a feline deity. So she decided that she would ask Bast, on behalf of Swipe.

She opened Swipe's cage onto the only table there; the long banquet table that had been there before. Where she had first seen Swipe about to forage. Clearly, it had been found in the wreckage. Perhaps righted by someone as they'd set up the secondary drones. Or, maybe the drones had been programmed to salvage it. Regardless, there was a chunk missing; it had split from the middle at one end and curved right. The base was still attached to the larger, remaining surface, so it still had four legs. But there was a whole curved chunk, shaped like a question mark, where about a third of the surface was nothing but air.

Released, Swipe went to bolt, then shortly paused, as though sensing that she had nothing to fear. She was, strangely and quite correctly, somewhere familiar and almost safe. She turned at a table leg, twisted her body around it, and looked up through the gap in the table at Astra.

She meowed.

The other thing with gods, with good ones who would help, was that they didn't really care if you got a few things wrong. If you were earnest, and true, and your intent was virtuous, they would pretty much answer the call because that was why they were there in the first place; they existed to manage and maintain the part of whatever realm they came from that existed here in the human collective unconscious. Perhaps another dimension or even planet, or time… but… it was elsewhere, but here as well, and they maintained it.

She prepared a small altar on the table. There was plenty of debris still strewn about. It looked as though the primary drones, elaborate, nimble and precise cranes of various sizes and mission-designs, had righted the balcony wholesale. Whatever items that had still been attached to it, or on, or around it as the secondary drones had lifted back the hard balcony structure from the lawn below, then reattached it in an initial crude weld, had been scooped up with it. There were still a few chairs, one or two were even in one piece, and a few shards of old ceramic serving platters. There were big flower pots, but she wasn't sure whether the pots had been here before. Maybe they'd been collected in the collapse and then scooped up, just generally with all the other stuff. Then there was the genuine debris; branches and chunks of wood, sections of brick and mortared stone, giant dirt divots and stretches of torn surface, grass still intact, all of which was now strewn everywhere across the balcony patio, like a bomb had gone off down there, and sprayed it all up here.

Astra had purchased something called a Cat Kit somewhere in the city on an emergency card she'd found in the stash with the shorg, which she now removed from her pack. She'd bought it clean because she hadn't wanted any connection with OneCom and the cat, and therefore the ritual.

She went about putting some raw meat, a ready-made saucer of milk, some kibble and some catnip from the Cat Kit around the soft basket she'd made from the bits of twig from the severed branches, and soil from the lawn chunks. Assuming Swipe had been from around here, she thought it all reflected the sentiment of something natural, from home, combined with the offer of a new home and someone to take care of her. She kept that intent in her mind as she arranged it all around an extendable scratch pole that also came with the kit.

All the while, Swipe watched.

Part way into it, she'd jumped off the table and for a second Astra's heart had sunk, but the chocolate feline had stuck around, exploring and weaving in and out of the four shattered doors. After a while, Astra realized she was hanging around the altar for the food, and the milk.

'Okay… Bast?'

She opened her mind, as best she could, and went within.

'Bast, I don't have much time. I've rescued this cat, from a dangerous situation that surrounded me, but was not really, truly my fault. But I rescued her and named her Swipe. I want to take her off-world. I think it would be good for both of us. If you give permission and she is okay with me communing with her, using the consciousness patterns that I have been using on her so far, I would like a sign. If there is a clear sign, she will come with me on my next mission. Bast, I ask with great love and affection for this creature, Swipe, a manifestation of the great friend and ally and companion of mankind that is the female domestic cat and an expression of the Great Feline Consciousness in general…'

Swipe meowed, loud and long.

Astra turned around.

Swipe was wailing as she walked about the restored balcony, moving in a strange figure eight.

Astra went over to her.

The chocolate cat was pacing around some black scorch marks…

They were blast marks.

From where Farraway had tried to shoot her.

They looked weird. Distinctive.

Swipe meowed again and rubbed up against her new military boots.

'Thanks Bast. I'll take good care of her.'
Then Swipe sauntered over, jumped up on the table and finally, after all that, had herself a hearty meal with a balcony view.

CHAPTER THIRTY-SIX

Swipe knew she was being admired.

Astra was happy to admire her.

The test was over and Astra was, as usual, the last one standing.

As usual.

Then, something odd happened.

She got a burst. Just as she had sensed, upon first seeing Swipe, that there was a connection, a consciousness ripple. She now had the same in reverse. Someone was… admiring her, flooding her with a burst of admiration, as she stood and looked down to the wreckage of the pool…

She turned around.

He was the most handsome man she had ever seen.

Standing in the second of the shattered doorways.

The doorways that had, not long ago, represented possibilities for her.

'I'm sorry.'

So this is what they mean.

Not love at first sight, nor lust at first sight.

Just instant chemistry.

She looked across the balcony and knew, this was her perfect man. If they did it, it would be great. If they hung out, it would be just as great. If they just spoke on the phone every now and then, they would be the best chats ever. But, if they didn't, if they did nothing with it, it would be a sin.

'I didn't mean to interrupt. I'm Cors. Cors Harrow.'

'Cors?'

'Yes. My brother hired you. I've brought the merchandise.'

Oh, God.

The man of her dreams was her worst nightmare.

EPILOGUE

She blinked.

She'd banged her head and passed out.

'Wake up!'

'What!?'

'Wake up, Hylar!'

'What!?'

'Hylar! We did it!'

'What!?'

'We got the ship! We got her! We're at the bottom of Sydney Harbour but it's okay! We did it! We dropped her off the platform!'

'Swish?'

'Yes, Hylar! Of course it's me! You've hit your head! You don't remember; you should be happy!'

'Happy that I've hit my head!?'

'No, that we dropped the ship and now she's ours! Well, *hers*, anyway...'

'Hers?'

'Astra's! The plan? We've got the ship, now we have to find Astra!'

'Astra? But she hates me...'

'*Hates* you? She *loves* you! Hylar, when you get things wrong, oh baby, do you, like, *really* get them wrong. We have to find Astra before that man they sent to seduce her kills her and takes all her secret psychic nature-tech. Then we have to get back!'

'Back? Back where?'

'Back to the dragons!'

'Dragons?' Hylar moaned. 'Ohhh... right. The dragons.'

'Amazon Seven, Hylar. We just stole the only ship in the galaxy that can take us back to Amazon *freakin'* Seven!'

TO BE CONTINUED…

Thanks for reading!

If you enjoyed reading this book, please feel free to go now and order, or pre-order, the next book in the saga from your favorite retailer…

If you really liked it, you might even like to leave a nice comment, or a favorable review somewhere.

The next book in this series is:
Amazon Seven – Book Two: Princess Executor

Thanks again, happy reading!

Acknowledgements

Enormous thanks and much love to Melissa Sheldrick.

Huge thanks also to Michal Dutkiewicz for the brilliant cover.

Thanks to Bronwyn Bean, Greg C. Grace, Pat McNamara, Dave Oz, Hamish Stokes, Melissa Stokes, and Francis White, for help, advice and encouragement.

Big thanks to Maggie Fiddian, Stan James, Gretel Newman-Sugrue, and again to Melissa Sheldrick, for creative input and editing.

Thanks finally to Adam Dutkiewicz for the formatting.

And just, thanks, really, to everyone who helped.

Thanks!

Edition 2.0 Notes

This edition differs from the previous ebook published via both KDP and Smashwords in that there have been some inevitable grammar corrections, some content edits and even a few outright changes.

A few small, extra details have been added, and occasionally subtracted, as the characters and the universe have grown in my mind, as I start writing Book Two. This has necessitated the more extensive world-building, and plotting of the Amazon Seven Saga in general.

Most notably – Hylar has become less forgiving, and Swish Worcestershire's role aboard *Hightail* has switched from LCA to LCC. (Enter the redoubtable Wing Spar.)

I'm sure there are a few other things here and there.

Like, Astra's outfit matches the cover now.

Stuff like that.

Such is the new publishing paradigm.

We now return to our regular programming.

Alex James, September 2015

About the Author

Alex James is a writer who lives in Adelaide, South Australia. He was born there on October 15th, 1967, and has lived there ever since.

Alex studied European History, Classical Mythology, Film Studies and Screenwriting under the Communications and Liberal Studies banners at the South Australian College of Advanced Education (now the University of South Australia) but kept dropping out and going back and never finished anything (at least not to his knowledge). He then dabbled with being an advertising copywriter, was apparently quite good at it, but did not enjoy it. He read Tarot for a while, wrote thousands of trivia questions for Imagination Games, and was a 'film culture' columnist and reviewer (paid) for the print version of the Adelaide *Independent Weekly*, before the internet made everyone a critic (unpaid).

Between 1992 and 2005 he wrote many, many, many outlines, treatments, concept documents, bibles, pilots and screenplays, for just about every active Australian production company there was. During that time, a few of these things even almost came close to nearly being made.

A confirmed telly addict who was binge-watching series on videotape decades before it was even a thing, Alex is also a life-long film buff, who has lost count of how many billions of films, and zillions of episodes of television he has seen. Alex saw *Star Wars* at age ten, arguably the perfect age, which led him immediately to *Doctor Who*, after which he never looked back.

Growing up on BBC series from the 70s and 80s, he was honoured in 2002 to be one of several to have a go at the long-touted revival of *Blake's 7*. These remain, when all is said and done, his favorite things, alongside The Alan Parsons Project, The Waterboys and All About Eve.

Alex is also a comedy aficionado, whose comedy heroes are too numerous to mention here, but will no doubt one day find their way into a dedication.

In his spare time, Alex still reads and watches. His influences as an author include Douglas Adams, Julian May, Clive Barker, Philip Jose Farmer, Elmore Leonard, and more recently Dan Simmons.

He listens to audio books, comedy podcasts, woo-woo radio shows, while drinking coffee, and walking his dog Romana, sometimes all at once. At the time of writing, he has not had a drink for five years, or a cigarette for three. He thinks he might be getting hooked on ice cream though.

Most recently he was an in-house writer for Angel-Phoenix, who published his first two novels, *The Pandora Sequence* and *Venus A.I.*, which were well-promoted at the 2013 San Diego Comic-Con and apparently did quite well.

Alex's most recent work has been published independently through Kindle Direct, Smashwords and IngramSpark.

Also by Alex James

Please visit your favorite retailer to discover other books by Alex James.

Out Now:
Terraguard – Book One: Maker of Rules
Dark Streets – Book One: Agents of Fear
Venus I.A.
The Sequence Saga:
The Pandora Sequence

Coming Soon:
Saga of the Urban Sorcerers – Book One: The Summoning of Barker Moon
Amazon Seven – Book Two: Princess Executor
Apricot Fox and the Cats of Saturn
Dark Streets – Book Two: Avatars of Wrath
… and *The Sequence Saga* continues…
The Sirens Sequence - Book One: The Pandora Inheritance
The Sirens Sequence - Book Two: The Pandora Arcana
The Sirens Sequence - Book Three: Daughters of Pandora

Connect with Alex James

Visit my website: http://alexjamesgalexy.com/

Friend me on Facebook: http://facebook.com/AlexJamesGalexyTales

Review me on Goodreads: https://www.goodreads.com/author/show/13206513.Alex_James

Follow me on Twitter: http://twitter.com/alexjamesgalexy

Connect on LinkedIn: http://www.linkedin.com/in/Alex-James

See me on Instagram: http://instagram.com/alexjamesgalexy

Favorite my Smashwords author page: https://www.smashwords.com/profile/view/AlexJamesGalexy